Advance Praise for
H●w The Str●ng Survive

The characters are compelling and telling at the same time. *How the Strong Survive* should give a Native reader a good sit-down and a Non-Native an idea of how Traditional Peoples live and think even though [it's] a fictional novel. Great Book!

Thomas Greywolf,
Founder
The American Indian Injustice Group

It really WAS a pleasure to read this exciting & fast-moving thriller with an intriguing point of difference! The book's protagonist — free-lance investigator Ben Pace — is a modern day *wichashawapiya* (Lakhota healer & seer), who happens also, during the vicissitudes of a varied life, to have acquired high-tech expertise!

Ben sees life from the fascinating indigenous Lakhota spiritual perspective: in terms of a system of cosmic checks & balances, and, imbued with a profound respect for the equilibrium of the forces of nature, established by the Creator, *Wakantanka* (The Great Mystery).

I especially appreciated the delicacy & restraint with which Newt delineates the love story between Ben & Teresa. Another very appealing feature is the sassy Lakhota humour in the interchanges of Ben with his spirit-guides!

Overall, the book is a nicely-judged blend of hard-nosed realism, even cynicism, on the one hand, with genuine spiritual vision, and informed idealism, combined with great sensitivity & high emotional intelligence, on the other.

Clive David Bloomfield,
Classical Scholar,

Irish Gaelic language teacher,
Lakhota language translator,

Active participator in Lakhotaiyapi forum (Yahoo!) devoted to serious study of Lakhota language & culture.

also by
Newton Love

NO ACCOUNTING FOR TASTE
A Nick Schaevers PI Novel

available from
RockWay Press

How
the

Newton Love

Emily,
Always believe in your
own dreams!

Newt Love.

Strong
Survive

a novel

RockWay Press

RockWay Press ❧❧ New Mexico

FIRST ROCKWAY PRESS EDITION

Library of Congress Cataloging-in-Publication Data
Love, Newton
How the Strong Survive, a novel / Newton Love
    Suspense, Crime, Detective, Political Thriller, Fiction, Novel,, Literature, *Lakhota*
    Spiritual Practices, Spirituality, Women's Studies, Violence Against Women Studies,
    Native American Authors,
    / Newton Love
    p. cm.
    ISBN 0-9776634-5-0
    1. Suspense 2. Crime 3. Detective 4. Political Thriller 5. Fiction 6. Novel 7. Literature
    8. *Lakhota* Spiritual Practices 9. Spirituality 10.Women's Studies 11. Violence Against
    Women Studies 12. Native American Authors
    Library of Congress Control Number: 2005938086

Cover artwork provided by Palo Alto (item number paa 184000036). From www.inmagine.com. Used with permission. Book & Cover design Alexandria Szeman & RockWay Press®
    Spirit Feather drawing © 2006 by Newton Love. Used with permission.
    Photograph of author © 2006 by Nance Love. Used with permission.

Published by RockWay Press
#01 Back Road, Studio Z, Madrid, New Mexico 87010-9727 USA

Distributed in bookstores in the USA, Canada, & the UK by Ingram and by Baker & Taylor; distributed worldwide online by Amazon.com, Barnes & Noble.com, Borders.com, Wal-Mart.com, Target.com, & RockWayPress.com

Visit our website at www.rockwaypress.com
Discussion questions available at www.rockwaypress.com and www.newtlove.com
Glossary of Native American terms and of *Lakhota* Moons at www.newtlove.com

10 9 8 7 6 5 4 3 2 1
Printed in the United States of America by Lightning Source

Dedications

To **Nance Love**, artist, mentor and partner: You encouraged me to complete my journey to author. You told me to take Delphine Cingal's dare, and turn the serial rapist genre upside-down. You are my "green lantern."

Delphine Cingal, Maître d' des conférences à l'Université de Paris II-Assas: In 2001, you read a draft of "No Accounting for Taste," and emailed, "This is the best first novel I have read in a long time. I worked on P.D. James and I think you could have the same qualities (psychology of the characters, construction of the novel?). You've got what it takes to be a great writer. I would like to make sure this novel reaches the maximum of your talent." You took me under your wing and taught me a lot about writing and friendship. You dared me to write a thriller based on my walk on The Red Road, with a lot of politics. This is that book, my first published novel. RockWay Press also bought "No Accounting for Taste," too, and it will be out soon. Thank you for being the first professional to "discover" me.

To **Alexandria Constantinova Szeman**, editor and publisher: I entered, but did not win, your 2004 novel contest. Of all your losers, I am the biggest winner, because you saw the flash of gold in the pan. You risked many hours tutoring me in how to use urgency, hoping I would blossom into a full-fledged writer. You were right about me. You are my Szeman-*Sensei*. May all your dreams come true.

Nance, Delphine, and **Alexandria** — thank you for believing in me. Now, let's have some more adventures!

Acknowledgments

I would like to acknowledge the help and assistance provided by **Grandfather** and his **Power Spirit**.

To **Maryland's Society of the Rose**, Huzzah! Huzzah! Huzzah! A round on me.

To my **Fellow Marines**: Strange drinks in strange places. As long as we have honor, we are kings. *Semper Fi.*

To writers: **Kinky Friedman, John Waters, Dashiell Hammett, Raymond Chandler, Cornell Woolrich,** and **Douglas Adams.**

To **Pat O'Connell**, who introduced me to the Maryland Writers' Association.

To the many members of the **Maryland Writers' Association**, who shared, mentored, and just hung-out as writers, thinkers, and co-conspirators in the arts during monthly meetings, poetry cafés, and annual conferences.

To **"The Novel Experience"**, a critique group inside of the Maryland Writers' Association, where I regularly go to take abuse and offer critiques.

To **Margot, CJ, Alma, Cindy, Gale, Vic,** and **Bridget** — Thank you.

To **Alexandria Szeman**, my Max Perkins. I hope to be your F. Scott Hemingway.

And most of all, to **Nance, Newton & Lois**, and **Annette & Joe**: I wouldn't be here without you.

Thank you all.

How the Strong Survive

a novel

Chapter One

Lightning struck the Maryland hilltop, igniting a blaze. Before rain quenched the fire, it burned the hilltop bare. It was quiet now. The wind sang songs of distant sunshine to the trees. Squirrels discussed the weather while the sparrows gossiped. It was the first phase of the Tender Grass Moon, or early April on the Gregorian calendar. I thanked *Wakan Tanka*, God, for the cleared land inside a forest close to Baltimore and Washington, DC. I built a home here to rest and recover.

Tall Brothers surrounded the hilltop, providing the squirrels with a tree branch beltway, and roosts for the winged ones. Many deer, raccoon, and other relations lived under their tall-trunked and leafy canopy. Most of the Tall Brothers were red, white and pin oaks, but included hickory, walnut and pine. Smaller trees like dogwoods, red buds and cedar were there too.

I smelled the sweet morning air. The small stand of Osage orange that I'd planted on the north side of the clearing were getting tall. The French called them "bow-wood." Of all wood, Osage orange is the most flexible. Members of the Osage tribe are pretty flexible, too.

I wasn't the only one in need of healing. My spirit guide, Raven Who Hops, had told me that people would come that morning to ask me for help. That task would show me the next steps on my own path.

The angle of the sun showed that it was time. I closed my eyes, opened my mind and listened with my whole heart. Wooden wind chimes bumped in the breeze, providing a quiet drum to my prayer. Beauty and peace filled the small hilltop. I sensed humans approaching. A minute passed before I heard their car. I opened my eyes.

A blue-jay whistled an alert and flew to a perch on the porch. I spoke in the old earth tongue.

"Winged Brother, what is it?"

"One of the big box-beasts comes."

"Stay and listen if you want, but it may be boring."

"Two-legged things are."

He flew away. I stood and walked the perimeter of the main geodesic dome to the east-facing front door. There was a knock. I opened it.

Four women stood in a diamond pattern on the large stone step. Each face wore a different emotion. The closest one looked serious. Behind her were two side-by-side. The one on the left seemed aloof, but she wasn't quite succeeding. The one on the right had a calm veneer, but the way she worked her left thumb's cuticle betrayed her. A flash of fear was all I glimpsed of the last, who prairie-dogged behind the others.

"May I help you?"

The nearest one answered.

"Are you Ben Pace?"

"Yes, and you are here to ask a favor." I stepped back, opening the door wider. "Please come in."

18

They entered while I watched. The one in back stayed close to the nervous one.

None of them appeared related, but they all looked similar. A police bulletin would have read "Be on the lookout for a female, five-foot-six-inches, 125 pounds, petite, with brown hair and small features."

The serious one wore a short-sleeved blue button-up shirt and blue slacks with sneakers. Random curls in various sizes framed her face. A coral nail polish matched her lipstick and her tan was an even bronze. Her eyes were green. Her right hand wore a gold shamrock ring with inlaid emeralds. Her left middle finger had an oval emerald set in a woven Celtic knot band. Her left pinky ring was a dragon with a ruby in his exposed claw. Her earrings were Celtic knots shaped into teardrops. She didn't wear a watch.

I could sense her pain, but also her strength. She seemed the type to take care of herself and others. Why would she need my help?

The aloof one wore black slacks and a crisp white shirt. Her basic red lipstick enhanced her untanned skin. A gold barrette fastened her coffee-colored hair at the base of her neck. Her eyes matched her hair. A large diamond solitaire graced her left hand and one-inch, gold hoop earrings glinted on her slightly detached earlobes. Three gold bracelets of varying thicknesses were on her left wrist. Her other wrist wore a plain, black-strapped, gold-coin watch. Her closed-toe but open-heeled shoes, belt, and purse could have been made from the same piece of black leather.

Everything about her said "money." Surely her family had a fixer on their payroll. Why seek me out?

19

While the nervous one was as tall as the rest, she had longer legs and a shorter torso. Tan slacks held a creased taper to a pair of oxblood penny loafers. Shoulder length chestnut hair fell in waves to brush the collar of her navy blue polo shirt. Her eyes were blue, and her earrings were pearl. An artistic medallion clasped her tan leather belt. Her lipstick was only a few shades darker than the skin tone visible between her freckles. No rings were on her long tapered fingers.

A *Lakhota* name for her came to mind: "Little Flower." I sensed a deep strength in her. The women puzzled me. What could tie them together and make them seek me out?

The fourth didn't make much eye-contact as she attempted to hide behind Little Flower. She wore baggy, grey sweats. Her brown hair and occasionally her brown eyes peaked from under a Baltimore Orioles baseball cap. Running shoes finished her outfit. She wore neither makeup nor jewelry. Here was one who was damaged and weak. Perhaps it was this one that I would help.

I ignored their whispers and stepped through the open flap of my *tipi*, crossing to the center fire-pit. I was sure that a full-sized great *tipi* was not what they expected to find inside my home. From the outside, it's an enclosed porch and three geodesic domes, from large to small. The inside of the largest was filled with a hide-covered *tipi*. Living in one helped my warrior-priest training.

On a trip to Montana, I had hand-harvested each of the *tipi*'s twenty-eight lodge-pole pine trees that leaned against one another in mutual support. The

20

interior was twenty-eight feet wide at the base and over two stories tall at the tie-off, with bare poles reaching above that to the dome's roof. Ten of the thirty-two hides that covered the poles were from my own meat-making. The rest were from the tribal store back home. I had tanned all but two of the thick fur hides inside the *tipi*. Of those two, one was a gift from my parents, the other a gift from fellow priest.

The serious one spoke.

"He said to dress as if we were going to a ranch. He wasn't kidding."

They looked around the *tipi*, maybe searching for a place to sit.

"There are no chairs," I said. "Perhaps you would be more comfortable in the kitchen?"

I got a few dirty looks. Perhaps I sounded sexist. I rephrased it.

"There are *wasiçiu* chairs in other rooms. The kitchen is the closest. In here, we sit traditional style." Comprehension did not cross their faces, so I added, "We sit on skins on the floor in here."

Little Flower asked, "Is a wah-see-chew chair comfortable?"

I smiled inside, but kept my face muscles slack. "*Wasiçiu* is *Lakhota* for 'fat stealer.' We use it to mean white society."

"Oh."

She looked sheepish.

"Do not worry, Little Flower. You cannot be wrong for asking to know more." I let my eyes smile as her own smile rekindled. "Visitors tell me that my chairs are comfortable."

They looked around to each other, then the serious one spoke.

"Perhaps we should try the kitchen."

"This way."

I left the *tipi* and walked the perimeter to where a second and smaller, but still large dome was joined. It held a modern kitchen, dining room, and entertainment area. One-quarter of it was an enclosed office area. There were windows at regular intervals up to the top, which let in a lot of light.

Traditional *Lakhota* homes and furnishings drew their design from the circle of winds and the roundness of the earth's horizon. I walked to the round pine table. *Lakhota* custom said I should sit first, but instead I stood and waved to the chairs. The serious one sat on the northeast. The aloof one sat on the east, Little Flower on the south, with the fearful one between them. I had the west half of the table to myself.

The serious one spoke.

"We need your help."

"Yes, I know. My spirit guide told me to expect you."

"Did he tell you our problem?" asked the aloof one.

I thought I heard a trace of sarcasm in her voice. No matter. My path did not include making people believe *Lakhota* ways.

"That's not how a spirit guide works. Never mind. You are here about something very important to you."

The serious said, "We're being stalked by a sick-o and we want it to stop."

We were all silent. I needed to know a lot more, but they would not want to tell those details to a stranger. I would let them know me first.

"Thank you for visiting me. You know my name, so please call me Ben. I am *Lakhota*."

"Do you mean *Sioux*?" Little Flower asked.

"That old word is not our name. It's all a misunderstanding. The Ojibwa called us *nadewisou*, which, in their tongue, meant 'by the twisting river.' The French shortened the word to *Sioux*. The name became a common reference to us. It is so deeply ingrained that we can't change it. It is similar to your saying 'German' when they say '*Deutsche*', or your saying 'Japan' and not '*Nippon*'."

"I'm sorry."

"It is nothing." I continued to open to them. "As a young man, the Army taught me to be a telephone lineman. After I got out, I came to Maryland and went to work for Bell Atlantic. Five years ago, a utility truck backed into the pole I was on. I fell."

I saw concern on their faces.

"It's okay. I am partially disabled but not dead. When Sitting Bull was young, he was shot in the foot. It healed wrong, and he limped his whole life, but he still could run faster and fight better than men with two good feet."

I permitted myself to smile, hoping it would help them to be brave.

"I am ready and able to help, but first you must tell me who you are."

Three of them looked to the serious one. She spoke.

"My name is Rita Cade. I own 'Shears Locks Combs,' a hair salon in Bowie."

She looked to her left, to the aloof one.

"I'm Maria Vacarro. I'm a pediatrician."

She looked to her left, to the frightened one, who shook her head, and then looked down. From her other side, Little Flower touched her hand and spoke to her.

"It's okay."

Little Flower turned to me.

"I'm Kelly, Kelly Larson. I do daycare in Glen Burnie. This is Lisa Towers. She's a little overwhelmed. She runs a crew for Nifty-Maid."

Lisa examined me from under the bill of her cap. They were all looking at me. I closed my eyes and sensed the room. Lisa and Maria's auras held fear, Rita's aura held apprehension, while Kelly's was one of anger or frustration. Perhaps she would be the one to tell me the specifics, but I couldn't ask her directly. I opened my eyes and spoke to their leader.

"Rita, how did you come here?"

"We took the freeway to the …"

"No, Spring Blossom, I meant, who told you to look for me?"

"I cut hair for some of the workers at the horse racing track in Laurel. I asked one of them if he knew someone who would kill a bastard for me. He said, yes, except after he'd heard the whole story, he laughed and said 'the bastard doesn't need killing; he needs to be savaged'. I asked him what he meant. He gave me your name and a map. He told me to not use a phone, but instead just pick a day and come. He said you seem to be here when you're needed."

24

That is part of having a spirit guide. They sometimes let you know what's on your schedule.

"Was his name Roy?"

"Yes, Roy Campagnella. How did you know?"

I would never admit what I had done for or with Roy. He always paid in cash.

"Roy and I share some history."

A look of wonder crossed her face. *Wasiçiu* faces display a running montage of their inner dialogue. Only their poker players and politicians practiced anything like *Lakhota* face control.. I turned to Maria, then Kelly and Lisa.

"Are you here for the same reason as Rita?"

Maria and Lisa nodded, with Lisa's head drooping low. Kelly spoke.

"We all want the bastard to suffer."

"What did he do?"

"He raped us. First me, then two women who aren't with us, then Maria, then a woman that killed herself, then Kelly, then Lisa."

Maria's voice held contempt.

"Those are the ones that we know of."

I now knew why they walked in the order they did. The ones with the greatest separation from their trauma were in front. As the most recent victim, Lisa kept back. I turned to Little Flower.

"Kelly, you show the most anger. Why?"

"The bastard humiliated me ... us. He made us beg to be let go, then told us that if we begged him to do it, he wouldn't kill us." She leaned forward. "I want him dead. I was going to buy a gun and shoot him, but they stopped me."

"You know that they are right, don't you? If you tried, you would just wind up in jail."

It was time to touch the wound.

"Why isn't he in prison?"

Lisa began to cry. Kelly and Maria tried to comfort her. Rita gave me a cold stare.

"His lawyers beat the DA in court."

"Were his lawyers lucky or good?"

"He had a whole firm of high-priced Baltimore lawyers. Didn't you see it in the news?"

"No. What put your case in the news?"

"The rapist, John Keagey, is a Kinkaed."

"The politicians?"

"Yeah, his family has a governor, a US Senator and six US congressmen, with the next generation waiting in state legislatures."

"We'll never get justice. The court's a joke that's on us," Rita said.

"Do you all want the same thing?"

"We all want him dead," Maria said. "Since he won in court, he's been simply horrible."

There were nods around the table. Kelly's eyes held rage.

"He waited outside my house after work one evening. He told me that he was going to make me his girlfriend again."

A tear rolled down her cheek.

"He said that he still has my panties."

Her clenched hands showed white knuckles. While Maria comforted Kelly, Rita and Lisa stared at me with rage in their eyes. I spoke into the maelstrom.

"I will help you, but you must help me to help you."

That brought quiet.

"Keagey and the Kinkaeds need to understand that the earth is not their private playground. At the same time, we must make sure that your lives are not made worse by our efforts."

"We're ready."

Rita pulled a brown paper bag from her purse and placed it on the table.

"There's ten thousand dollars there. If you need more, we'll find a way to get it. We're not as rich as the Kinkaeds, but we will pay you to take care of this."

"It's not part of the *Lakhota* way to require payment for a deed that must be done. Our way holds that the strong and brave must serve the weary and weak. I cannot be a good *Lakhota* man while there are people in the village who are hungry, cold, or afraid."

I picked up the bag of money and placed it in Rita's hand.

"Perhaps we will share expenses, but you do not need to pay me to be a man."

"So, you will kill him for us?"

"No, I will do something much worse than that."

It was quiet in the room.

"I will need phone numbers."

I took four cards from my wallet.

"Here is my information."

Rita put the money into her purse and pulled out a folded sheet of paper.

"Here's ours."

I took it and set it on the table.

27

"Now that you have come to me and I have promised to help you, each of us has taken steps on a path that we will now walk together. Progress brings comfort, but don't let it show. We are now at war with the Kinkaeds. Our strongest weapon is surprise. You must not change how you act toward him. Don't tip him off that something is coming. Okay?"

A chorus of agreement filled the air.

I continued, "We need a plan to not end up in trouble. I need time to think."

I looked each one in the eyes.

"We must not let anyone know what we are doing. You all can continue to associate, but you don't know me. We will be strangers that meet and talk, nothing else. Understand?"

I received another round of agreement.

"If Keagey bothers you, call the police or whatever you usually do. Only call me as a last resort. For this to work, you can't let anyone know about me. When I contact you, I will say the *Lakhota* man's greeting '*Hau*' to let you know it's me. It means both 'hello' and 'how are things going?' "

"Like the Hawaiian word '*aloha*'?" asked Maria.

"Yes, except we don't use it for good-byes."

I stood and walked to a drawer in my utility closet. I returned with four cheap cell-phones. I passed them out.

"Here, take these. These are throw-aways. The phone number is on the piece of masking tape on the phone. Use these for our business until we are finished. When we are finished, soak them overnight in bleach before you discard them in a public trashcan. Don't act surprised when I call. I will tell

28

you when and where we can meet, or ask you to pick a place and time. Never discuss anything over the phone."

I smiled the grin of *Iktomi*, the Trickster.

"You will have your revenge and solution."

Rita must have sensed that I was finished. She stood up, triggering the same action in the others.

"Is it okay if I use Rita as my primary contact?" I asked.

They all nodded.

"Then I suggest you go to lunch, but don't celebrate too much until Keagey's been dealt with."

I started for the doorway that led back into the *tipi* dome. I ignored the conversations behind me as they followed. The view through the open windows reminded me of the Great Spirit's kindness. I walked in his beauty. I walked in his strength. As I walked, I radiated his peace, painting the walls with love.

My blue-jay friend was in a tree near one of the open windows.

"Are they leaving? Their big box beast smells."

I chuckled then spoke in the ancient tongue, "Yes, Winged Brother, they leave."

"Good."

He flicked his tail and flew away. Kelly caught up to me and touched my arm.

"Did you just talk to that bird?"

"Yes, Little Flower, but don't tell anyone. They might doubt your sanity."

"I can hardly believe I saw it."

"Perhaps your world changed a little today."

I said the eastern sky blessing in my head and opened the front door. Kelly hung back looking out the window. Rita stepped forward and shook my hand.

"It's good to meet you. When will you call?"

"Soon, Spring Blossom. Be patient."

Maria shook my hand.

"Thank you."

I let a small smile come to my lips and eyes. She smiled back then left. Kelly stepped in and hugged me. Lisa joined the hug, then began to cry. She hadn't said a word the whole time she was here. I put my arms around their shoulders and connected to the hilltop stone under my home, drawing the ancient strength of the Stone People up and around us. The women jumped a little when the energy bathed us. I spoke into Kelly's hair.

"Don't worry, Little Flower. The Great Father's strength is now on us. All will be well in time."

Lisa leaned back, her eyes sparkling from more than tears. She tried to speak. After a failed attempt, her mouth silently formed the words "Thank you" before she stepped outside. Kelly looked into my eyes.

"Are you a wizard?"

"No. I'm a disabled telephone lineman."

"And I'm a warrior princess."

"Yes, I know you are. Now go. I have research to do before I can make our plan."

She stepped away, but turned back.

"Are you married?

"No. Now go."

I turned to plan how John Keagey would beg for death before he went to prison.

30

Chapter Two

John Keagey's silver spoon had fed his sense of security for long enough. Soon he would know the taste of fear. I needed a plan to expose him, while protecting us, and needed it soon.

I stepped inside, went to the middle dome, and crossed to my office. Two windowed exterior walls and four interior walls enclosed a hexagon-shaped space lined by shelves over a wide counter that circled the room, even under the windows. The shelves held more artifacts and fetishes than books. The tabletop doubled as a desk and workbench. I used the part under the northwest exterior wall as my desk. On the eastern interior wall counter sat computers that hosted part of the Indian Heritage Web-Ring.

I tapped a phone number from memory. At the beep, I pressed my phone number then cradled the hand set, ending the call. My spirit guide, Raven Who Hops, said my nickname.

"*Mahto*."

"*Hau*, Raven."

He became visible on the windowsill.

"*Hau*. So, what do you see ahead?"

"The renegade is protected and grows arrogant in his imagined security. His relatives' misuse of power disrupts the present and disturbs the future."

Ever the tutor, Raven asked, "What must be done?"

"Harmony must be restored. The power must be rebalanced."

"You are learning well. Can you see how this will help you complete your training to reach the second level of Stone Dreaming?"

Raven loved pop quizzes.

"No."

"Center and listen."

I emptied my basket of expectations and opened my heart to learn. It came to me.

"Before I can progress, I need to do more than just understand the strength of the Stone People. I must learn to use it."

"Yes. The power of the Stone People will help you remove the renegade's obstruction to the flow of *skan*. power. The universe must flow smoothly, without turbulence."

"Yeah, eddies in the space time continuum and all."

He cocked his head but didn't laugh.

"We will talk later. You have a call."

He hopped from the windowsill to the ground, then toward the trees before hopping into flight and vanishing. The phone rang.

"*Hau.*"

"You beeped. What's up."

It was Roy Campagnella.

"You set me up on a blind date but didn't tell me."

"I figured your raven friend would make sure that you were home when they came by."

"You presume much."

"Yeah, I know. It's a problem I need to work on. So, what do you want?"

I grunted.

"I ought to count *coup* on you. You know it's against *Lakhota* custom to tell strangers where people live."

"You think you can hit me and dance away before I smack you back? I'm not easy to count *coup* on. Besides, Rita's no stranger. We've been friends for a million years."

"Wow, you look only half your age."

"Wise-ass. So, you want the skinny or what?"

"We should eat together," I said.

"I can get free this afternoon."

"How about some buffalo?"

"Sure. We swept there a few days ago. There aren't any listening devices to spoil our fun."

Chapter Three

The steady stream of tourists through Ellicott City obliterated shopkeeper memories of faces. The town is as anonymous as a public telephone booth. It was a perfect place to meet Roy.

Ellicott City is closer to Baltimore than Washington DC and looks older than it is. The small downtown of Civil War era buildings is perched on hillsides uplifted by an ancient granite intrusion. Huge slabs of it lay exposed on the slopes of Main Street. Gentrification had given the tiny town a facelift, filling the old buildings with artful and clever boutiques. The tiny theater became a gift shop, while a tribe of antique dealers filled the furniture store with consignment merchandise. The rest of the town followed suit.

The Ellicott Mills Brewing Company is in the old hardware store. I don't drink, but it serves buffalo steak. They cook them right, so they're tender, not chewy. Their buffalo stew is almost as good as my mom's.

Roy and his crew were regulars, so they made sure there were no listening devices. With the National Security Agency and the Army Intelligence headquarters nearby, Roy's sweeps appeared to be legitimate. The wait-staff was too busy to remember faces.

I was already seated on the first floor with a pot of tea and a steak with vegetables when Roy walked in. He saw me and walked over, waving to the bartender on the way. The bartender called out .

"Marzen?"

"Yeah, thanks."

"*How*, Chief. I'm only staying for a beer."

"*Hau*. You still don't say it right. *Hau*, not 'how'."

"Sure Chief, like you say. So, were the women hot or what?"

"They are hurt. Are you blind to their pain?"

"No, but I'm not blind to their beauty either. I wish I could have helped them, so I could let them express their gratitude, but I can't get involved in any domestic situations."

Roy cared; it was in his eyes. I let it go.

"I think of them as my sisters."

"I thought you would say that." He paused. "So, you took the job?"

"Yes."

"And now you want the skinny?"

"Yes. Here comes your beer."

Roy and the bartender exchanged greetings as he put a pint of amber ale in front of Roy then left.

"When I gave Rita your name, I knew you'd do it. What do you want to know?"

"Who and where is this Keagey punk?"

"I did some checking around when Rita asked me to have it done. Keagey's not a good chip off the old block. The Kinkaeds are all Harvard Law, but little Johnny's a trade-school dropout. He does something at a little ISP and web-site company in Annapolis called 'An Apple Less Web Designs'."

35

"An Internet Service Provider?"

"Yeah. The only reason little Johnny works there is the Kinkaeds pumped a pot of money into it."

"Is he the boss?"

"Are you kidding? He couldn't manage a ménage-à-trois. They stuck little Johnny in Annapolis so his aunt could keep an eye on him from the Governor's Mansion."

He grinned.

"What happened with the case?"

"The DA rushed it to trial before the case was solid. He claimed it was so it wouldn't affect the election, but the fix was in to get a trial that Keagey could beat and not wait for the evidence to make one that he couldn't."

"Were there other victims?"

"The scuttlebutt guess is six victims who haven't come forward. He must be fixated on some woman in his past, because he keeps to the same physical type."

"Did the police have any hard evidence?"

"His attorneys convinced the jury that it was inconclusive, that it didn't physically tie him directly to the victims. After that, it was 'he said, she said' with a Kinkaed versus the unwashed. His lawyers smeared the women as gold-digging trailer-trash."

"The police didn't find his stash?"

"Maybe he didn't keep souvenirs."

"The women said he takes panties." I paused. "I need to know; did he do it?"

"Oh, yeah. The cops and the lab guys are sure it's him."

"He's probably just a weak, spineless coward who can't get a date, so he plans and rehearses. Only then would he feel powerful enough to overcome petite women. He needs a stash to feed his fantasy of power."

"My, my, my. You've got a hard-on to get little Johnny.

"He perverts the path to the future and disturbs spiritual harmony. He is an obstacle that must be removed."

It was Roy's turn to grin like *Iktomi* the Trickster.

"I knew you were going to go savage on him."

"Perhaps you don't know me as well as you think you do."

"Yeah, yeah. Do you need anything? A safe-house, maybe?"

"No. I can set this one up as clean as the Little Yellowstone River on a lazy summer's day."

"Great." He looked at his watch. "Hey! I have to run." He downed the last of his pint. "Good luck, Bear-man."

"Walk in beauty, Roy."

On his way out, he put some cash on the bar, and exchanged a few words with the bartender.

I finished my meal in silence. My waitress brought the check. I left her a good tip. When we give, we signal *Wakan Tanka* that we are available for blessing.

I stepped into the Maryland twilight. The smell of auto and diesel fumes was heavy in the air. It reminded me of what I had left in the Dakotas. Back on the Rez, we had clean air and water, but also a 90% unemployment rate, rampant alcoholism, obesity, and diabetes. We had swallowed so many *wasiçiu* lies that we had become fat and sick from them.

37

I walked to my Jeep Cherokee. It was turquoise-sky-blue — the color of *skan:* power. I'd paid extra for a tan leather interior. I drove home, parked at the bottom of the hill, and walked up. The animals and I didn't need to smell it on top of our hill.

I walked through my house, opening the windows in the main dome, through the kitchen in the second dome, and hit the answering machine in the office. I tapped the volume up then continued to the smallest dome. It was divided into four bedrooms off a central hallway. I used the first one on the right, but I slept in the *tipi*. The bed was comfortable; I just preferred *tatanka*, buffalo, fur on the floor. Perhaps my clothes enjoyed a modern closet and dresser. While I undressed and selected a robe, I listened.

"Ben, This is Rita. I know you said not to call, but I had to. Thank you for meeting with us today."

A chorus of background voices sang out, "Thank you!"

Rita continued.

"We feel as if we have hope again. Please contact me soon. Goodbye."

It was the only message. That was fine with me. I needed solitude tonight to dream with the Stone People. I had questions for Raven Who Hops. I needed time to listen to the quiet depths of *Wakan Tanka*. Tonight would be a very busy night of stillness.

Chapter Four

I found the center of my peace. I let my soul feel the winds of time. War clouds were gathering in the future. I would be ready for them.

I parked in front of Shears Locks Combs in Bowie. It was just down Route 3 from Stonehenge Gardens. They supply the construction and landscaping trades with interesting stones from all over the world. Several of them were now in my yard and some are shelved in my office.

I got out of my Jeep and walked into the hair salon. The reception area had four large comfy chairs with magazine-covered tables in between. The chairs were covered in a rose, floral print. Mirrors in gold picture frames hung on light teal walls. A Bentwood coat rack stood by the door. The cash register sat on a glass-topped counter that displayed hair-care products. A vase of white carnations sat on a short column by the right wall.

Behind the counter, the cutting room floor was clean, except for right around Rita, who was working on a woman in her chair. They looked up as I entered. Rita started to greet me, but I interrupted.

"Hi. A friend said to ask for Rita. He said that she would know what my hair needs."

"I'm Rita. What would you like?"

"My friend said that if you just washed my hair, you'd know what it needs. Can I have an appointment?"

The other hairdresser chimed in.

"I'm not busy. I can take you right now."

Her look might have meant she wanted to wash more than my hair, but she was probably just looking to drum up some business.

"Thank you kindly, ma'am, but my friend insisted that I see Rita."

Rita spoke to her customer.

"I'll be right back, hon."

She walked to the desk near the door and ran her finger down the schedule book's open page.

"I'm clear after two. Is that all right?"

"Sure. That's fine."

"What's your name?"

"Ben."

"Okay, Ben, I'll see you."

I left the shop and drove to the dip in MD-450 between Bowie and Crownsville. I parked on the side of the road, took a bottle of water from the case in the back of the Jeep, and walked south along the trail. I didn't have far to go. A few minutes hike along a wooded path brought me to the bank of the South River, under an ancient red oak. The trail's end was a small piece of land jutting into the water, offering a nice view.

I sat with my back to an oak Tall Brother and looked around. The opposite shore was about ninety feet away. The water stretched a half-mile upstream to the left, before disappearing around a tree-lined bend. Downstream, the opposite shore became more distant as it stretched away. My eyes tracked downstream, considering the little tributaries that cut through stands of trees, automatically estimating which one would have the best fishing.

No urban noise reached my ears. An occasional car could be heard on the rural Route 450 to the north where I'd parked. This land was zoned agricultural, but I wondered how long the politicians would resist the developers' bribes. Streamside town-homes would fetch a lot of money.

Cool draughts of air sluiced south through the channel. Alone, I checked my watch. It was ten till noon. I would wait here. I took a pouch of pemmican from my pocket and bit off a chunk. The flavors rushed around my mouth making the saliva flow. It was my own recipe.

I buy my *tatanka,* buffalo, from a rancher named John Kelloms on Maryland's Eastern Shore. He lets me hunt, kill, and dress the bull on his property. *Lakhota* hunters are with their food-animal as it dies. We hold his head in our hands and look into his eyes. We bless him and thank him for allowing his life to pass into ours, for feeding our family with his body. We breathe his last breath into our own lungs. In respect of his sacrifice, we use every part of the *tatanka* as either food, clothing, or tools.

Frank Rosensteel, a meat-cutter in Baltimore, helps me process the *tatanka.* We grind the leg muscles fine and mix it with mashed blueberries, cranberries, minced apples, salt, pepper, and a bit of white sage. I spread it flat on dehydrator drying racks on my enclosed porch. The finished pemmican is stored in my freezer with the other cuts of meat.

41

Some of it hangs in my *tipi* as traditional food. I eat pemmican during my seasons of prayer. I replenish the *tipi*'s stock of meat from the freezer as needed, but my solitary appetite hardly makes a dent in the food provided by a single *tatanka*.

Grandfather, the Great Spirit, is kind. I have plenty to eat. I have time to tan the hides and to make moccasins and clothing from the hides that don't become bedding or *tipi* covers. While my fingers are busy, a lot of prayer can be made.

I drank some water and chewed, re-hydrating the meat. Pemmican is so much better than the *wasiçiu* beef jerky with all its chemicals. Once, I tried some of it. The label said "pemmican," but the list of ingredients looked like it contained ground-up *wasiçiu* government agencies: BHA, BHT, were there as preservatives, and maybe dehydrated BATF, BIA, FDA, and some powdered IRS were in there, too.

A breeze stirred the surface of the water. A fish jumped and caught a bug. Ripples spread out on the surface, heading for the distant shores. Even the simple act of a fish feeding sent subtle pulses of impact in all directions. How could people imagine that their actions don't affect others?

I needed to attune to my path. I needed to sensitize myself to the gentle guiding presence of *Wakan Tanka* and his power spirit *Taku Skanskan*. I placed my water on the ground and purified my mind.

I had been learning new rituals. I thought I'd try one. I began to sing a soft summoning song. I heard motion in the tree above me. I ignored the two squirrels that ran over to look. Squirrels are cute and funny, but they sure put the "ding" in "dingbat."

42

Their appearance wasn't proof that I was performing the summoning ritual correctly.

With my mind, I reached deep into the earth. I felt an underground stream. Water is stronger than rock. I drew strength from it and let it flow through me. I chose not to broadcast, but to simply resonate in it. Soon the summons saturated my being.

I sensed other animals. Without moving, I opened my eyes to slits. Across the water, a doe and two fawns came out of the trees and down to the water. While the children drank, the mother watched me.

I moved my eyes right. Two beavers poked their heads above water. One floated on his back while the other climbed on top. For a moment, the second beaver's head was about fourteen inches above the water and looking at me. I did not move.

I continued to resonate with the summoning rite. A presence to my right made a small cough. I opened my eyes and turned my head. One of the beavers smacked his tail before they were both gone. I continued to turn my head. A red fox spoke.

"What do you want? I was sleeping."

"I am sorry, Red Mother. I was practicing my prayers and spoke the summoning ritual."

"Yes, yes. Well, it worked. What do you want?"

"Nothing, Red Mother. I was only practicing. I learned it recently and wanted to see if I could use it."

"You woke me for that?"

"I am sorry, Red Mother. I didn't think."

The red fox sat.

"Never mind. It is good to talk to a two-legged. You aren't as ignorant as your brothers."

"I am a star-child of The Great Father and Earth Mother. We are *Lakhota*. The ignorant ones are not our lodge brothers. We call them *wasiçiu*, one of our terms for 'strange ones'."

"They certainly are strange."

"Yes," I said.

"If there is nothing you need, then I will go back to sleep."

"Thank you, Red Mother. In the future, I will only summon if I need council."

"If I hear, I will come." She cocked her head. "It has been longer than can be said since one of your people spoke to mine. Why is that?"

"The *wasiçiu* drove the Red Nations from the land. The *wasiçiu* know nothing of the ancient earth tongue."

"Where you live, do your kind and mine talk?"

"Only a few of us. Most of my people are sick with *wasiçiu* ways. I am one who hopes to heal them."

"Good luck, Red Brother. The other two-legged are evil and it will take strong medicine to defeat them."

"I don't think they mean to be evil. They are simply ignorant and self-centered."

"Maybe you know them better than we do. We just avoid them. Wait till I tell my kit-brother that I spoke to a two-legged. He won't believe it."

"The *wasiçiu* don't believe we talk to animals. Sadly, a lot of *Lakhota* don't believe it either."

"It was good to meet you, Red Brother. Walk in beauty."

"Walk in peace, Red Mother."

"You know our customs? Now, I know kit-brother won't believe me."

She snuffled in laughter as she trotted into the woods. I checked my watch. It was 1:00. It always seemed as if I had been in a time-warp when I was done meditating.

I was sweaty and hungry. I had no more pemmican, so I told my hunger to be quiet. The first of the *Lakhota* ways — denial of the body — is to strengthen the spirit. Life is hard. That is why we honor bravery.

I stood, picked up my things, then walked back to the car. I smiled at the bass that swam in the lake, keeping pace with me. I wished for them to have many bugs over their water tonight. *Taku Skanskan* would have to grant it; I did not know any bug-calling rituals.

When I got to my Jeep Cherokee, I took a satchel from the back seat. A small medicine pouch provided powdered sweetgrass and cornflower that I rubbed between my palms, warming and crushing it further, releasing the fragrance. I rubbed it into my underarms, then wiped my face and hands with a cloth before wiping off the herbs. Placing the towel on the seat to dry, I started the car, turning it west toward Bowie.

It was now the time of the beginning.

There was no turning back.

Chapter Five

We're alone," Rita said. "I gave Rose the afternoon off. Tuesdays are always slow. We won't be bothered."

"That's good, but just in case someone comes, maybe you should do my hair?"

"I'd love to. Bring your long hair over here."

She took my hand and led me to the rear of the shop. She pushed me toward a chair with a sink behind it.

"Sit."

She put a towel under my neck before removing the black elastic band from my braid.

"So, what's the plan? When do we kill the bastard?"

"I have no plan at the moment. I am still studying my enemy."

She stopped unbraiding my hair.

"But I do have some general thoughts."

I tried to sit up and look at her, but she pushed me back down.

"Be still and talk. Let me do your hair."

"We cannot kill him. His people would require someone to punish."

"If we can't kill him, what can we do?"

"He stole power from you. To reclaim your lives, that power must be taken back. We must act in such a way that leaves him and his people in a condition that they either cannot or will not continue to escalate this war."

"I like how you call it a 'war'."

"The real conflict is larger than your battle with John Keagey. Every action and choice in life creates the future. Through many means, the Kinkaeds have accumulated wealth and power. Their fortune started with profits from running booze during Prohibition. In other words, from illegal activity. Which they're still apparently practicing. In any event, alcohol was one of the things that helped to remove Indians from having any say in the future of America or the planet."

With my hair loose in the sink, Rita turned on the water, adjusted the temperature, and wet my hair.

"The Kinkaeds misuse their power, which perverts the future. They're more concerned with staying in power than with anyone's health, especially with women who are raped and violated or with the Indians on Reservations."

She stopped the water and applied shampoo.

"My life is dedicated to reversing that inequity," I said. "Warrior Priests guard the earth's balance to protect earth's future."

"And I thought you were just a pretty face."

I leaned my head further back and saw her large grin. I chose to follow her lead into lightness.

"Our paths are linked; I must help you win your battle so that I may also fight my war."

"What are we going to do?"

"We must encourage him to make moves that put him in a place where we can spring a trap, leaving him no place to turn. We must also make sure that his people don't, won't, or cannot help him."

Rita rinsed my hair.

"How're you going to do that?"

"I don't know yet."

She began a second lather. Her hands felt wonderful on my scalp. I became aware of her smell and the swell of breast that bumped my shoulder. I reminded myself that though I was a man with lusts and passions like every other man, it was more important practice denial of the flesh in order to serve *Wakan Tanka* and my people than to serve my little big man.

"Maria said something about 'the women we know of'. Were there other rape victims?"

"Probably."

"Was he on trial for any of them?"

"I only know about the ones in the trial that he beat."

"You're yanking on my hair."

"Oh, sorry."

She let go.

"About your hair — what do you wash it with?"

"Soap."

"What kind of soap?"

"Dish soap."

"Dish soap? The kind you wash dishes with?"

"Yes."

"Dish soap? That's not for hair."

"Aren't all liquid soaps the same?"

"I sure hope you know more about traps than you do about soaps. You can't use a harsh detergent like that as a shampoo. It strips out the hair's natural oil and moisture. Color, too. No wonder you have split-ends."

"Nobody notices. I keep it in a ponytail or a braid."

"A frizzy ponytail or braid. Just because you don't hear any comments doesn't mean people don't notice."

"That bad, huh?"

"Your hair could be a great asset. If you got it into condition, women would pay you a lot of attention. They'd want to touch your hair to see what it feels like."

"That is more distraction than I can afford right now," I said, all the while knowing I wanted some of that distraction and attention.

"At least let me trim the ends so that it doesn't look like a bad perm. Besides, that's our cover, right? You were recommended to me. To do your hair."

She pulled on my shoulder. As I sat up, she put the towel over my head and began drying my hair. After she'd finished, she tossed the towel into a white canvas basket on wheels, and lightly slapped me on the back of the shoulder.

"Come on, Chief. I'm going to cut your hair."

"Cut my hair?"

"Just a trim."

"A very slight trim."

"My specialty, Chief."

Rita led me forward to her chair. Its vinyl felt cool on my arms.

"Now, what were you saying about Maria and her comment?"

49

"Just that if we could tie him to other rapes, then he could go to trial on the new charges. I need to understand why the DA lost. Then I will know what I need to find for the DA on next case."

"Apparently, the jury felt that the he didn't prove the case. The way the jury understood it, the DNA could have belonged to a lot of people, so the fit for Keagey was a coincidence."

"Let me guess. The defense made sure that nobody on the jury had any science background."

"The jury foreman was a green grocer. I know more chemistry than he does. Two of the others didn't finish high school."

"That doesn't mean they're not smart," I said.

"It means they're not educated."

"They might read on their own."

"After the first day, most of them slept or yawned constantly during the DNA evidence."

"That's not good."

"No. The jury believed Keagey's lawyer. All the evidence was circumstantial. Nothing tied Keagey to the crimes. They admitted that he'd been at the scene of the crimes, but not on any specific dates. His being there didn't tie to the rapes."

She was combing my hair pretty fast and hard.

"My questions seem to be upsetting you. Let's change the subject while you're working on me."

"Was I tugging?"

"Yes. A little."

She laughed that musical laugh again. She leaned around the back of the chair to look at me.

"By the way, Chief, who cuts your hair?"

"I do."

50

"I should have known. What do you use? A dull knife?"

"I sharpen it before I use it."

"You're joking, right?"

"No, I always sharpen my knife before I use it."

Her laughter was like the song of birds. It was good to hear her laugh. Good to hear that, after what she'd been through, she could laugh.

"No wonder your hair's so ragged," she said. "Next time you cut it, use a straight razor."

"I can't. It has to be my knife for the rituals. A straight razor is foreign to me, so it can't be used."

"I'll be using scissors and a straight razor. Are both of those all right?"

"Yes."

I paused to create a mental shift in our conversation. A shift in our relationship. Rita combed, separated, and trimmed tiny sections of my hair.

"When we trigger our trap, you all will need alibis. They have to be stronger than stone. Do all of you have someone that will work with me to set up personal alibis?"

"Yes. We've already closed ranks once. Before the troubles, we all had a lot of friends. Afterwards, most of them dropped us like we had a contagious disease. That's how we found out who our true friends were."

"People are that way. They avoid things that are too hard for them to handle."

Rita came around from the back of the chair and looked at me, her head cocked, comb in one hand and scissors in the other.

"What did they have to 'handle'? We were the ones who got raped."

"A lot of people desperately cling to their illusion of safety. The rapes exposed their delusion."

"But why'd they dump us? We didn't do anything."

"No. But your rapes shredded their imagined security. They chose fantasy and illusion over the flesh-and-blood reality. Those people you thought were your friends are poorer for it."

She retuned to trimming my hair. Because she had the chair turned away from the huge mirrors as she worked, I couldn't tell how much of my hair she was cutting off. When I tried to look down at the floor to see the falling pieces, she put her hand on the top of my head.

"Don't move."

I kept still.

"If it makes you feel any better, Rita, those people who withdrew from you and the others probably didn't do it consciously. They were reacting to their unexamined emotions, not to their intellectual processes."

The comb jerked a little in my hair.

"I feel a lot better, Chief. Really, I do. That makes being dumped by your friends so much easier."

I stayed silent and still.

"Would you like to cut my hair when you're less angry?"

"When am I going to feel less angry? What's the matter? Are you afraid I'm going to cut it too short?"

"Your anger might make you … less attentive to your task."

She stopped, and I heard her take a loud, deep breath. She held it a few seconds before she released it. After she did that, she began combing and cutting my hair again, more slowly.

"Do you have relatives or close friends whom I can draw on?"

"Yes," she said.

I listened for a few moments to the cutting of my hair — the *wasiçiu* way of cutting hair. The clip of the scissors followed the comb's almost silent gliding through my hair as she separated it for cutting.

"We must be better prepared than our enemy. We must anticipate his options and eliminate them. We must make sure that it can't be proven that you were involved."

"You sound as if you're good at this revenge stuff."

"It's not revenge. This is justice. We will restore the balance of good and evil that the Kinkaeds have upset."

She started to blow-dry my hair.

"Please, don't dry it."

She put the blow dryer back into its chair holster.

"Should I just comb and braid it then?"

"Yes, please."

As she parted my hair into three sections, pulled it back over my ears and shoulders, I could feel her fingers on my neck for a moment. Her voice sounded thoughtful as she gently braided my hair.

"I've always believed that taking the law into your own hands was wrong."

"That's because your culture is based on ideas like Hobbes' theory of the social contract."

"What's that?"

"Hobbes said that the government makes a deal with the citizens. If the people surrender some freedoms, then the government will protect the people's remaining freedoms. If you surrender the freedom to walk anywhere you please, then the government will protect your freedom to not have your home invaded by someone who wants to walk in on you."

"What was your major in college? Philosophy? Political Science?"

"I never went to college, but I've read many books. I study your culture to know my enemy."

"Your enemy?" she said, stopping her movement. "Am I your enemy?"

"No. You are my friend."

"Do you only hate white people you haven't met?"

I chuckled.

"I don't hate anyone. *Wasiçiu* society — or more precisely, the government and their policies — is my enemy. It's the enemy of many people. For instance, *wasiçiu* ways were used to set Keagey free. *Lakhota* ways would never have allowed that."

"Then it's okay to take the law into our own hands?"

"That depends on who you are. You are in your culture. I am from mine. "

"And?"

"That's the social contract. Your 'government of the people, by the people, for the people' is a codified version of the contract. They 'govern with the consent of the people'."

54

"What does that have to do with us?"

"When the people believe that the government is not protecting their designated freedoms, then they believe that the government has breached the social contract. The government's inaction forces citizens to protect their own freedoms. By twisting the law to protect only the rich and powerful, the government breaks the contract with its people."

"I've been thinking things like that ever since the trial ended. And this guy — Hobbes? — he thought of it a long time ago. And I thought I was coming up with something 'original' and 'ground-breaking'."

"You were. And you did it without any help from Hobbes. That shows how intuitive and smart you are."

Her fingers brushed my back occasionally as she deftly did my hair. I could see Rita's face in the large mirror in front of me. Her face remained pensive.

"We are products of our cultures," I said. "Anyone from your society would feel that way. Your government let you down. It manipulates the law to make people do what it wants. In your grandparent's time, the people were citizens. Now you are sheep sheared by taxation to support the ruling class in luxury."

"That's the truth," said Rita, glancing around at her shop.

"The government has become a house of tyrants which rewards itself and its supporters, but use, abuse, and neglect the rest of us."

"You're saying that since the government, meaning the Kinkaeds, manipulated the trial to get the 'not guilty' verdict, the government broke its contract with me and the others that Keagy raped?"

"Correct."

"Which means we have the right to extract our vengeance?"

"Justice."

"What does your culture say about taking the law into your own hands?"

"My people never let go of the law. Look at when Sitting Bull led us against Custer. All he could do was say 'the US Army must be stopped. Tomorrow I will fight them.' He could not order anyone into battle. If the *Lakhota* didn't want to fight, Sitting Bull would have stood alone at Custer's Last Stand. Everyone had to make up their own mind. Even at the most crucial times, we don't surrender our freedoms."

"But you're on reservations. Didn't you join our social contract?"

"We are the only nation to have forced the US Government to sue for peace to end a war. We signed treaties agreeing to their surrender if they would leave us alone on our lands. We won the war, but the wasiçiu won the peace. Those treaties were violated more times than an Army Post prostitute."

"So your contract is void too?"

"The deal is off between the US Government and me."

"Are you an anarchist?"

"No. I just want the government to take their controls off my people, so that we can actually have the freedoms and protections that are ours by right and treaty."

"Like what?" said Rita as she finished braiding my hair and tied the end.

"A US Federal Judge named Royce Lambert forced the government to admit that it had abused its custody of our tribal lands. In violation of our treaty, they allowed corporations over the last 125 years to extract more than $240 billion of mineral and timber wealth from our sacred lands without paying us."

"Did the judge make the government give it back?" she said as she took the protective covering from around my shoulders and shook my hair from it.

"No. Despite our protests, the BIA approved the plundering ..."

"The B-I-...?"

"Bureau of Indian Affairs."

"I didn't know there was such a thing."

"There is. But the royalties owed to us by the corporations disappeared into people's pockets. The GAO estimates that the *wasiçiu* government stole more than $14 billion from our trust funds."

"No wonder you hate the government."

She took a broom and began sweeping up the sections of hair she'd trimmed. It didn't look like she'd taken too much off the length, but piled together, it seemed like a lot of hair.

"So, here I am — a *Lakhota* priest fighting injustice where I can. I practice a very focused form of civil disobedience. I protect women and children. I protect the weak from the abuses of the mighty. I attempt to push the world into spiritual balance, correcting our path into the future. I look for every opportunity to force the US Government closer to honoring their treaties with the Red Nations. Keagey is a small step, but it's one step in the right direction."

She stopped sweeping the hair into the dust-pan and looked at me.

"Is that why you're helping us?"

"It's not the only reason," I said, standing up.

"Too bad there aren't more like you."

"There are, but we are too few to make much impact."

She dumped the hair into a trashcan near the back of the salon, lowered the chair with the foot-pump, then straightened the counter in front of the mirror where she'd been cutting my hair. She put the comb, the straight razor, and the scissors in a line.

"My elders and peers back on the Rez think I'm renegade."

"Why? I'd think they'd all want to be like you."

"They don't approve of my actions, but I can't just sit on the Rez and pray. Or drink. I am content to fight the battle in my own way."

Rita handed me a mirror to see her finished work.

"I'm glad you're on my side."

"I will always be on this side of the struggle."

I used the hand mirror to view my hair in the wall mirror.

"It looks good. What do I owe you?"

"You're going to fix Keagey's wagon for free and you want me to charge you for a shampoo and a trim?"

"Yes. I insist. How much?"

"A plan by next week."

"I might have a plan sooner."

"Then that'll be my tip."

Rita walked to a shelf and took a bottle. She put it in my hand.

"No more dish soap."

"Okay."

"If I catch you with scruffy hair, I'll ... I'll ... scalp you. Oh, my God, you know that was just a joke, don't you?"

I laughed while I walked out to my Jeep. As I backed out, I saw her watching through her glass door. Rita would have her plan. I vowed that this abuser and his family would learn that women were not property to be violated, destroyed, and then discarded as worthless.

Chapter Six

I needed information and help getting it. I needed to know the sorts of things that aren't found in libraries or on the Internet. I needed Max. He had access to records systems not open to the public.

Most people don't know that the bail bondsman lends his own money when he posts the court-required bond. To stay in business, he had to know what people owned and owed so he could decide how to lend his money. If the suspect skips, the bondsman may have to eat a loss. They are very clever about discovering assets owned by their clients and information needed for a skip-trace.

I met Max when someone I knew needed to post bail. Since then, I had done some work for him. He had a small office on West Street in Annapolis. I parked behind the open-pit Greek restaurant, then walked around to the front of the building.

I rang the bell and in a moment, the door buzzed loudly. I pulled it open and entered. I heard Max's gravel voice from the back.

"Here comes trouble. I'll be out in a minute, Chief."

I stood in his dingy waiting room. Clients who hoped you could arrange liberty from lock-up must not care if your office wasn't bright and cheerful. Max covered his walls with pictures of him and his friends with weapons. There was a framed set of Max at the target range. The left picture was a tight group of bullet holes on a torso silhouette target and Max with an AK-47. The right picture showed another tight target grouping and him holding a Glock 9mm.

The rest of the pictures were primordial. There were a few of him and his friends handgun-hunting wild boars on Catalina Island. There were pictures of them bagging deer, elk, and waterfowl with rifles and shotguns. If a picture is worth a thousand words, these pictures said a lot about Max and his friends: they could track down a bail-jumper and kill if required. I hoped it helped Max's business.

"How you been, Ugly?"

"Better than you, Double-Ugly."

"It's not hunting season. What're you up to?"

"Nothing. And you have a really bad memory today."

"Gotcha. One of your justice-for-the-little-guy kicks. What don't I know?"

"John Keagey."

"Kinkaed cousin. On trial a few months back. Serial rapes. 'Not guilty' on a bunch of technicalities. Money changed hands. Promises were made. Not that I'd know anything about those kinda things. Ah, rich and powerful. Must be nice. You never can do anything wrong."

Max went to a coffee pot and poured a cup. He offered it to me. I declined. He took a pull from the mug.

"You taking on the Kinkaeds?"

"Someone should."

"The DA did. He lost."

"What do you expect from a DA who's in the same political party as the Kinkaeds?"

"Figured that on your own, did ya?"

I raised the right corner of my mouth. Max gave me his whole grin. It looked five inches wide.

"What information do you not want me to get for you?"

"Everything."

"Whoa. That's a helluva lot of stuff I'll have to forget," he said before his grin gave way to a raised eyebrow. "I won't be getting a call from jail, will I?"

"I am a ghost who scares a child."

"Sound of the wind in the trees, eh?" said Max. "Like the Bernadette Russo case?"

"Don't recognize the name," I said, my face as relaxed as a sleeping cat's.

"I can meet you for dinner. Next door around six okay?"

"Sure."

"See you, Ugly."

"Okay, Double-Ugly."

I left as Max went into the back. I walked to my car and drove to Quiet Waters Park. It's a huge greenspace just south of Annapolis, with a lot of forest trails and a panoramic view of the South River joining the Chesapeake Bay. The park's amphitheater hosts outdoor concerts in nice weather.

I showed the guard my season pass and drove to the southwest lot. I parked near the trailhead and walked into the woods.

"Raven Who Hops, may we speak?"

I spoke in *Lakhota* in case anyone was around. If someone heard me, they might think I was chanting to myself.

"*Mahto.*"

I turned to see my spirit guide hopping on the trail toward me, then up into a tree branch.

"You would talk?"

"Yes. Thank you for coming."

"What is on your mind?"

"I believe that I know my plan, but I don't see how to use the power of the Stone People in my task."

"Think. What are the first ways of the *Lakhota* and of the Stone People?"

"The first of the *Lakhota* ways is denial of the flesh. The first of the Stone People ways is impermeability."

"How could they go together?"

"I don't know."

"If I tell you, then the knowledge will not be yours. To lead your people, you need your own connection to eternal knowledge."

"Can you suggest a meditation?"

"Enlightenment must rise from within to connect you to the great mystery. When the time is right, you will know what to do."

He cocked his head.

"This is a good time for you to practice some medicine. There is someone here who needs help. Find him and do what you think is best."

He dropped from the tree into a graceful glide to the ground, where he took two hops and jumped into nothingness.

I closed my eyes and rotated a slow sensing around the circle of winds. When I aligned on the Red Road, the road which goes north to south, my mind pulled toward the south. When I aligned with the Black Road, from east to west, my feet seemed to sink into the earth, feeling free when I rotated off-axis. Throughout my circle, I felt for a calling. I found one to the north of me. I focused on it and opened my eyes. I began walking. The calling led me to a large oak. I stood close and was still. I tried the few words of the trees that I knew.

"Tall Brother, may I help?"

"Are you a priest?"

"I walk The Way, but I am at the beginning."

"You will do."

At least that is what I thought he said. I knew so little tree speech. I repeated a phrase I knew.

"May I help?"

The tree spoke at length with me. I guessed at the problem.

"Tall Brother, I know only a few words of your tongue. If I understand you, you are having trouble breathing?"

"Yes."

"I will see what I can do."

I looked up and down the tree. In its crown, I saw a tangle of vines spreading over the top branches.

"You are covered with vines. Their leaves overlay yours. You can't eat or breathe."

"I thought that I could feel something keeping my branches from proper motion when I dance to the windsongs. Would you take them down?"

I pulled my knife and stepped to his trunk. There were a dozen Virginia creeper and furry poison ivy vines clinging to the bark of the old tree. I began to cut gaps in the vines. The creepers oozed while the poison ivy sap flowed from the cuts. I was careful to avoid it.

"Tall Brother, I cut the stalks of the vines that covered your crown. This year you will be able to eat and breathe freely. You will dance to the windsongs."

"Thank you. "

"Thank you for letting me help. You have helped me along my path."

"I sense Stone People strength in you. Do you know them?"

"Yes," I said.

"So, do I. They flake off little pieces of themselves to create soil. I draw the pieces into my roots and use them to build my body."

"The Stone People's imperviousness helps you?"

"Yes. We use it to harden ourselves against insect attack. We use it to stand up tall under the heavy weight."

I carried my knife back to the parking lot. From the rear hatch of the Jeep, I opened a can of mechanic's goop and rubbed it onto the knife. I grabbed some paper towels and walked over to the trashcan. I shook the knife off into a trash can, then wiped it clean. I put it back in my boot sheath.

I checked the time: 5:30. There was that time warp again. I got in and drove back to Chris's Open-Pit Greek Restaurant and my meeting with Max.

My period of civil disobedience had begun.

Chapter Seven

At peace, I prepared for war.

Nature is a circle; the horizon is one, the sky another. We seek harmony and so live our lives in cycles, in round *tipis* and lodges. The sun and moon dance in circles, so our lives revolve with the earth in a sympathetic circadian rhythm.

The sun had completed another circle and was again high in the sky. After the dawn prayer and bathing rites, I spent the morning studying the task ahead. Fasting sharpened my mind, giving me an edge to work the information I had on my target. Before noon, I was full of facts and figures, but lacked a kernel of truth on which to build a plan. I left the office and entered my *tipi*. There, prayer and meditation would pave the way.

Sitting cross-legged, I would search for it. I settled on the thickest hide. I emptied my life. I soaked in *skan*, knowing the smallness of my place in the universe. I let the universe shape me. I melted in the cool heat of the highest power, Grandfather, *Wakan Tanka*. I awaited *Wicasa Wakan*.

I waited to see what He would have me know. He owed me nothing. My few years of devotion would not impress him but for the women that he had led tome, I believed that Grandfather would hear my prayer.

Taku Skanskan led my mind through fields of ripe thoughts. He led me through the quiet canyon of souls. I saw how the Tall Brothers looked inside their wooden bodies. I saw the Stone People dancing for the sun and rolling in the moonlight. I saw the earth that was before, and the earth that was now present. I knew how it would begin, and the sign of the right time.

How different we are from the *wasiçiu*. They wake up and repeat to themselves how the world ought to be, then go out and try to make it so. *Lakhota* wake up and see how the world is, then fit themselves into it. *Wasiçiu* cut roads through mountains, then clear the landslides. If the mountain wishes to spread out, *Lakhota* just walk further around. We don't tell the mountain how to live or where to stand.

Wasiçius make plans and follow them. They might even try an old plan that worked once for them before. The condition of the earth inside the universe doesn't fit into their calculus for action.

That is very foreign to *Lakhota* life. We walk in the moment, but live in eternity. Every medicine is adjusted for the moment it is administered. Every breath supplies the *skan* of the moment from the eternal source. The earth turns, seasons change, and so do the people. The wheel of chance moves to a new position. The universe aligns to another focus.

Lakhota medicine is made for the world of the moment. Each realignment of the large path requires careful planning and the knowledge of the exact moment that the realignment could take place. *Wakan Tanka* did not give me the date and time that I would act. Instead, he attuned my heart to that moment in time. I could feel it approaching in the future. I didn't know how far away it was, but I could see a flaming arrow in my mind's sky. I would watch its flight. When it struck ground, it would be the moment to act. My medicine would be ready and potent.

I sat alone as the Power Spirit's joy seeped from me. I felt the guarding presence of my guide Raven Who Hops. He did not intrude, but stood watch while I was away from my body. When I slipped back into my body, I felt Raven withdraw.

I felt the strength and size of the bear as I stretched. Bear medicine has been a part of my life since I was young. I stood, making deep impressions in the fur. The floor creaked under me as I walked to the office cloaked in bear-ness. Though I enjoyed the feeling, I shed the bear magic. Oversized paws would have been awkward for handling a computer keyboard.

I studied archived newspaper reports of the trials. I studied detailed maps of Maryland, learning the routes between the rape sites and Keagey's home, between the rape sites and his workplace.

I now had my plan. I knew how to rebalance the local harmony. As ripples on a lake, the effects would reach a long way. This would be good for the cause, but only if we could remain anonymous. To do that, I would have to perfect the women's alibis. I called Rita's shop.

"Shears Locks Combs. May I help you?"

I used a southern accent. I tried Texan, but it probably sounded more Georgian than anything else.

"Rita there?"

"Just a sec."

I waited on hold while some county music played in my ear. Rita came on the line.

"This is Rita. Can I help you?"

"*Hau*, it's your friend, but don't say my name."

"What do you have in mind?"

"I need you and your closest friend to meet me. Pick some place where you never go, but where there are a lot of people and it's noisy. Call my cell phone number when you decide. Do you think that you can make it tonight?"

"Yes, I think so. Let me see what I can do. I'll get back to you."

I called Kelly next.

"Bowie Boys and Girls."

"May I speak to Kelly?"

"This is Kelly. Who's this?"

"*Hau*. This is your friend, but don't say my name."

"What's up?"

"I need you and your closest friend to meet with me. Pick a place where …"

"I've been waiting for you to call," she interrupted.

"We're supposed to be strangers. You aren't expecting my phone call."

"Oh, right... sorry."

"Don't be sorry, but be aware that it might be noticed. You need to be careful what people overhear. There must be no sign that you or anyone you know have any plans brewing. I need to talk to you and your closest friend. Use your throw-away phone to call my cell phone when you know when you both can meet me."

"I will."

69

I tried Maria next. My southern accent might be improving with practice. She was in a meeting, so I left a message for her to call Rita for the news.

Lisa didn't answer the phone. She probably was out on her cleaning rounds. I left a message on her answering machine to call Rita for the news. It wasn't good to leave my voice on her machine, but I had few other options. I had to initiate the operation.

I called Rita again.

"Shears Locks Combs. May I help you?"

"Rita there?"

"This is Rita. Is that …"

"Don't say my name. *Hau*, Rita. Say 'hi' and the name of someone who calls you at work."

"Hi, Teresa."

"I couldn't reach Maria or Kelly. I didn't say my name. I left messages for them to call you for news. Please ask them to call my cell phone to tell me when they can meet me with their closest friends."

"Why can't we all just meet together?"

"I need to meet with each group separately so that none of you will know what the others' alibis are. The less you know about each other, the better for you all."

"It's a little late for that."

"We can do the best we can from now on. Now I have to go."

I checked my watch: 3:30. I changed into khaki trousers and a navy-blue golf-shirt. It seemed to be the unofficial uniform for Annapolis men. I used a mirror to practice a look of mild amusement and empty thoughts. Men at malls seemed to look like that.

I grabbed a stakeout pack, walked downhill to my Jeep, and drove to the Annapolis Mall. I parked in Applebee's lot on the road that George Washington traveled to resign his commission: The General's Highway intersected Defense Highway at the mall. My target worked in a converted house that was about a half-a-mile down Defense Highway from the mall, on the north side. I pulled out my Army surplus field glasses and settled in to wait.

A convertible Mercedes was parked in front with two other cars. I zoomed the field glasses and read the license plate. It matched the information I'd gotten from Max.

I was practicing breathing exercises when Raven Who Hops appeared in the passenger seat.

"*Mahto*, I see that you wait for your target."

"He's not high enough on the evolutionary ladder to answer a summoning rite."

"That was a good one," Raven laughed.

"I don't have a day job. Maybe I could get a night-gig at a comedy club in Baltimore."

"I don't know if they would understand *Lakhota* humor."

"No, probably not."

"You did fine with the Tall Brother in the park, despite the communication troubles. Perhaps now you will study your languages?

"The tree-tongue, too?"

He gave me a beady-eyed look.

"Okay, Raven."

"So, Bear-man, do you have your plan?"

"Yes. Would you like to hear it?"

71

"Perhaps later. We have something else to discuss. Do you know how to use the first of the Stone People ways in your task?"

"I think I do. A Tall Brother told me how the Stone People magic helps them stand up tall and strong. They eat small flakes from the Stone People to make their bark hard against the bites of insects. The strength of the stones helps them hold their crowns to the sky."

"How will you use the Stone People ways?"

"I could harden my skin so that it would be more difficult to hurt me."

"Perhaps it is the insect's teeth that hurt when it bites the stone magic and not the skin that is hard?"

"I will attempt to discover the nature of the magic after I learn to use it. Remember, I am less than three tens. You are ancient. You've had a lot of time to build your knowledge."

"Yes, but you started on your path late. You are behind where you should be. I thought I would try to speed you up by doubling your lessons. You are capable of faster progress, even though you won't learn patience as well."

"If I manage to remember while I am fighting with someone, I'll try to observe the magic's flow and effects. But you understand that I might be concentrating on staying alive."

"Perhaps your target won't be strong enough to require your complete attention. In the meantime, you can practice alone."

I looked at my spirit guide.

"Practice the rituals here? I'm trying to watch for Keagey leaving work, so I can follow him. How am I supposed to Stone Dream and keep a lookout?"

"Not the dreaming. The magic. The first of the Stone People ways: impermeability."

I looked back to Keagey's car. It was still there.

"Tell me what to do."

"You would know if you had thought about it, but I'm the one who wants you to make rapid progress." He sighed. "Remember your training. Remember the Stone People you have met and their presence while they told you their stories. Feel what it's like to be one of them. Take that stone-ness and wear it as your skin. Now what do you feel?"

"Heavy. It's similar to walking as a bear, but different. I'm heavy and immobile."

"Push the stone covering from one side to the other. Wear it all on one side, while the other is normal. Keep your concentration firm but in the background. Use your normal hand to feel your stone arm. Try to put a fingernail into the skin."

"It won't go in."

"Try the stone skin hand on your normal arm, but do it gently."

It was hard to move my stone-hand. I got the hand there and just rested a fingernail on my arm. I felt the pressure.

"You can practice while you watch the target's car."

"Why was it so hard to move my arm?"

"You are still inexperienced with the magic. In time you will learn to be as hard as stone while using

Wakinyan's magic of the winds to fly further when you run and jump. Can you guess how?"

I thought about the Stone People as I glanced through the field glasses at Keagey's car again.

"I can apply the stone qualities separately. I don't have to wear them both at the same time."

"You need to be able to wear either or both in an instant and shed them as fast. With experience, you will be able to wear as little or as much as you need. When you're a full priest, you will be able to put stone magic around things, animals and people other than yourself. That level of magic is available only to the most steadfast. If it is ever misused, *Inyan*, The Rock, will remove your access to his power. His Stone People will not talk with you. Remember that the second of the *Lakhota* ways is truth."

"I will never violate my oaths or my quest. I will walk in truth. In peace. In strength. In beauty."

"It is good that you renew your pledge at every increase in your power. Your destiny is great, but you must be worthy of it, or your feet will lose the path."

"My life isn't my own. It belongs to *Wakan Tanka*."

I looked through the field glasses. The car was still there.

"You have about a quarter hour to practice before your target comes out."

I didn't look toward Raven because I knew he would simply vanish. That was his way. I spent the time practicing my new exercises. I learned to change the ratio of weight and hardness, but I still couldn't make one without the other.

Then I saw Keagey leave the web business and walk toward his car. I drove around to the traffic light heading out of the mall. Keagey drove out onto Defense Highway, then turned right onto The General's Highway heading east, where the road's name changes to West Street.

My light turned green, so I turned on West, following him. He stayed to the right and took the ramp onto the westbound 50 freeway. I was three cars back as we made the merge from the on ramp to the freeway. I stayed back, not knowing his destination. He could either take the 97 north toward Baltimore, or continue west toward Washington DC.

Keagey changed lanes to the left. I waited. Tailing someone by yourself is very hard if you don't want to be noticed. After a count of ten, I changed lanes left, too. I hoped that Keagey wasn't looking in his rear view mirror then.

We passed the 97 exit. Luck was with me. Keagey and the car behind him turned on their signals to exit onto the loop over to the Aris T. Allen Parkway. I swung in behind. At this point I guessed that Keagey was heading for home. He lived in a condo overlooking Back Creek in the Eastport district.

It turned out that I was right. Keagey went through to Forest Drive. Where Bay Ridge met Forest Drive in Eastport, he pulled into a lot and parked. I parked a little distance away and watched him enter a big liquor store. About five minutes later, he came out with a sack. From the shape and size, I guessed it was whiskey. He was probably on his way home to get drunk while watching porno.

Keagey drove out of the lot and crossed Forest Drive on Bay Ridge heading into Eastport. When he turned right at an Episcopal Church, I pulled to the side of the road near the corner. I watched him down the long street until he drove past the guard's gatehouse at the condo entrance. I turned down the street and drove to the condos but turned right on the street there. I went up two blocks and turned around. I drove back and parked on the side of the road about a block away from the gatehouse. I doubted I would have any action before I met Rita for dinner.

I settled in for the wait.

Keagey didn't know it, but his life had just changed.

Chapter Eight

My cell phone beeped.

"*Hau.*"

"It's Rita."

"Are we on?"

"Yes. How about the Hoppin' Frog in Laurel?"

"Do they know you there?"

"No. We've never been there."

"I'm about 45 minutes from Laurel. Where's the Hoppin' Frog?"

"It's on US-1, just south of Laurel as you're heading toward DC. It's on the right. It's got a big sign. They tell me you can't miss it."

"I'll be there as soon as I can, but it might be an hour or more with traffic."

"That's okay. I have to go pick Teresa up at her place. We'll see you there."

We said goodbye as I started the car. I hoped Keagey wouldn't do anything stupid until I got back to watch.

I pulled into the Hoppin' Frog's lot. Judging by the cars, this was an ecumenical crowd. People who worshipped the almighty dollar were parked near ones who either didn't worship at that church or had taken a vow of poverty.

I parked next to a Lexus and walked in. Happy Hour was in full swing. Longneck beers were a buck, drafts were two, and well drinks were three. Too bad I didn't drink. I walked through the bar looking for Rita.

A counter covered the longest wall with the hard liquor racked in back. Corona piñatas worked on their tans in the neon glow of Budweiser beer signs. Three buxom mixologists were pouring for the mostly male clientele.

Two brunettes tag-team appraised me as I entered. They checked me out as I checked the room for Rita. Nearby, a shorthaired elf, probably from College Park, was learning how to blend a margarita in her mouth, assisted by two other elfin co-eds.

The wall booths and tall tables had views of plenty of TVs showing every sport I knew of and some that I didn't. The young men in the bar were so entranced by sports broadcasts that they were oblivious to the dramas playing in front of them at the bar. The place was clean and cozy, with pleasant indirect lighting.

It seemed to be a nice enough place, as watering holes go. I wondered what *Lakhota* life would be like if my people were able to drink with impunity.

I stopped that train of thought. The second of the *Lakhota* ways is truth, so we accept who we are and the world as it exists. And the fact was that, like many people in other cultures, our genes make it hard for us to process alcohol.

The pitiful state of life on the Rez was only made worse by white-rage-induced drunken brawls. My people needed to accept our predisposition for

78

alcoholism, cast out the *wasiçiu* poison, and return to the *Lakhota* Way.

Reality may not always be what we wish or want, but it is the beginning of truth. Some of my fellow healers were attempting to cure alcoholism with new blends of herbs, and some of them were making progress.

Like a coyote at a dog show, I crossed the bar full of *wasiçiu* men and women while they worked their wiles on each other. They were here to pay and play. I was on a quest to realign the spiritual harmony of a local zone of the universe. We couldn't have been further apart if we'd been born on different planets. I enjoyed the cultural panorama before me as I continued my search for Rita.

Chafing dishes steamed with happy hour snacks, while platters of cold items stood nearby. Tonight's free foods were mystery-meat balls in red sauce, chicken wings in buffalo sauce with bleu cheese dressing, and crab balls. Crudités with ranch dressing shared a space with various types of bland cheese squares. I put some vegetables on a paper plate and carried them into the reception area.

I looked over the shoulder of the hostess and read the names. No Rita or Cade. I stepped back and then around to the front of the hostess station.

She wore a one-piece dress that fell from shoulder to ankle in one flawless flow of fabric. Usually I avoid noticing younger women, but this one made an impression on me like a meteorite on a marshmallow. She spoke.

"Hi. How many tonight?"

It's a good thing that *Lakhota* practice face control. She wouldn't know how I much responded to her charms.

"Three, non-smoking. The name's Cade. C-a-d-e."

It was a risk using Rita's last name, but it would look more suspicious if the police investigated and found she'd used a fake name.

"Thank you. It will be ten to fifteen minutes."

I stepped way, putting a carrot stick into my mouth as I went. In case I'd missed her name on the list, I walked into the restaurant looking for her. She wasn't there. I walked back to the front and then outside. I stood next to a bush and waited.

The big planting pot that held the bush was almost as big as the evergreen in it. The bush seemed happy enough about life in a pot. Maybe Mr. Spruce thought of it as a mobile home. I didn't ask him. Now wasn't the time to make a house-call on a small Tall Brother.

I finished my vegetables and stuck the folded paper plate in a back pocket. I nodded my head at people who made eye-contact with me as they went inside.

A modern replica of the 1950s T-bird coupe pulled in. I had a nice view from the rear. The driver's door opened and a pair of pumps below beautiful legs hit the pavement. As she stood up, her outfit accentuated the curves of a woman while her high-heel flexed her perfect calf, that matched the toned thigh that disappeared into a modest but sexy black skirt.

She faced away from me as her companion came around the coupe from the passenger side. This one

80

looked like Rita but wasn't. I looked back to the driver as she turned. I was stunned to discover that Rita was the one who'd been driving.

I looked at Teresa. She was beautiful, too. She walked like a model, with her weight hitting hard on her feet, making her breasts flounce and her hips sway as she walked. *Lakhota* women don't walk that way.

Her top shimmered in the parking lot lights. It caught then released her curves as she walked toward me. Her navy-blue skirt was modest yet still sexy.

I enjoyed the view, but forced myself to be calm by reminding myself of the *Lakhota* denial of the flesh. We made introductions all around. Teresa had the same last name as Rita. Sisters? Cousins? I wondered if she were single.

Rita asked, "How long is our wait?"

"We should be almost ready. Why don't we go check?"

When we stepped inside, the hostess saw me.

"There you are. I was about to come looking for you," she said as she took three menus from a rack. "Follow me."

The dining area was about forty by sixty feet, with high ceilings full of exposed ducting painted in shades of the primary colors. The wall-booths were low-slung and covered in forest green leather. The tabletops were even darker, probably Hooker's green. Two aisles of tables that matched the booths divided the rest of the room.

As the hostess led us back to a booth near the window, I thanked *Wakan Tanka* for guiding events. We would have a perfect place to talk. She settled us

81

in the booth, telling us that our server would be by soon.

I sat on the side facing the back wall. Teresa and Rita sat facing the room. That would be fine. I had more reason to remain anonymous, and the two women were dazzling enough to make me invisible. They both smiled at me.

"Both of you look lovely," I said.

Rita looked down. Teresa spoke.

"Tonight's the first night that Rita has felt ready to dress-up since ... everything happened."

Rita lifted her head.

"I owe it to you. You're so strong and confident. You make me believe that I might get part of my life back. You helped me feel I could be a woman again."

"You will regain much of what you lost. We will make him give it back."

"How?"

"Soon I will show you. We *Lakhota* understand a lot about the spiritual side of nature. While the great minds in your culture researched science, our greatest minds researched man's place in nature and in the universe. While your scientists discovered the power of splitting an atom, we discovered the power of *Wakan Tanka*, the Great Mystery."

After we'd ordered our drinks from the waitress, I looked from Rita to Teresa and back.

"We are vessels of power. *Lakhota* learned how power transfers between beings. We understand the destructive power of violence, aggression, and abuse."

Rita winced when I said it. Teresa drew a sharp breath. Perhaps I shouldn't have started right in.

There was nothing to do but press on. I reached across to touch Rita's hand.

"We also understand the healing nature of sharing, blessings, and gifting."

I chin-gestured over my shoulder.

"By the way, you need to warn me when someone is coming. We need to keep all this under wraps."

"Okay, but why did you need me to bring Teresa?"

"I have our plan. You will regain your lost power."

"I was teasing when I said you had to get a plan by the end of the week."

I watched Rita and Teresa as they talked over the menus after I suggested we should decide on our meals. It was nice to be at a table with two beautiful women. I hadn't taken an oath of celibacy, but I'd been neglecting my study of dating rituals for my devotion to mystic rituals. I wondered what either of them would say to my putting a robe around us while we talked outside a *tipi*.

After the women had decided what to eat, Rita restarted the conversation.

"So, what's the plan?"

"Don't worry about that: I'll handle it. I will call you when we are ready to checkmate him. In the meantime, we must prepare your alibi."

I looked into Teresa's eyes.

"Can Rita depend on you?"

"If I thought I could get away with it, I'd kill the little bastard for her."

She looked to Rita and held up the little finger of her hand. Rita held up hers. They interlocked little

83

fingers and shook hands. Two voices said, "Sisters to the end." with conviction.

"We need you to create a rock-solid alibi for Rita. You can't admit you did it, even if you're pressured."

"I'd die before I let my sister down."

"Good, because Rita and I are going to make the little bastard wish he'd never reached adulthood."

Simultaneously, their two voices said, "Good."

"So here's what we need to do …"

Rita put her hand on my arm.

"Here comes the waitress."

I nodded. The waitress put a glass of Chardonnay in front of each of the women, then put a cup of hot water in front of me. I reached into my pocket for my powdered horsemint and chamomile. Tonya was all smiles.

While the two women ordered, I studied the room. Women filled most of the tables and booths in the restaurant, while throngs of grinning men surrounded the few women in the bar. In here, the women were ignoring the few tables of men. Not dating may be lonely, but it has less rejection. After I gave my order, the waitress left.

I opened my herb bag and put a big pinch into my hot water. I left it to saturate and put the pouch back in my pocket. Teresa picked up her pear-shaped wineglass and drank a sip. She looked at her glass, perhaps enjoying the color, then licked a small drop of wine on the rim.

I felt an inner stirring at the sight of her tongue. I looked to Rita who was watching me watch Teresa. I let my face show a small smile. She met my eyes, taking a deep breath as she smiled back. Her eyes held mine, but I still noticed the rise and fall of her breasts.

Yes, I was a man, and though I had a mission, I knew that my days of denial were numbered.

"What's in the pouch?" Rita asked.

"It's just some medicine for my back."

"A home remedy?"

"I'm a *Lakhota* medicine man."

"Herbs and things like that?"

"I have a prescription."

I turned to Teresa

"Can you fix yourself up to look similar to Rita?"

"Rita could cut my hair like hers and I could dress to look like her, but I won't fool anyone who knows either of us well."

"You won't need to. Here's the sequence. When I call Rita to meet me to take care of business, she will drive over and trade cars with you. Rita will meet me. You will drive to the mall in Rita's car and shop for clothes that will fit her. Don't try them on, just buy some for later. She needs to use your credit card, Rita. Teresa, can you sign Rita's name as she does?"

"I can practice up and forge her name well enough to pass a test."

"So Rita, can Teresa use your credit card?"

"No joy-riding."

"I promise."

"Teresa, you need to go to several stores and buy an item or two at each shop. By the end of the evening, have about three dresses and several skirts and blouses. What you're really doing is collecting date and time stamped receipts. After shopping, drive to Rita's and go inside with the clothes. The neighbors will think you're Rita."

After our food arrived, and we'd taken our first bites, I turned to Rita.

"When we're done, you'll go home. Your neighbors will think you're Teresa, whose story is that she had a bad blind-date and came over for consolation. Teresa, you should spend the night. I'll try to make it happen on a weekend, but just in case, be prepared to spend the night."

We ate for a few minutes after the waitress came back to see how our meals were. We complimented the chef, and the waitress left, satisfied.

"Rita, the next evening, you will go to the mall and return almost all of the clothes. You should keep a few things. At the mall, your story will be that you felt more secure trying the clothes on at home, so you just took a bunch home. You're bringing some of them back for returns. Make sure you make an impression on the clerk. Engage her in a small conversation. Whatever impression Teresa made the night before will solidify onto you. Oh and don't forget to change Teresa's hairstyle to something else afterward."

They sat quiet, looking at me, the forks back down on the table, their wine glasses emptied. Teresa spoke first.

"I'm in."

"Teresa won't have an alibi."

"She has the blind-date. So what if it can't be verified? She met him accidentally. The cops can't prove he doesn't exist. The phone number he gave her was a wrong number. He lied about his name and where he was from. Besides, the cops won't be looking for Teresa. But just to be on the safe side, Teresa should make a call to some number from her cell phone and claim that the wrong number was the one that the blind-date gave her."

"Why would anyone be looking for me?"

"They won't if you follow my instructions when we are teaching the little bastard to not play with fire. If we stick to my plan, the cops won't be able to connect you to anything. They might suspect something, but they won't be able to prove a thing."

"This sounds too good to be true."

"How do we know you can be trusted?"

"Teresa, how can you ask that?"

"She should be asking that. It is her right to be your protector as well as her own, just as you are hers and your own."

The two exchanged a smile.

"You can trust me because before I finish, I will be guilty of several Class One felonies. If I turned any of you in, the cops would flip you to get to me, and jail is the last place I want to be."

The women nodded. They picked up their forks and began eating again. When the waitress asked if they wanted more wine, both nodded.

"I will neither fail you nor betray you," I said when we were alone again. "You have my oath as a *Lakhota* priest. This is a sacred vow."

I wished for a puff of the pipe to show my breath, but these two wouldn't understand the significance of the *Chanumpa*, sometimes called a "peace pipe." When we make our breath visible, we must tell the truth or evil will happen. By breathing out the smoke, we promise to tell the truth.

"There are just two more things I need you to do."

"What's that?"

"Don't tell anyone about your alibi. This meeting never happened, right?" I said, and they nodded. "Rita, can you save a couple of big bags of hair cuttings?"

"How big?"

"Big. Try to get men's hair in there, too."

"We don't get as many men as women, but I think I can do that. What do you need it for?"

"I can't tell you now."

"Is there anything you want me to do?"

"Perhaps something will come up later, Teresa."

The rest of the meal went fine. I learned about them and they about me. We were having so much fun that I didn't notice the time. When Tonya brought the check, we'd been there over three hours. Both of them reached for their purses.

"Don't. I've got it."

"You're doing all of the work, taking the risks, and you won't let me pay you for anything. At least, let me get the meal."

"It's amazing what a guy will do to impress beautiful women."

Rita blushed as Teresa laughed. I left the waitress a good tip. Gifting increases power. When we stood to go, Teresa was close to me. I liked it. Rita was even closer. I liked that too. She kissed my cheek.

"You don't know how much this means to me. I could never repay you."

"Consider it a gift from our Great Father, *Mitakuye Oyasin*, 'all my relations.' We are all children of the Great Father's very large family."

"You are so sweet. Thank you."

She squeezed my hand then started for the door. I did too. Teresa put her arm through mine as we walked. She hugged me before they left. While I enjoyed her breasts crushing against my chest, I felt her feeling my ponytail. Without a word, she turned and walked to Rita.

As I walked to my car, I heard my name and turned. Rita and Teresa blew me kisses. I reached into the air, caught them and brought them to my heart. I gave them a wave then got into my Jeep.

It wasn't good that I was thinking like some of the men I didn't respect — wondering how I might get and enjoy some of that feminine gratitude.

That kind of thinking could get me — or someone else — killed.

Chapter Nine

The arrow in my mind's sky had not moved. I was ready to strike, but my clients were not.

Two days had passed. I spent much of that time outside of buildings that Keagey was inside. He hadn't done anything that seemed strange. Perhaps he was on good behavior.

Lisa Towers had called the day before to set up a meeting. She was going to bring her sister Emily to the Coyote Cafe in Bowie. It was up Route 3 from the 50. At least it was closer to my stakeouts than Laurel. I left Keagey at his work and drove west on 50 to Bowie, swinging north on Route 3.

I pulled into the lot. The building was 1970s functionality crossed with a 1960s Baptist Church. It was a neat and tidy cowboy sports bar, just the sort of place I'd expect Lisa to pick. I looked around. I couldn't see her anywhere. It was still early, before 5:00. Except for the waitress and bartender, the place was empty.

The waitress approached.

"Would you like a table?"

"Yes, a table for three, non-smoking."

"Is your party complete?"

I was standing by myself. Perhaps she couldn't count, or maybe she thought I had a multiple personality disorder.

"Everyone else will be here in a minute. May I wait at the table instead of in the lobby?"

"I don't see why not. Follow me."

She led me to a table just inside and to the left of the entry. I had a view of the parking lot and the outside of the front door.

"Thank you. This will be fine."

Just as I sat down, a tan Nissan pulled into the lot. Lisa got out of the passenger side while a woman I assumed to be Emily got out on the driver's side. If this was Emily, they didn't look enough alike to be mistaken for sisters. While Lisa was a petite white brunette, the second woman was tall, thick and mixed race, probably black and Vietnamese.

They were talking and didn't notice me until they got to the door. Lisa saw me, raised her hand, and made a small wave. Her sister turned to look at me. She didn't smile, but she didn't frown either. Perhaps she was a poker player.

I stood in anticipation of being introduced. Before the hostess could intercept them, Lisa and Emily walked to the table. I spoke first.

"Lisa. I'm glad you came. Is this your sister?"

"Yes."

Her voice was small, but loud enough to be heard in the empty room.

"Let me introduce Emily Towers. Ems, this is Mr. Pace."

"It's nice to meet you. Please call me Ben."

"It's nice to meet you too." She didn't return my smile. I guessed I wouldn't get to call her "Ems."

I wanted this to go well, so I started by pulling their chairs. Emily went first and sat nearest the door.

91

She motioned Lisa into the chair next to her, away from me. I had just sat again as the waitress returned. We ordered wine and hot tea.

The restaurant ritual had moved on to phase two. I turned and faced the two Towers.

"This is nice, but it's not what I asked for."

Lisa looked around the empty room. Emily gave me a dirty look.

"You asked to meet Lisa and her closest friend for dinner. So here we are."

"I asked to meet in a crowded place. There's no one here but us."

"That's not the message we got from Rita."

It wasn't *Lakhota* to play the blame-game. It didn't matter whose fault it was, it had happened. I gave them another small smile.

"No matter. We will make do."

Emily's face lost its sour expression. Lisa quit looking like a repo-man had foreclosed on her bluebird of happiness.

I sat forward and explained in a soft voice, "I wanted a crowded and noisy place so we could talk without worry to our privacy. Here it will be hard for the waitress and bartender to not eavesdrop."

Lisa's voice was still small.

"I messed up," she frowned as she turned and looked away.

"No, you didn't, Lees. He did," Emily said in a normal voice, perhaps in defiance to my request.

The path of peace was the one to take tonight. I spoke again with quiet tones.

"You are right. It was my mistake."

92

The strategy was good. Emily spoke, this time in muted tones.

"We didn't know that you wanted a crowd, but it will probably work out okay. This place usually fills up after five."

"They don't know you here, do they?"

"No, not really. We eat here once in a while, not that anyone would notice. Why? Is that important?"

I lowered my voice to where the sisters had to lean in to hear it.

"I don't want anyone to remember us meeting. If they know you, then they will look to see who you're with, so they can have conversation material with their other friends." I used a quiet falsetto. "I saw Emily the other day. She was with her sister and some Indian." I switched back to my normal but quiet voice. "We don't need that. In order to do what Lisa and the others want, we must make sure that nobody will remember us being together."

"Okay," Emily said.

I had her interested, but her sister would be the one to make her commit. I turned to Lisa.

"We want to remain anonymous. That way, when the nameless little bastard runs crying to his mommy, he won't know who to tattle on. If he does suspect anyone, we will make sure that you have an airtight alibi."

It was time to ask for their commitments. I asked Lisa first.

"Do you trust Emily?"

"She's my sister."

I took that to mean "yes." I faced Emily.

"Can she depend on you?"

"I've been her big sister my whole life. Our parents were childless, so they adopted me. I was a Vietnamese War orphan. About a year later, mom got pregnant. We've been sisters since then."

"Yes, you're loving sisters, but if a policeman were to ask you if you helped create Lisa's alibi, could she count on your protection?"

"After how they let John ..."

"Please, no names. Use 'the little bastard' instead."

"After how they let the little bastard go free, they can all rot in hell. Did you know that he was waiting outside Lisa's house one evening? That's when I asked Dad for one of his handguns. If the little bastard tries that again, he'll get a choice of holes to pee through," she said before she leaned over and gave Lisa a hug. "We're going to get this guy, just like that bully in third grade when we kicked his ass all over the schoolyard."

It sounded as if Emily thought she was going to be with us for the event. That wouldn't work. If she were there, Lisa was sure to hold back. Lisa looked down, then up at me, then to Emily, then back to me. I couldn't read her face: it had too many emotions competing for display space.

A couple of guys came in and headed for the bar. One detoured to the jukebox. "All My Ex-es Live in Texas" echoed around the room. I cleared my throat.

"We're going to make the little bastard wish he had never passed puberty, but right now, we should choose something to eat."

The drinks arrived, and we completed the choosing food ritual just as the waitress returned, all smiles, probably because there wasn't any math this time.

"So, have you decided, or do you need another minute?"

While the girls ordered, I sipped my horsemint and chamomile tea. Emily ordered the crab dip. Lisa chose the chicken wrap. I asked for a bleu cheese burger with grilled onions. After the waitress left, I pulled us back to planning.

"Emily, it sounds as if you're ready to confront the little bastard."

"Yeah. When do we do it?"

"Soon, but you can't go."

"Why not?"

"This is Lisa's task. She was by herself when her spiritual power was stolen. She alone can take it back and she has to do it in her own way. Besides, she needs you to set up her alibi."

"How do I do that?"

"I have an idea, but I need help from you with some of the details. Help me figure this out."

I got two nods. Lisa's face showed that she was curious. It was an improvement over her earlier expressions.

"The basic idea is that when Lisa takes off to meet me, you start taping a cable TV news program at the best picture quality. When Lisa comes home, you play the tape on the TV while videotaping Lisa and you doing something, anything. The important thing is to get Lisa on tape with the news broadcast. It will be proof that she was at home with you when the little bastard was getting his wagon fixed. You should also make sure to set the date and time in your video camera to be the same time as the news broadcast."

Lisa said, "That sounds great."

"Yes, except I don't know what and why you are taping yourself. If there isn't a good reason for you to be doing it, then it will appear that it was done on purpose to create an alibi. If they suspect that, then they will get their high-tech forensics people to bust it. We need to make them believe that you had no idea that you would ever need the videotape as an alibi; you just made the tape for another reason."

Lisa looked to Emily, who looked back. Their confusion was obvious to me, as they looked at me like a dog looks at shoelaces. There was silence.

"Perhaps you have a relative that isn't local? You could be taping something for them to see?"

They both smiled to each other and said, "Grams."

Emily turned to me.

"Our grandmother lives in West Virginia. She's 92 and doesn't travel much. She lives with Aunt Sheila. They are always sending us things, crafts and stuff. We could videotape Lisa and me looking at them and putting them up around the house."

Lisa chimed in, "If we got some sweaters, we could try them on so Grams could see us in them. Grams is always knitting us sweaters."

"Good. Then we have our plan, right?"

"Right."

"Will I need an alibi?" Lisa asked. "I mean, will the police be looking for me?"

"Yes, you will need an alibi. I doubt that you will use it, but there is a slim chance that you might. We need to be ready for that, just in case. I doubt the police will be looking for you, but they will have to suspect someone. When we confront the little bastard, we will leave him alive, but shaken. He will be very sorry for what he did, but he will re-gain courage when his people surround him. When they go on the warpath, we need to be sure they can't prove that any of us were there. I know how to do that."

"How?"

"You'll just have to trust me. The less you know about the plan, the better it will work. I'll call you and tell you when to meet me and what to do."

"Okay."

The waitress came with our food, asking me again if I wanted anything else to drink. I shook my head as she turned to the women and asked them.

"Lisa, there is something that I need you to do," I said.

"What's that?"

"Can you save about six used vacuum cleaner bags from your cleaning crew?"

"What for?"

"I need them."

"What's in this for you? You turned down a lot of money. Why?"

"I have my reasons."

"Which I'd like to know," said Emily, in her protector mode. "I don't trust anyone that I don't understand."

"Your sister and the others were harmed when precious things and privacy were stolen from them. Their spiritual power was stolen, too. The same people who protect the little bastard have been raping

97

and stealing from my people for over a century. The Great Father directs my path. I serve him to right wrongs. Your circumstance is just one of the situations that I must attend to as I walk my own path."

Emily and Lisa stared at me. I read surprise suffused with confusion on their faces. Lisa's mouth hung open.

"I have a Don Quixote complex?" I suggested.

The tension broke. They both laughed like I was a funnyman. Perhaps I should try to keep it light the rest of the night, I thought.

"You're scary," said Lisa. "How did you get into this business?"

"I wanted to try money-laundering but didn't have enough for a full load."

They both laughed again. I was on a roll. Maybe I should try stand-up comedy.

I could hear Raven's voice in my head, "Stick to your studies, Little Bear."

I told myself to remember that my "soldiers" in this dangerous mission were amateurs, neophytes who knew nothing of rebellion and war. We lacked the time to teach them to be cunning and skillful warriors.

They had no idea how dangerous it was to take on a political syndicate like the Kinkaeds. I had to allow for that in my plan.

Chapter Ten

P atience. Patience. Patience. I repeated the third
Lakhota principle to restrain myself from acting
too soon. Yes, I wanted to act — now — but every
action creates ripples that often have unexpected
consequences. The medicine must be administered at
the right time, when it is most potent, when time
aligns the universe. Then the ripple effects will follow
their course and have desired results. I would wait,
then strike the enemy — hard.

I spent two days tailing John Keagey. He spent
time on mundane errands such as going grocery
shopping and to the post office. On the second night
he went to the Arundel Mills Mall. The Annapolis
Mall was fifteen miles closer to his condo, but what
did I know about being a serial rapist?

Keagey sat in one of the food courts, watching.
After a while, he would select a petite brunette and
follow her. I followed him. He wasn't as good at it as
I was. One of the women he followed noticed him
and pointed him out to a security guard. He ducked
for cover.

Except for the one who reported him, he would
tail the women until they left the Mall. After that he
would return to the food court to start again. Each
woman he targeted looked similar to my new sisters.
The little bastard was cruising for another victim. I

hoped he would lead me to his trophy house soon. He had to be stopped before he raped again. Due to double jeopardy, he'd never be convicted of the rapes of my four friends.

The police had searched Keagey's places but found no stash. If I could find the stash, he'd get a trial on any other rapes he had committed. I planned on tricking him into revealing the location of his stash.

During Keagey's work hours, I worked at building a gadget that would help me get inside Keagey's head. I almost had it finished when my cell phone rang. It was Kelly Larson. She and her friend Linda could meet me that evening at Mike's Crab House in Riva. I made sure that they weren't well known at Mike's. We set a time. I went back to work.

If the gadget worked, it would be a good spook-tool. I'd found the plans on the Internet. It was similar to a rifle, except that it shot sound waves. You could focus it on a wall, then press the trigger and talk. The gadget put your voice on one of the two sonic amplifiers. Each one produced a 200 kHz tone, but of opposite phase from the other. The high frequency sound was beyond human hearing. When the two beams of sound hit a wall, the carrier waves canceled each other out, leaving just the voice. When used with an audio telescope to listen, I could hold a conversation with the person who thought the wall was talking to him.

Since I didn't want to attract suspicion, I didn't build the original rifle design: I built it into a box. The voice telescope on top looked like a flashbulb reflector. The whole thing could be mistaken for a home-made, old-fashioned camera. Or so I hoped.

I had just finished bore-sighting it when it was time for me to leave for Mike's Crab Shack. I took the gadget with me and walked down the hill to my Jeep. I hoped to be on stakeout after dinner.

I negotiated the back roads to Crownsville, then drove south to the Truman Parkway east, then turned south on Riva Road. I crossed the South River bridge and swung left on the access road that took me to Mike's. A couple of miles down river in the same place under the Solomon's Island Road bridge was the Surfside 7. Both were good, but I preferred the Surfside to Mike's. Oh well, it was Kelly's choice. I parked and went in.

Mike's has a package store attached to the landlubber side of the building. They sell beer, wine, and soda, with gourmet and deli foods to go. You can get restaurant take-out, too. It's a well known provisioning point for picnics and outings in the area. Besides the usual car traffic, Mike's gets a good deal of amateur sailors, too. There are three long docks on the South River, and the marina next door has a gas station.

I walked past the store and entered Mike's. It's split into four sections: the bar, interior dining, exterior covered dining, and open-air seating. Every seat had a view of the waterfront, while some were part of it. The first room was interior seating and the hostess stand. Nobody was there at the time. To the right was the bar, which had almost as much room as the first dining room. The decor was dark wood furnishings with lighter wood paneling. The mood was a modern twist on Hollywood's version of a Shakespearean public house.

I walked through the room and then the bar, taking a look outside. It was still a little cold in the season for most folks to sit outside, so the open-air seating was empty. Under the roof of the patio, the propane heaters were pumping BTUs into the semi-interior space. Thick plastic sheets hung as outside walls, holding most of the heat in. The roofless part of the patio had a magnificent view but nobody wanted the cool temperatures.

I spied Kelly at a table in the back, by the building's exterior windows. A woman sat opposite. I was almost there when Kelly spotted me. She waved and gestured to the place beside her in the booth. I slid in.

"Hi, Ben. This is Linda Monroe. Linda, Ben Pace. I was just telling Linda how you are going to take care of …"

"No names. Just call him 'the little bastard.' You never know who knows whom around Annapolis."

Kelly lowered her voice.

"You're right. As the capital of Maryland, the politicos are here, too. Sometimes, we forget that."

Linda added, "We wish they weren't here."

"I know what you mean."

"I told her how you were going to get revenge…"

"This isn't about revenge; it's about providing justice for you, while gathering evidence for another trial that the little bastard will lose. You will attend an event to re-acquire your self-respect through taking back the spiritual power that was taken from you."

Linda still didn't look happy. I shouldn't have allowed the conversation to get this intense before I'd had a chance to prepare them to hear the hard parts.

"It's too early to get into all this," I said. "We need to see how you are with things before we lock down on the details. Besides, we should eat and relax, get to know each other."

"You're right," Kelly said.

"Are we getting crabs?" I asked.

"Maryland crabs don't start running until July," Kelly said.

"Other crabs don't taste the same," Linda added.

"So, we shouldn't order the Dungeness legs I saw on the board as I came in?" I asked.

"Some people do," Kelly said.

I took the hint.

"What do you suggest?"

"They have good burgers. The big one comes with a T-shirt if you eat the whole thing."

"I don't eat that big. Besides, we don't want to attract attention."

I picked up my menu and started browsing. Kelly and Linda offered suggestions ranging from the chicken pasta to the bar-b-qued pork sandwich. I chose the seafood pasta *fra diavolo*, which probably meant "pasta from hell." Kelly had the chicken pasta while Linda had the chicken Caesar salad.

Kelly was able to catch the eye of our waitress and wave her over. After she finally arrived, she took out her order pad.

"Hi. My name is Becky. I'll be your server tonight. Can I start you off with a cocktail?"

Yet another Stepford Waitress.

"I'll have a Chardonnay."

"Me, too."

They all looked to me. Didn't I already see this movie? Was every *wasiçiu* restaurant scene the same? Did *wasiçiu* women always order Chardonnay? Didn't any of them drink anything else?

"Sir?"

"Hot water, please."

"What kind of tea do you want with that? We have ..."

"Just the hot water, please."

"With lemon?"

"No. Just hot water."

"Hot water?"

"Hot water."

"Okay, hot water. I'll get your drinks right out. In the meantime, our specials are in the menu on the insert. If you have any questions, just let me know."

"Actually, we're ready to order," I said.

"Your food?" she asked.

I hoped that we hadn't put the waitress too far off of her routine by skipping ahead to the ordering. Only a few of the outside tables were filled. Perhaps that would help her cope. After she'd taken our orders and left, I tried to get the conversation at the table onto a more pleasant track than the one we'd been on earlier.

Linda had lost some of her "deer in headlights" look, but still appeared apprehensive. If I couldn't manage to get her "petrified deer" persona out of this line of conversational traffic and onto the shoulder, I might have my first road-kill. I couldn't afford to have anyone in our inside circle defect and roll over for the police.

I turned to Kelly. I hoped that if I drew Kelly out, Linda would self-disclose, giving me an opportunity to understand who she was and how to motivate her to stay in the fold.

"I hardly know any of you, Little Flower. It would help if I did."

Kelly smiled when I used the name I'd given her when she'd visited my *tipi*.

"You called me that name again."

"It seems to fit you."

"Why do you call me that?"

"The Great Spirit suggested it to me when you visited my *tipi*."

"I like it."

"I'm glad. Tell me about yourself."

"I do day care in Glen Burnie. I started there after my husband Ryan died in a car accident. Being around all of the babies and toddlers kept my spirits up. I was just getting back on my feet and beginning to feel like myself again when ... when ..."

"We understand. Tell me about your hobbies."

"I don't have any. Not anymore. I used to be an artist. I had paintings in several galleries and had just finished my first show in New York when Ryan died. I had just begun to paint again when ... Now all I do is sit at home every night with every light in the house on. I've been so depressed."

"Did you see a counselor?"

"Yes, but there is only so much that can be done by talking. Linda started to come and get me so that I wouldn't just sit at home."

Linda's smile was back. She reached and held Kelly's hand.

"We grew up four blocks apart in Waverly," said Kelly. "We met in Kindergarten."

I turned to Linda.

"Where's Waverly?"

"Northeast of Baltimore. But inside the beltway."

"Do you like it there?"

"I did, but it's a rough neighborhood now. Lots of violent crime."

I dug for the tea in my medicine pouch.

"That's sad."

"Unfortunately, the police are too understaffed to provide beat-cops anymore," said Kelly. "A lot of neighborhoods in Baltimore that used to be nice are overrun by thugs and gangs."

"My mother grew up by Patterson Park," said Linda. "It used to be nice. Nowadays, you can't walk there after dark."

"It's as if the police just pulled back and let the criminals run free. If you complain, they tell you that you are free to move out to the suburbs."

"It's so frustrating. Vagrant criminals have more rights than the local citizens. If someone breaks into your house with you there and you shoot them, you will be the one going to jail, not the guy who broke into your house."

"You may as well hang a sign on your home that says, 'Please burglarize my home'," said Kelly. "Maryland Law protects you while committing the crime.'"

I would strike a flame to the fuel they had stacked.

106

"I understand your anger and frustration. You've been let down by those who you trusted to protect you. They manipulated the rules to benefit criminals and special interests, while short-shifting regular citizens."

Kelly said, "I wouldn't be surprised if drug dealers were funding election campaigns."

Before I could feed the fire more, the waitress returned with our meals.

"Anything else?" she said.

"Not yet," I said, and she gave me a funny look.

We ate for a few minutes before I spoke again.

"If the politicians were smart, they'd know that addicts need money to buy drugs, so they'd want to make sure that the addicts were protected while they commit burglary and strong-arm robberies. That way the drug lords make sure their addicts have money to buy drugs and everyone has the protection of politicians who are paid-off with campaign contributions."

"It just makes you sick, doesn't it?" Linda said, sighing.

Now, it was time to get their commitment to our plan, but the waitress chose that moment to bring refills of our drinks and ask how everything was. There were two teabags — one black tea and one herbal — and a slice of lemon on the saucer beside the cup of my hot water. I handed the teabags back to her. She blushed as she apologized. I felt bad for my Stepford Wives reference. Being a waitress meant keeping many lists in your head with notes to help keep it straight, and our waitress was covering a lot of tables. The complexity of the task made it natural to follow a routine where possible. They weren't being mindless robots when they appeared to operate from exactly the same script. They were just being efficient. I was wrong to have thought the way I did.

With Linda watching me closely, I put a large pinch of the tea from my medicine bag into the new cup of steaming water before I turned to my dinner companions.

"It's not often that a citizen can do anything to help put criminals behind bars."

"What do you mean?" said Linda. "I thought that's what you were going to help us do."

"Kelly and her fellow victims asked me to get revenge on the little bastard. I agreed to help them, not for revenge, but so that we could find evidence against him, so that he would be convicted for the other rapes that weren't in the first trial."

"He raped other women?" Linda asked, turning to Kelly. "You never told me that."

"The police are almost certain, but they lack the proof," I said. "I'm going to find it and give it to them."

"He raped other women," Linda said. "Oh, honey, I wish you'd told me."

"You couldn't have done anything," said Kelly. "Besides, what difference does that make?"

"A lot," said Linda. "It means he's not just a rapist. He's …"

"… a serial rapist," I said, and Linda nodded. "That makes him much more dangerous."

A cool breeze rustled the plastic tarps.

"There is another part of this plan that must be done. Kelly and the others need to take back the spiritual power that was stolen from them."

I started looking back and forth between them.

"Kelly burns every light in her house because the little bastard made her afraid. The others are also in pain."

Linda reached out to comfort Kelly who'd covered her face in her hands.

"I know a way for Kelly and the others to regain much of their former lives. There is a *Lakhota* ceremony for recouping spiritual power stolen from someone. When I have secured the proof the police need and have captured the little bastard in a citizen's arrest, I will have Kelly and the others join me, where we will perform a ritual that will return their confidence to them. They will no longer fear the little bastard."

"That's wonderful."

"I can't tell you how much this means to me."

Kelly was near tears.

"Don't thank me until I deliver." I paused. "I need your help to accomplish our goals. I need you to bring a few soiled diapers from your daycare. We need them for the plan."

She nodded and I turned to Linda.

"It's certain that he will attempt to make trouble for Kelly and the others. We can't let him win."

I waited.

"Okay," Linda said tentatively.

"I will make sure that Kelly and the others cannot be directly identified by the little bastard, but it is certain that they will be in the initial list of suspects."

Kelly and Linda both fidgeted in their chairs.

"It can't be helped. It's obvious that his victims have a motive. What we need to do is to make sure that Kelly has an unshakeable alibi. I know how to do that, but we will need Linda's help."

Linda raised her eyebrows.

"What's in the powder you put in your hot water?"

Did she think she had me caught in a trap? I couldn't back out; I could see suspicion in her eyes.

"Powdered horsemint and chamomile. Why?"

"What's horsemint?"

"It's a *Lakhota* remedy for muscle pain. A few years ago, I broke my back when I got knocked off a utility pole. It still bothers me."

"Sorry for being nosy."

"It's okay. A lot of *Lakhota* ways must look strange to outsiders. Now I'm curious. What did you think I was putting in my tea?"

"Drugs or something. Look, I'm sorry. I'm just careful, okay?"

"That's fine by me. After all, we just met, and you are looking out for your friend. You don't know me from anyone."

"What do you want me to do?"

I turned to Kelly.

"I checked the area around where you live. Do you have a Giant grocery store card?"

She nodded.

"Good. This will work if you both agree to it. Linda, when Kelly comes to do her part of the ceremony, you will take her car and bankcard to the Giant in Eastport. They have a bank money machine

110

in the west wall of the store. It doesn't have a camera and the store cameras don't point there. Withdraw some of Kelly's money, then start shopping. The bank transaction will be the first of the time-stamped alibis for Kelly."

Linda said nothing.

"Next, you take your time going up and down the aisles, doing Kelly's shopping. Make sure you buy her favorite ice-cream and her favorite topping, maybe hot fudge. At the check-out, pay in cash but use Kelly's Giant card to get the store discounts, making the second time stamped alibi for her. If we are lucky, the cops will use the card events and not check the store videos to visually verify that Kelly stood at the register while her card was used. Next, drive to the Blockbuster video rental and take your time picking out some good chick-flicks. That will give her another time stamped alibi receipt.

"Drive over to Kelly's condo and put her groceries away. Kelly will come home in your car. You will probably want to talk, but Kelly, you have to make sure you watch the movies before you return them, so that you can answer questions about their story line. Maybe you can just rent ones that you've already seen. Make sure you take the receipts. Smudge your fingerprints around on them, then lose them in the bottom of your purse."

I turned to Linda.

"Can you do that for us, Linda?"

"Please, Lin," said Kelly. "Do it for me."

"And I'm not going to get in trouble? You're sure?"

"All you're doing is some shopping for your friend and giving her the receipts. No matter what, you are innocent. Still, you should keep this to yourself."

"Please? For me?"

Kelly's voice made me want to do it for her. We waited in silence.

"Okay."

"You're doing the right thing helping your friend, Linda. You're also protecting the women that I watched the little bastard stalking at the mall."

"Oh, my God, no!"

"Yes. He hasn't done anything yet, but I watched him trawling for his next victim."

"I wish you would just kill him," Kelly said before she took a long drink of her wine.

"No, we will put him in prison where he can be somebody's girlfriend."

"That's poetic justice," said Linda, while Kelly nodded in agreement.

Chapter Eleven

I wondered whether things were slow in order to teach me patience or to wind my spring for the strike. Regardless of the reason, waiting was what I had to do.

I'd been on the case for nine days, seven of those days tailing John Keagey. So far, his only bad behavior was following women around in malls. He had yet to visit his stash of personal items stolen from his victims. I decided to play with his mind.

I waited at the confectionery supply across the street from where he worked. I stood behind my Jeep with the voice thrower focused on the wall of An Apple Less Web Designs. I said a few words of *Lakhota*. I heard them in my earphones. The gadget worked. I played with the focus while I whispered *Lakhota* prayers and listened to them in my ears.

I had just tightened both sonic projector mounts and made a test when Keagey walked out the door. I pressed the mike key. In a soft but taunting falsetto, I spoke.

"Johnny. Oh, Johnny."

Keagey whipped around, his eyes wide, his mouth open.

"Johnny, why won't you play with me again?"

Keagey whirled around.

"Johnny, I've been lonely. Please play with me."

"Where are you? Let me see you."

He was looking at the wall. At least his ears were working.

"Oh, you're no fun. You know how much I liked it with you. I like it rough. But if you won't play, I might have to get another playmate."

Keagey looked around for a few minutes. I stayed quiet. He moved slowly to his car, his head swiveling as he fumbled for his keys, got into his car, and immediately locked the doors. He drove quickly out of the lot. I was about to follow him when my cell phone chirped.

"*Hau?*"

"Hi. It's Maria Vacarro."

"*Hau*, Maria. What's up?" I said as I tailed Keagey.

"Robert and I can meet you tonight, if it's not too short notice."

Keagey was just three cars ahead of me. We were in the right lane heading south on General's/West.

"Tonight's fine. Where would you like to meet?"

Keagey continued in the right lane, which meant he was going for the freeway.

"Do you know Ego Alley in Historic Annapolis?"

"At City Dock?"

"Yes. Can we meet you there at six?"

Keagey turned right onto the freeway on-ramp. I followed.

"Six's fine."

If Keagey was heading for his condo, I was prepared to get past the guard. I trailed Keagey to where he turned off Bay Ridge and drove down to the guard shack at the entrance of his condominiums. I stopped at the top of the street. While Keagey drove the last few blocks home, I opened the hatchback and lifted a tarp. I pulled out my "Roccanelli's Pizza" car-roof sign and anchored its magnetic feet onto the Jeep's roof. There was no such pizza place in Annapolis, but I doubted that the guard would notice. I drove down the street and stopped at the guard shack.

"I gotta pizza to deliver."

I always talked funny around potential witnesses.

"Go ahead."

I drove on. Maybe the guard was there to keep the riff-raff out, but to let the pizza in. That was probably the nature of security in Annapolis. I followed the route I'd seen Keagey drive. I started looking for addresses as soon as I made the first turn. Finally, after having to retrace my route a few times, I found Keagey's condo.

I parked across from it and got out. Nobody was around, so I stood behind the Jeep and focused the sonic contraption on the wall, then panned to the plate-glass window of his unit. In my headphones I heard what sounded like a television, but with a muted double-toned sound. I'd read about this effect on the web-site where I'd gotten the drawings to build my gadget. I was listening to sound on the other side of double-paned glass.

That meant that any voice transmission I made wouldn't be clear enough on the inside of Keagey's condo to talk to him. Single-paned windows would have worked, but who has them anymore? I was lucky they weren't triple-paned and argon-filled. If I'd had a laser-echo device, I might have been able to listen, but that still left the task of putting the tormenting voice where Keagey could hear it. That wasn't possible with my level of tech.

I packed it in. That was probably good, since I didn't want the guard to send out a search party. I put the gadget away and drove out. When I stopped at the guard shack, I waved to the old coot. He just nodded his head a little, then went back to watching his television.

I drove up to Bay Ridge and turned right. A block later, I pulled into a shopping center and parked. I got out, stored my fake pizza company sign, then drove the little distance through Eastport to the Spa Creek bridge that took me into the historic district of Annapolis.

I drove around Annapolis' City Dock and turned right into the waterfront lot. The Ego Alley Bar & Grill slid by on the left, while the narrow body of water it's named for slid by on the right. The little slip of water was so narrow and visible to the town square that it was said "you have to have a big ego to bring a big boat into this little tourist alley." The name "Ego Alley" stuck.

How ironic: I was meeting with Maria and Robert to plan her freedom just a few yards from where Franklin, Jefferson, and Adams signed the Treaty of Paris ending the Revolutionary War at the Annapolis City Dock.

The yachts tied to the bulkhead were beautiful in ornate teak and fiberglass. Huge sailboat masts towered over luxury powerboats. Annapolis is often referred to as the "no visible means of support" town since everyone seems to be out on boats and never at work.

I parked in front of the Harbor Master's office and walked the boardwalk back to the Ego Alley. I sat at one of their outdoor tables. The weather was nice. Perhaps Maria and Robert would like to sit outside. It would take a while for someone inside to notice me outside, but that was okay. I watched people walk around the quaint village.

A big black bird swooped in and landed on the luggage rack of a Chevy Suburban parked at the curb.

"Are you going to feed me something or what?"

I spoke in a soft voice, trying to not make a scene.

"Raven, since when do I feed you?"

"Humor me. I don't feel like doing the 'only you can see me' magic right now. If you feed me something, it will be a cover story while we talk."

"What have I got to feed you?"

"Go next door to Storm Brothers Ice-cream and grab a sack of broken cones," Raven suggested.

"You're always ready with a fast answer."

"What do you want me to do, learn to stutter?"

"What?"

"Never mind. Just get those ice-cream cones."

I stood.

"Big handfuls."

"Don't be a spectacle," I said.

I left before Raven Who Hops could get me in trouble for talking to an unregistered alien. I saw the box with the sign that said, "Free Bird Food." How did he know this was here? I took one of the bags and put three big handfuls into it.

"What took you so long?"

"Since when do you eat earth food?"

"Just start breaking off pieces and tossing them over here."

He raised his head and opened his beak. While I broke and tossed pieces, he whistled bird calls. A few dozen finch, sparrows, and pigeons flew in from all directions to eat. People started to look. A few took photographs.

"You just wanted me to feed the birds."

"It's been a slow spring, and the little ones are on their way."

Raven Who Hops returned to the roof of the car while I tossed cone-crumbs to hungry, tiny-winged brothers and sisters.

"How do you think you're doing with your task?"

"Progress is slow, but I can't move on the target until I have the alibis set for the others."

"You will complete that tonight."

"Perhaps …"

"Mom! Look! He's talking to a crow!"

I looked toward the youth. I switched to American.

"*Lakhota* don't talk to Crow if they can help it."

Raven chuckled as the boy gave me a confused look.

"He's a Raven, not a crow."

"Like a Baltimore Raven?"

"Kind of. Except those Ravens are men who play football. This is a real raven."

"Not really. I just look like one," Raven corrected in *Lakhota*.

I spoke *sotto voce* out of the side of my mouth.

"Don't bother me when I'm talking my way out of your getting me into trouble."

I turned back to the boy and spoke in American.

"This raven is my friend."

"Your friend?"

"We've known each other for a long time."

"How'd you meet?"

"He … just came to me."

He started pulling on his mother's sleeve.

"Can I have a raven like he has?"

The mother started to drag the boy away.

"We'll see, dear."

"Please!" was all I heard before they were out of earshot.

"Thanks for making trouble for me," I said.

"It's good to talk your way out of situations. It builds character."

"I don't think you're very funny."

"Maybe not, but you sure were. You should have seen the look on your face. Just feed my little friends, and then the people you wait for will arrive."

He hopped off the car into traffic, making a Mercedes-Benz screech to a halt. He continued across the road and up onto the bulkhead of Ego Alley, where he hopped into flight and climbed without beating his wings. When he cleared The Sign of the Whale shop on Compromise Street, he vanished.

"I might have guessed you would be feeding birds."

Maria Vacarro walked up with a tall man. His dark hair had a perfect haircut, and his clothes were tailored in an understated way. He wore smooth leather boots that disappeared into tapered black trousers. His light blue Oxford shirt was crisp and open at the collar. His navy blue blazer was unbuttoned, showing his flat stomach.

Maria's hair was once again in a perfect pony-tail, which allowed her diamond earrings to catch the last of the sunlight. Tonight she wore navy-blue slacks and a white blouse covered by a long leather coat. I had seen couples like them in the breeders' circle at the racetrack where Roy Campagnella worked.

The birds scattered as I stood up.

"Maria, how are you?"

"Fine, thank you. This is my friend Robert McKinnon."

After he glanced at my ponytail, he met my eyes.

"I am happy to meet you."

I put out my paw for a shake.

"Likewise."

He reached out and we shook.

"You are an Indian. Are you Blackfoot?"

"No, but they are cousins. Why?"

"I raise horses. One of my trainers is Blackfoot. I'd swear he can talk to the horses."

"He probably can."

These two were obviously part of Maryland's horse set.

"You should come to my ranch on the Eastern Shore and meet him."

Perhaps he lived near John Kelloms' buffalo ranch.

"Is that where you live?"

"No, Maria and I live in Gibson Island."

I knew of that rich enclave, and noticed that he didn't share their address with me. He turned to Maria.

"You must be cold. Let's go inside."

Robert was closest to the door, so he opened it and motioned us in. Maria went first, with me following. The sign on the roped-off stairway read "Closed for a Private Party." We stepped past it into the main room. It had a Caribbean motif, with surfboards and rum banners covering the walls between jute nets with colorful stuffed fish and painted floats, while a sign over the bar read "Only Sailors get Blown Offshore."

A tropical fish tank sat below the wine rack in the back. Ten tiny tables and a cozy loveseat with a coffee table filled the whole room. The rest of the room was filled with the curved bar with tall stools.

As Robert closed the door, Maria spoke to a woman with wavy blond hair.

"Hi, Bridget. There's three tonight."

"Maria! How've you been?

"Fine. How are you?"

Bridget stepped close and kissed cheeks with Maria. Robert stepped up and did the same. She gave me a once- and then a twice-over. I returned the favor. Her skirt showed her legs from mid-thigh down to her pumps. Her blouse was a dress version of a tropical island print. She was too thin for my tastes, but I wasn't there to find a date. I was supposed to be remaining anonymous. Another plan shot to hell.

"Hi. I'm Bridget Frankel. This is my club."

Her eyes flashed over her smile. Her long-fingered right hand reached for mine.

"I'm Ben. It's certainly colorful."

Her hands were warm and strong. Her long and lithe neck muscles disappeared into the open collar of her shirt. A single charcoal freckle on her left clavicle stood in stark contrast to her ivory skin.

"Thank you. I hope you like it."

She turned to Maria and touched her wrist.

"Sweetie, I have to go upstairs. Angie will take care of you."

"Have fun," Maria answered.

A young woman in tan slacks and a blouse like Bridget's came over. She gestured to the half-full room.

"Sit anywhere; I'll bring you menus."

She walked away, leaving us to choose a table.

Robert smiled

"Our usual table is open."

They both looked to the small loveseat against the wall with the low table and two chairs opposite it. It was as if a small living room sat in the middle of the eclectic little bar.

"That's fine with me. Let's sit."

I crossed to it and sat in one of the chairs facing the loveseat. Robert and Maria sat together.

"So ... here we are," she said.

"Yes, but this isn't the right setting. I thought I said to pick out a place where people didn't know you, where it was crowded and noisy."

"I never heard that. Rita told me to pick my closest friend, someone whom I could trust, and to go to dinner with you."

"When did you talk to Rita last?"

"Last week. Why?"

"That would have been before I gave Rita improved instructions." I looked at them both. "It's too late. Bridget, Angie, and the bartender have all seen us together."

"Is that a problem?" Robert asked. "Why shouldn't we be seen with you?"

"It's probably overly protective, but I was trying to make sure that there were no witnesses that could put any of our group together.

"You're not a felon, are you?"

"Robert!"

Maria stuck up for me. That was a good sign.

"I haven't even had a parking ticket."

He looked indifferent.

"I'm glad you asked, though." I looked to Maria. "The idea was that we would get together and plan Maria's alibi for when you join me and the others. If we did it in a noisy bar where you aren't known, then it would be hard to find witnesses who could put any of us together before we do our operation."

"Oh. I'm sorry." She paused. "What do we do now?"

"We've already been seen. Even if we went somewhere else, we couldn't change that fact. All we can do is hope that my plan is perfect and that the cops will never investigate, so they'll never ask Bridget if she saw you with anyone unusual."

"I wish I'd have checked in with Rita again."

"Don't worry. If there is any blame, it is mine for not providing better instructions." I still sensed the blessing of the Great Father. "We should continue."

Robert spoke, "What do we need to do?"

I lowered my voice.

"First, we should all speak softly. Next, we need to cut our conversations whenever anyone comes near. Since my back is to the room, you will need to be the look-outs. If we get someone incoming, use some normal conversation phrase like 'How's work?' to warn me. We can ad-lib until they are gone."

Maria said, "Incoming."

Understanding dawned just as Angie appeared at my elbow.

"Here are some menus. Can I start you off with a cocktail?"

Maria started.

"I'll have a Chardonnay."

"I'll have a pint of your house ale."

They all looked to me.

"Do you have herbal tea?"

"We have a box of Stash. I'll bring you a pot of hot water and you can pick your own from our stash of Stash."

She faced Maria and Robert.

"I'll get your drinks. In the meantime, our specials are in the menu. If you have any questions, just let me know."

After Angie left, Robert said, "You were saying we should not let anyone know what we're planning. What is the plan?"

"Maria, can you trust him?"

Her eyes filled with tears, but didn't overflow. She took an embroidered kerchief from her purse and dabbed them dry.

"Yes."

"Maria and I were getting serious. I had just started to carry around a diamond ring, looking for

124

the right opportunity to ask her to marry me when that damned John …"

"No names. 'That little bastard' will do to identify him."

"I was about to pop the question when that little bastard … It's been tough on Maria. It's put our relationship on hold. I'd do anything to fix this. I want our life back."

"If things work out according to my plan, Maria will reclaim a lot of her old self."

"Just tell me what you want me to do," Maria said.

"Me, too," offered Robert.

I looked at Maria.

"All you have to do is meet me when and where I say, bring some head and shoe covers, as well as some surgical gloves with you from the office. As you're leaving, call Robert to do his part."

"I can do that."

"What's my part?" he asked.

"You get to go out on a date with your sweetie, only she won't be there."

"I don't understand."

"You drive to the mall and buy two tickets to a movie, keeping the receipt and tickets. Next, go to the food court and buy dinner for two, something she likes and something you like. Keep the receipt. Throw away as much food as you like, but don't give it to a panhandler. Witnesses might remember that."

"That's it?"

"Be careful handling the movie tickets. Tear one off leaving your fingerprints on it. Hand it to the ticket-taker and keep the torn stub. Go a little ways in, then turn around and leave. Take out the remaining ticket by the edges and hand it to the ticket-taker on the way in the second time and keep the stub in your shirt pocket or someplace safe."

I looked back and forth between them, but continued speaking to Robert.

"Watch the movie. Keep good mental notes. When it's over, drive to Maria's. She should be home by then. If not, just wait inside for her."

"I should give her the second ticket stub, right?"

"Right."

I turned to Maria, who said, "So, how was work today?"

I caught it this time.

"Fine. The same old stuff. How about you?"

Angie put the drinks on the table.

"What can I get you?"

I hadn't even looked at the menu. Maria and Robert were regulars. I'd wing it when it was my turn.

Maria went first.

"I'll have the coconut shrimp."

"I'll have the Caribbean Goat Stew."

I looked to Robert.

"What was it that I said sounded good?"

Robert blinked twice.

"It was the Island Burger, wasn't it?"

"Yeah, that was it."

I turned to Angie.

"I'll have the Island Burger well-done, even a little burnt. No mayo or dressing, but lots of veggies."

"Lettuce and tomatoes … how about pickles? It comes with caramelized onion shreds."

"That's fine."

"I'll get your food order in. It won't take long. Another pint, Robby?"

"Sure."

When Angie was gone, Robert said, "The Island Burger is just a cheeseburger made with Gouda. I hope you like it."

"I'm sure I will. Now, where were we?"

Robert had the thread.

"We were covering the second ticket stub."

"Right. Maria, you need to start keeping receipts and ticket stubs and that kind of thing in the bottom of your purse. That way if you get asked, you will have your alibi ticket stub in there with other ones. It will look suspicious if the only receipt you have is the one for your alibi."

"That's not a problem. I already save all my receipts for my bookkeeper."

"Good, you will have no trouble convincing the police that the movie stub is just another receipt. Perhaps to sell it even better, you should let her keep the dinner receipt, too. The date and time stamps will make your alibi air-tight, as long as you swear that you were together and you both can answer questions about the movie's plot. Take her to see the same movie the next day in a nearby town to make sure she knows it. If my plan goes off without a hitch, then you will never need to use that knowledge."

"What is that plan?" Robert asked.

"Can't tell. The less anyone knows about it, the better it will work. I need to count on the spontaneity of the four women. None of them can know about it beforehand."

"There's nothing we can do to pry it out of you?"

127

"Not a thing."

"Then we should change the subject to something we can discuss."

Everyone was curious. If they knew the plan, they would be shocked. Anticipation from not knowing would build their energy.

They would need it.

Chapter Twelve

I needed strength, too.

Lakhota ways are rooted in family life. Though I lived alone, I was still a member of my family, my band, my tribe, and my nation. My home was my sanctuary where I drew strength from those roots. The time was coming when I would be tested. Only deep roots would withstand the storm of war.

The Winged Brothers always wake up before the sun. The rooster crows at dawn, but if you've been awake early, you know that the Winged Brothers are awake long before that. They fly around in the twilight before daylight breaks the eastern line.

Each morning since ancient times, our holiest priest prays the sun up from the ground. Later the same day, he prays it down into the earth. We know that the sun will rise and set without our prayers. We aren't stupid. Praying the sun up and down each day isn't about making the universe function properly: it's about our fulfilling our own function in the universe.

Lakhota priests still pray the sun up and down. Every morning I pray the rite, usually on my Crownsville hilltop. No matter where I am at dusk, I chant the core blessing of the sunset, if only to myself.

The morning prayers were complete. I waited in patient hope the Great Father would bless me with a vision. Instead, he granted a time of peace. *Taku Skanskan* moved his presence on to another place. I soaked in the peace.

The largest of my domes sat just west of the center of the hilltop clearing. The second and third, in descending size, were connected, making a line to the northwest. A doorway of each dome looked east toward the rising of the sun.

I sat naked on a skin on the ground in front of the first dome's door. I knew every tree and stone in view. A footpath led to the northeast, where the trail joined the driveway leading down to the road. A small gravel circle marked the space where cars could be parked. A small fence corralled the metal-box beasts.

Lakhota cherish the sacred hoop, and thus make everything we can a circle, including our homes. It's funny how the *wasiçiu* make everything a square: a square meal, a square deal, even their homes and businesses are inside squared structures. The *Lakhota* often wonder what it is about the square that the *wasiçiu* worship.

The fire that had cleared the hilltop left an almost perfect circle open to the sky. A Cherokee construction company came from North Carolina to Crownsville and did most of the heavy work while I was still in physical therapy. They were as sensitive to Earth Mother as I was. We disturbed as little as possible while building the domes. What had been harmed was restored. Except for the three domes, the car corral, and the sweat-lodge, everything was as it had been before we started.

Many Tall Brothers stood on the slopes around the clearing. Most were white oak, with a few pin oaks near the driveway. I planted various medicinal herbs around the clearing. The red birch and eastern red cedar I'd planted along the northern rim were doing fine, and the Osage Orange on the southwestern rim were getting tall.

The hilltop was attuned to *Wakan Tanka*. The trees and rocks were happy as sunlight warmed their sides. The wheel of life had a new cycle of the sun to use. Everywhere were the sounds of natural morning movements.

It was time to start my day. I stood and walked to the east-facing front door. The sun was above the horizon, shining into my home, my *tipi*, and my heart. I closed the door and walked naked around the outside of the dome to the south-facing porch, passing through it to the outdoor shower.

I used the knife hanging on the wall to sharpen the edges on the eastern red cedar scraping sticks. Replacing the knife, I raised my lifestone and kissed it. It had begun to become chalky white at the edges. The piece of raw Kingman turquoise dropped to my chest on its leather thong.

My prayer of cleansing puffed in the cold air while cold water wet my skin. It wasn't a running stream, but it would do. I ignored the chills and scraped my skin with the wooden blades that I had just sharpened. In deference to Rita Cade, I used some of her shampoo on my hair, then rinsed it until the ponytail no longer made suds.

I stopped the shower, then used my hands to brush off what water I could. I entered my dwelling through the porch and walked around to the *tipi* flap, where I donned a doe-skin robe that hung from a peg. It drank the excess moisture from my skin, warming me after the morning ritual of cleansing the body, mind, and spirit, while immersed in a cold stream.

I gathered my used clothing and walked the perimeter around to the kitchen dome. In the laundry area, I opened the folding doors that hid the washer and dryer to start my laundry.

While it ran, I made some horsemint tea. Looking around my home, I was again struck with the sincerity and authenticity of my present life. When I was an impatient youth, I had left the Rez seeking a better life among the *wasiçiu*. I got older and secured a steady source of income. The nature and amount of that income had changed because of the accident, but I still had a steady source of *wasiçiu* money. Now I was living in more luxury and creature comfort than my whole band.

My heart ached. I missed my family. I shut the thought out. I knew that I couldn't focus on dwelling in my center with the poverty and rampant alcoholism on the Rez. I had to stay in Maryland until I completed my training journeys.

I had always known that my life wasn't completely my own, even when I tried to deny it. I was defined within the context of my culture. After the accident, I admitted my selfish indulgence. I had an obligation to my people and to *Wakan Tanka*. I resolved to return to the path I had left.

But I didn't know how to find my way back. I did the only thing I could think of: I returned to our sacred land to fast and pray on *Mahto Paha*.

Wakan Tanka sent Raven Who Hops to me as a guide. I listened to his council and learned of the way that I'd left. My feet were now on the Red Road, and they were leading me back to the Rez.

"You think of home."

I was used to Raven's appearing without warning, even behind my back. I answered without turning.

"Yes."

"And what do you think?"

"When I was younger, I didn't want my path. I left my people behind. Now I have all of this." I gestured around the rooms. "I was selfish. I thought only of myself."

"I know."

The tea kettle whistled. I poured the water over the herbs in the teapot.

"Long ago, when the *Lakhota* were free," Raven spoke, "they hunted in all directions. At the end of a winter encampment, the bands would separate in the spring and travel to different hunting grounds to make meat, clothing, and *tipi*s. Sometimes a young man would be led off on his own, rather than to remain with the existing bands."

Raven hopped onto the countertop as I checked the steeping tea.

"When a young man received a vision to go his own way, he would take his family to where *Wakan Tanka* led him. The next winter encampment allowed everyone to see how the other groups had done over the season. If the young man's family had much meat,

133

many fine hides and clothing, thick new blankets and *tipi* coverings, then the people would see that *Taku Skanskan* had given power to him."

"I think Uncle told me some of this," I said before I picked up the strainer for my tea.

"Over the winter, others would think about where they would go in the spring and whom they would hunt with. If the young man was deemed wise, then others would join the new group when it left in the spring. *Lakhota* recognize *Wakan Tanka*'s presence and power in our leaders. We follow only those who deserve it."

I strained a cup of tea and took a sip. Raven changed which eye looked at me and cocked his head.

"*Lakhota* follow by conscious choice, but those who lead do so by intuition, inspiration, valor, diligence, and sacrifice. All great men serve *Wakan Tanka*, helping him care for his people and the Great Island."

I swirled the tea in my cup.

"What does this have to do with my thinking about the Rez?"

"You left to seek your path. You hunted in new meadows. You have made much meat, clothing, and shelter. You learned how to make *wasiçiu* money: you've sent much of it to your parents, who, with that money, are able to deliver traditional food to shut-ins all over the Rez. In your own way, you are performing an ancient rite. In a way, you've started your own band, although you may not realize it."

"I'm not a leader. I don't want anyone joining me."

"Too late," said Raven.

"*Lakhota* don't tell other people how to live their lives. I will not do it."

"Follow your intuition," said Raven. "Let the *Lakhota* choose for themselves if they would follow you."

"I'm not starting any new traditions. Everyone must live his own path."

Raven tilted his head back then lowered it.

"How long has it been since you've seen your cousins, aunts, uncles, sisters, and brothers?"

"I've been gone a long time."

"You must return, so that you can see how you have changed. You must also allow them to observe who you've become and how *Wakan Tanka* has blessed you with power."

"I have no power."

"This summer, you must dance with the Sun. You will have four eagle claws in your chest. You must sweat, bleed, and endure to show *Wakan Tanka* that you are dedicated to your path. If he accepts your pledge, then you must accept the vision he gives you."

I stared at Raven Who Hops for a long time. I put down my teacup.

"I am last," I said. "I have nothing, eat nothing, until the people are clothed and fed."

"*Mahto*, you know the ancient pledge of a leader?"

"My uncle taught me that when I was younger, before I knew what it meant."

"Do you pray it now?"

"Yes. Though none depend on me."

Raven hopped around to come closer to me. He stood next to my teacup.

"All *Lakhota* depend on medicine men. Your path, *Mahto*, is to restore old ways and heal old wounds. It is a deep medicine for a whole nation."

"I'm not a leader. I only committed to walk the Red Road."

Raven stepped back a few paces and spread his wings to full span, reminding me of his size and power.

"*Lakhota* aren't like *wasiçiu* bosses who command others to do their bidding. We aren't shepherds herding their sheep to go in the direction we wish. *Lakhota* decide what must be done, then pledge to do it. We commit to the path and to the future. We perform the task, regardless of the risk or cost, alone if necessary. It doesn't matter if anyone follows."

"You're not a leader if no one follows," I said, but Raven didn't laugh.

"Your Stone-Dreaming is tuning your heart to *Wakan Tanka*'s. That is why you think of home."

"This is my home …"

"Your house is beginning to feel out of place. Your hilltop has begun to feel foreign. Soon, *Mahto*, you will leave all this. You will take your *tipi* home to the *Lakhota* lands."

"Raven, you tell me to let *Wakan Tanka* guide me, but then you tell me what to do."

"I tell you what you will do," Raven corrected, "because it is already in your heart."

"In the meantime," I said, straining more tea into my empty cup, "I have the task of realigning the local energy balance, of setting right how these women were wronged. What? No advice?"

Raven flew to the coat-rack by the backdoor and admired himself by the mirror there.

"To lead your enemy into your trap, you must know what motivates him, what he desires, and what most entices him."

He preened a few feathers.

"Then I can snare John Keagey in his own trap?"

Raven turned his head to the right to get a better look at that side in the mirror.

"You must be careful to not spoil the evidence you leave for the police. It must bear his fingerprints, not yours."

"You wouldn't happen to know where he keeps his stash of souvenirs, would you?"

Raven smoothed his chest feathers before he turned gracefully on his perch to face me.

"I know many things, but I am not at liberty to say. This is your task, not mine. You must walk the distance."

"I had a feeling you would say that."

"*Mahto*, you are fun to watch. You knew I couldn't give you the answer and yet you asked anyway."

"Is there any help you can give me?"

Raven hopped back to the countertop, settling his glossy wings smoothly at his sides.

"When you make the walls talk to your target, it will be more effective if you name the voice 'Billy'."

"Who's 'Billy'?"

"His imaginary childhood friend. It's a *wasiçiu* thing. *Lakhota* have the spiritual universe to talk to," Raven said, lifting his right claw and flexing his talons. "*Lakhota* don't need imaginary friends."

"I've heard that the Celts have some lovely naiads and dryads to talk to. Maybe I should trade you in for one of those."

"None of them know much about *Lakhota* ways. Although naiads do give life to lakes, rivers, springs, and fountains; the others live in the woods. All serve the Great Fathers on the other side of the world …"

"I've heard they're very beautiful."

"I doubt they have more than a vague idea of *Lakhota* traditions."

"I'm only making fun, Raven," I said.

"Go ahead. Throw me away for some soft and curvy water-tart. Or a bare, leaf-covered tree-tart. Forget about me and all I've taught you."

"I wasn't serious, Raven. You know that."

"Yes, you were serious."

"Only a little," I said. "Forgive me."

Raven hopped onto my shoulder.

"You will find a mate soon enough, *Mahto*."

"I didn't know I was looking for one."

"Yes, you did."

I put my empty teacup in the dishwasher. I sighed, feeling Raven's feathers against my skin.

"It is lonely, *Mahto*, the waiting."

I nodded.

"Waiting is the only safe way to find your life-partner. Walk your path. When you find a woman traveling a path close to yours, get a little privacy, and then speak your heart."

Raven Who Hops went into flight, passing through a closed window, flying south before he vanished.

138

Meanwhile, I had many tasks to complete before I could meet my mate, as my spirit guide said I would.

After we found each other, she would come with me back to the Rez.

She would watch as I danced in the high summer's sun.

Chapter Thirteen

The universe must be rebalanced. You will soon meet your mate, and dance a Sun Dance."

But hurry up and wait. If achieving full priesthood weren't so important, I would simply cut Keagey's throat and be done with it. Instead, in trust, I waited.

I sat across the street from An Apple Less Web Designs, waiting for John Keagey to leave. He still had made no moves to visit his treasure stash of personal items taken from his victims. Today, I hoped to change that.

I sat in the cargo area with the rear hatch open. Earlier in the day, the manager of the confectionery supply had come out to ask me what I was doing loitering in her parking lot. I waved my old US Army ID and told her I was monitoring Defense Highway for any suspicious or terrorist activity. She asked if I was with the FBI. I told her no, but I couldn't reveal whom I was working for. She gave me a big wink and a knowing look before she went back inside.

I had the voice-thrower focused on the wall of the web design shop that Keagey's family had bought into so he could have a job. After a long time, he walked out the door. I stood and pressed the microphone key.

In a soft falsetto, I said, "Johnny. Oh, Johnny."

Keagey stopped and turned to look at the wall.

"Johnny, it's me, Billy. Why won't you play with me anymore?"

"I don't know any Billy."

He turned his head away, but not his body.

"We used to play together all the time when you were little. Johnny, please play with me now."

"My therapist helped me to stop hearing your voice. She says you don't exist."

"They used drugs on you, then kept you drugged until way past puberty. That's why you drink so much. That's why you don't play with me anymore. They don't love you, Johnny. Not like I do. They're only trying to control you. We were happier without them, weren't we?"

He looked back to the wall.

"Why should I believe you? You don't sound like Billy."

"You haven't listened to me for a long time. I thought you had forgotten me."

"They told me that it was bad to listen to you. I don't want to be crazy."

He glanced around, probably checking for witnesses who might see him talking to a wall.

"Don't worry. I won't talk when anyone else is around."

"Why won't you talk to me at home?"

Think fast, Injun, I told myself. I couldn't tell him the truth: that my voice-thrower wouldn't penetrate the double-paned glass of his condo. I hoped my explanation would work.

"Your attention and excitement were what made me strong before. I'm still weak from being ignored for so long. I only have enough power to talk outside, where I can use the earth's energy. Maybe after I grow stronger, I can be with you everywhere."

"Is that why you won't talk to me in the car?"

"I am too weak to move very fast. I also can't stay for very long. I'm not strong enough yet."

"Can I help you get strong?"

"The excitement you have been having is what made me strong enough to make contact."

"You mean, the trial?"

"No. I mean, when you were so strong and manly with the women. I felt your strength and power. It rekindled my own."

"You mean my mastery of women makes you stronger?"

"It makes both of us stronger. When you make them beg, you are a man. A real man. Not what they want you to be. When you're a real man, that makes me stronger, too."

Keagy switched his briefcase from one hand to the other and cleared his throat as he looked around again.

"I came to ask you to be strong for both of us."

A big lie is often easier for people to believe than a little one. At least, that's what Joseph Goebbels said. Not that I was emulating him. But lying to an enemy is allowed.

"It is wrong how your family drugged you and told you to not talk to me. Especially when I could have helped you with your enemies."

Keagy turned around and faced the wall.

"I know those who help your Uncle Seamus and Cousin Fred. No one made them give up their childhood friends"

"I knew they were the ones doing it to me. I'm going to march right up to Uncle ..."

"You can't do that. They will know that I'm the one who told you their secret."

"Yes, yes, of course."

"They will force you back into therapy. They will either drug you, or brainwash you into giving up the strength and power you have been acquiring for yourself."

"You're right. Yes, absolutely right. I can't tell them anything. They're all against me. But I'm too smart for them now. And ... you will help me, won't you?"

I made my voice softer.

"Yes, but I'm too weak to eavesdrop on your uncle. I must grow stronger before I attempt it. His invisible friend is too strong for me to hide from until I get stronger."

"Your voice is fading."

"I am weak. Do something manly. It will give me strength."

A good salesman stops selling when the sale is made, waiting for the mark to complete the transaction. I shut off the voice-thrower and put it away. I closed the back hatch and then walked around, entering the driver's seat. John Keagey continued to talk to the wall for a few moments — probably asking it what he should do that was "manly" enough — before he hurried to his car. I started my engine and followed.

I was lucky that Keagey was a fool. Any normal person would have spotted me tailing him. Not the idiot I was following. The fact that he swallowed the whole line of bull that I'd fed him without even burping said volumes about his lack of mental health. His mind was beyond sick: it was polluted.

I tailed him toward Eastport. I thought he was going home, but he continued past the Hilltop cutoff, ignored the shortcut at the Annapolis Fish Market, and drove past the liquor store where Forest Drive merged with Bay Ridge. When he turned left at the Giant, I thought it was a grocery run. Instead, he turned into the condos west of the shopping center.

He was heading for Kelly Larson's. I watched him drive past, then brake and signal for a turn. I pulled over and parked on the street short of Kelly's parking area. Keagey made a U-turn then pulled over and parked. I leaned down in the passenger seat and peeked out over the dashboard.

Keagey climbed out and crossed the street. He walked into a group of buildings. I got out and hurried to the rear where the grass and swing-sets were.

I started scanning stairwells. I got a hit on the third one: Kelly's. It appeared that Keagey had knocked on her door. I hid near a hedge and watched. After a few minutes, he unzipped his fly and began training his trouser snake right there in the open-air stairwell. I pulled my cell phone out and found the number to Kelly's throw-away cell phone. I pressed *send*. I waited through three rings before she answered.

"Hello."

"*Hau*, Kelly. Don't say my name."

"What's up?"

"Are you free to talk?"

144

"I'm on my way home. I'm alone."

"How far away are you?"

I watched Keagey. His hand was in a hurry while he stood still.

"I'm just getting onto 97 in Glen Burnie. Why?"

She was about a half an hour away.

"We have a situation developing."

From my distance, I couldn't see the details, but Keagey was weaving enough for me to believe he was singing soul music.

"What situation? Is it tonight? Are we ready?"

"No, not that situation."

Keagey was doing shallow knee-bends. After about six of them, he straightened his clothing and zipped his fly.

"Why did you call? Are you safe?"

Keagey started to descend the stairs, so I walked for my car.

"No troubles and no danger, but you might want to know what I just saw."

"Am I in danger?"

"No, but it's gross. You have to play this exactly how I say."

I was at the street and saw Keagey crossing to his car. I didn't think I could make it to my car without being spotted, so I stood back against the wall waiting for him to drive past. With luck I wouldn't lose him.

"When you get home, walk to your front door. Look on the door, the knob, and the ground for any goop. If you see anything, call the police. Tell them what you see. Tell them that you suspect it was left there by your stalker."

Her sharp intake of breath told me a lot. Unfortunately, that's when Keagey drove past.

"Hold on a second. I have to move."

Keeping to the cover of the parked cars, I ran for my Jeep. I got behind the wheel just as Keagey reached the stop sign at the beginning of street, heading back the way we'd come. I tossed the cell phone onto the seat so I could use both hands. I started the car and pulled a U-turn. I grabbed the cell phone again as I drove in the direction Keagey went.

"Are you still there?" I asked.

The voice on the other end of the phone sounded wet.

"Are you telling me that the bastard just shot his wad on my front door?"

"That appears to be the case. I was too far away to see the fluids, but the body movements gave that appearance."

Traffic on the main street had held Keagey on this side-street long enough to let me be only a third of a block away as he turned. When I turned, he was only four cars ahead of me. The cell phone was silent.

"Kelly, talk to me. Don't have a wreck. Say something."

"Can't you just kill him and get this over with?"

"You know, I can't. If you get the cops out and they take a sample, then you can have DNA proof that's he's breaking your restraining order."

"I won't be able to eat tonight."

"At least I warned you so you won't step in it or touch it. Do you have a flashlight in your purse?"

"Yes."

"Good. We can't tell anyone that I am helping you, so you can't say anyone told you they saw it and called you, because they would want to interview the witness."

Two of the three cars between Keagey and me were turning right like Keagey. He turned right at the Bay Ridge light. Since it was red, the next cars had to wait for breaks in traffic to turn.

"Tell the cops that when you went to put the key in the lock, your flashlight showed you something shiny. When you looked close, it looked goopy. You thought it might be semen, and that meant your stalker had been there. Tell them you will file a complaint."

"That won't do any good."

"Do it anyway. I will call you later to see how it went."

By the time I got to the front of the right turn lane, the light had turned green. I made the turn. I tried to spot Keagey, but he was gone. I pulled over to the side of the road.

"Remember, Kelly," I said into the cell phone, "don't do anything until the police come and do their job. After that, bleach is best for sterilizing everything."

I turned around and headed back to the Giant. I had sat for only a few minutes when I saw Kelly drive past and turn into her subdivision. It was almost fifteen minutes before a police car rolled past. The driver looked to be an early-thirties, white male.

I waited. In another five minutes, a second patrol drove to join the first. This one appeared to be a late-twenties, black man. I wondered who else would

147

show up. Twenty minutes down, an unknown number to go.

In another ten minutes, an unmarked police car with lights flashing but with no siren, zoomed down the road and turned on Kelly's street. The car's party hat went dark and a white gent who seemed fifty, with a flattop haircut and a sour-looking disposition, hurried into Kelly's building carrying some kind of a bag. I wondered what warranted the arrival of a *wasiçiu* Big-Belly.

I didn't have long to wait to find out. In less than five minutes, all three cops came out with the older plain-clothes guy bringing up the rear holding what appeared to be a trash bag. If I were closer, I might have been able to see how much they had in the bag. My cell phone rang.

"*Hau*?"

"Ben, it's Kelly."

"How are you doing?"

"They just left."

"What did they do?"

"The first cop was nice and took my statement. The second cop started taking samples. When I told the first cop who my stalker is, he called his dispatcher while the second cop asked me about the neighbors and if I knew anyone who would do this. I told him that it was Keagey. No one else would do something like that."

The cops managed to turn their cars around and were en route, most likely to a hot cup of coffee and a warm donut.

"Why are you upset?"

"The third cop showed up, a Lt. O'Maeghle. He even spelled it for me. He tossed a roll of paper towels to the first two cops and told them to clean up the mess."

"You're kidding, right?"

"No. Lt. O'Maeghle told me it was probably some punk kids that they would never catch. I told him that if he would just check the samples, they would match the little bastard."

"I'm sorry that I didn't take your advice, Kelly. You said it wouldn't do any good. I see now that the police have become co-dependents of the Kinkaed addiction to power. You told me, but I had still hoped for decent support from law enforcement. I will have to revise my strategy to make sure that what we uncover can't be swept under a rug."

Keagey had just upped the price I would pay for his scalp.

I hoped I could take a few cops down with him.

Chapter Fourteen

It takes an hour to properly sharpen a boot knife by hand. It takes many hours to handcraft a weapon. It made sense that crafting my plan to take down Keagey would take weeks to prepare. I was finally making progress, but I wanted more.

I had already prayed the sun up from the ground and showered when Raven Who Hops came. I was finishing my morning tea while dressing. I spoke first.

"*Hau,* Raven."

"*Hau.* How goes it?"

"Slowly, and you?"

"Fine. My other tasks for *Wakan Tanka* go well. You are not a disappointment either."

"I wish Keagey would reveal where he hides his trophies."

"Perhaps you don't understand your target as well as you should."

"How can that be? He's a simpleton who's haunted by delusions of mediocrity. His mind needs a three thousand episode oil change."

Raven hopped closer to me.

"Perhaps like the tree that falls in the woods when no one is there, he moves and makes sounds, even though nobody is there to observe."

I buttoned my shirt.

"You're saying, he's been there, but not when I was following."

"Yes. Think, *Mahto*. Why does he keep souvenirs?"

"They support his fantasies? They remind him of his conquests? They stimulate him by reminding him of his cruelty."

I tucked my shirt in my pants before I took another sip of tea. My back ached a bit when I leaned forward to get the cup. It probably ached because of all those hours in the car watching Keagy.

"There is more."

Raven hopped onto the robe-stand and looked me in the eye.

"Why do you wake-up before dawn?"

"To walk the lizard because I drink too much tea?"

"Why can't you *Lakhota* be more serious," said Raven, "like the *Dakhota*?"

"Buffalo Woman always did like them best."

"Tommy Smothers, you are now."

"Hey, how do you know so much about *wasiçiu* culture?"

"Answer my question."

"Okay, Sour-Man. In the morning, I pray to *Wakan Tanka* to align my life with the universe."

"To draw the power you need for the day?"

"Of course."

Raven cocked his head, waiting for me to continue. When I didn't, he hopped closer to me.

"Where does John Keagey get his morning power?"

I raised an eyebrow.

"His trophies. Of course."

"He may not realize that his rituals are prayers to *Iya*, the Chief of Evil, but they are. *Iya* drips a bit of power on John Keagey each time he handles his souvenirs, and then Keagy is again secure enough in his illusion that he can sit safely in a cubicle next to women co-workers."

I looked at Raven Who Hops, nodding.

"When he awakens, empty, after a bad dream, he goes to his trophies to re-inflate his ego. I need to track him in the morning."

"Yes."

"You're helping me for a reason. But you won't tell me, right?"

"Yes."

I was dressed. I walked my cup back to the kitchen. Raven hopped along behind. After putting the cup in the dishwasher, I turned to Raven.

"If you aren't going to help me any more than you already have, why are you still here? Are you just taunting me?"

"You'd deserve it, but no, I remain for another reason."

Raven looked at me. I looked at him. Time passed. He outlasted me. I spoke.

"I'm supposed to guess?"

"You should be able to sense it."

I felt around the room. I felt my aching back, and my clothes against my skin. I closed my eyes and felt the room again.

"Nobody here but us chickens, boss."

"Look deeper, *Mahto*."

I closed my eyes to feel for my connections to the universe. They were solid and flowing. Raven was challenging me to learn and grow. That meant something must be for me to feel. I started through my indirect connections. My link to my father and uncle were strong; through them I could feel the stones of the Standing Rock Rez. I felt toward my mother.

"Something about Mom."

"What?"

"I don't know."

"Call her."

"You know that less than a quarter of the people on the Rez have phones. She's one who doesn't. It's a poverty hell-hole."

"You sense there is something not complete in your connection through your mother."

"I don't sense pain … there's a … weakness in her presence."

"No immediate danger?"

"No."

"Try to reach her spirit. Also, try your father and uncle."

"What do they have to do with any of this?"

"You have learned enough this morning. Try putting a simple message on your connection."

"It's over a thousand miles."

"That is no impediment."

I closed my eyes and felt for my connection to Mom. I drew close to it. I thought of her love for me and put mine on the channel to her.

"You chose to send love. That is a wise first choice. Now get ready to listen."

A flood of emotions washed through me. I couldn't process more than a few of them. I felt love and joy along with concern.

"Don't think. Just feel. Let your heart respond. Understand later."

I concentrated on Mom. Our hearts touched. After a few minutes, the flow ebbed to a pleasant back and forth.

"I feel the rocking-twisting that I feel when *Taku Skanskan* moves me."

"Exactly the same?"

"Not exactly. It's like I'm floating, only slightly rocking."

"Tell me how your mother is."

"Mom is resting after a mild heart attack. She is thrilled that I know the ancient way of connecting. Now we will always know how the other is doing. She will call my cell phone tonight after supper. Our love is strong and her work goes well on the Rez."

Raven came closer to me.

"Can I talk to anyone in this way?"

He answered without turning his head toward me.

"You can sense anyone, but you can only communicate with people who have learned to be aware at that level."

"Why do so many avoid the *Lakhota* way?"

"*Lakhota* or *wasiçiu*?"

"*Lakhota*," I said. "If they knew the joy from resonating with Wakan, they wouldn't take *wasiçiu* drugs or drink firewater."

He went with me to the front door then outside.

"Your path is that of a restorer."

"I like 'restorer' better than 'leader'," I said, gently and slowly stretching my arms, shoulders, and back.

"The first becomes the second," said Raven before he flew to the west.

I breathed deeply after I finished my stretching. Then I walked down the northeastern slope to my Jeep.

It was a little before six in the morning when I parked on Cross Street outside the entrance to Keagey's condo association. I settled in to wait. I didn't want to start a connection to my uncle or dad then have to cut it off when Keagey rolled out.

Instead I searched for the connection from me to Teresa, Rita's sister. Teresa had been in my thoughts a lot lately. I didn't know if that was good or bad.

I felt for the tendril between her and me. It wasn't as thick as the one to Mom, but it was thicker than the threads connecting me to everyone else on earth. I felt Teresa's spirit.

A bit of happiness. Low-grade anxiety. I sent a pulse of affection to her to see what would happen. After a delay, a slow flow of warmth came back toward me. Interesting. I might have to investigate when I had a chance. But it would have to wait.

Keagey's car was approaching the speed-bumps coming out of the condo's lot. I started the Jeep and prepared to follow. The dashboard clock showed 6:54. I let him get a head-start, then went after him. He lived about four miles from his job. It couldn't be more than a few minutes drive. Either he had an early meeting or Raven Who Hops had given me some good advice.

Keagey turned right, heading toward the historical district. By the time I turned onto Bay Ridge, he was six cars ahead. I prayed aloud in *Lakhota* while I tracked my target.

> I stand in my heart.
> Though I ride an iron dog, I stand in my heart.
> I stand for the weak.
> I stand to straighten a path.
> I stand.
>
> Listen, *Inyan,* hear my voice.
> Listen with your son, *Iktomi.*
> I stand asking for your look, a glance to my task.
> I stand in hope of the Trickster's help.
> I stand for *Wakinyan* to look my way.

Wakan Tanka's presence filled the car, carried by *Taku Skanskan*. Faint swirling pulses of brightly colored energy filled the Jeep's cab, rotating right to left.

I trusted.

I accepted.

I relaxed.

The energy faded as we approached Sixth Street. Keagey turned left toward the Spa Creek Bridge. There was another light before the bridge. If I didn't make that light with him, I might lose my target.

I chose not to worry.

I relaxed.

If the universe aligned for me, so be it. If it didn't, there were other days.

When I got there and turned, I could see Keagey's car stopped ahead. In a short distance I had to stop, too. The driver of the car ahead of me shut off his engine. He got out and began stretching his leg muscles.

I rolled down my window.

In my best *wasiçiu* voice, I asked, "Pardon me. Why are we stopped?"

"The drawbridge is up. They're letting big boats in and out of upper Spa Creek."

"Will it be long?"

"No, just a few minutes."

I cranked my window closed and waited. I turned an inner eye toward the strand linking Teresa and me. It still felt warm and friendly. I focused on it and thought of her mocha brown eyes. I felt a surge of my own emotions that must have transferred to Teresa's tendril. It took almost a minute, but I felt feedback from her. I didn't know if she was responding to me or to the emotions flowing to her subconscious.

It's hard to know what an untrained *wasiçiu* could sense. Probably as much as an untrained *Lakhota*. Many *wasiçiu* came from Celtic stock. They might still have ancestral connections to ancient ways, even if they don't practice them. Other *wasiçius* had gypsy blood, or traced from ancient tribes like the Sumerians that roamed Europe before the Christianized Romans burned their form of Hellenized Catholicism on the world, trying to eliminate every spiritual practice considered "pagan."

157

There was a chance that one or more of those ancient peoples were part of Teresa's heritage. If so, perhaps she knew it was I who'd sent her a throb of attraction.

I didn't get a chance to find out. The drawbridge lowered; traffic began to move. The man ahead of me stopped stretching and saddled up. Keagey's car began to roll. Car by car, progress rolled back toward me. As Keagey crossed the intersection, I was in motion, too.

As I reached the light, it turned yellow. I went with the car ahead of me. I couldn't see the traffic light overhead, but I believe I cleared the intersection before the light changed. We rolled over the bridge from Eastport into Annapolis' Historic District. Yacht clubs and boat-yards bordered the basin. From the bridge I saw the Naval Academy's sea wall and grounds before I descended into streets and buildings dating from the 1600s.

Keagey drove into the traffic circle at the city dock and went a little more than half-way around before driving uphill on a road that led to a steepled church. It was a challenge watching both Keagey and the traffic, but I managed. Two cars between us pulled off before we made it to a light in the middle of the uphill street. The light turned red.

I was amazed that Keagey hadn't turned rabbit at the sight of a turquoise Jeep Cherokee by now. He was either a blind fool or felt so secure in the capital of Maryland that he never checked for a tail.

I didn't care. I just wanted him to lead me to his stash that the police had never found.

The light turned green, and the small convoy drove its way up the hill and around Church Circle. Keagey took the second right between two old buildings. I couldn't read all of the signs as I went past, but I caught one that said the building on the right was the Governor's Mansion. The Senate's offices were on the left.

Keagey turned left on Roscoe Rowe Boulevard. I was only two cars back when I turned left. We drove over an unnamed creek and onto the next Annapolis peninsula. This one had more churches and government buildings. On the left-hand side, a courthouse obscured part of the Navy and Marine Corps Memorial Football Stadium.

We waited at the Taylor Avenue traffic light. In case Keagey might be looking, I tried to look like a weary commuter on my way to work. After a time, the light changed, and we started off.

Keagey still hadn't spotted me. Instead he drove with the flow of traffic, keeping to the right lane. When we reached the next light, he turned right onto Melvin, then right again onto one of the small side streets. I was too busy trying to avoid being obvious to catch the name. Keagey cruised the narrow lane while I pulled over to watch.

He drove past three small office buildings before pulling into the lot of the fourth. I sat in my car, hoping to see whatever I could, wishing I was closer.

But I didn't dare get any nearer. If he saw me and suspected his hiding place was compromised, he might clean it out before I had a chance to see what he was hiding.

Keagey walked to the door, using a key to let himself in. I turned into the lane, drove past the building, looking for a parking place that would also provide some cover from Keagey when he reappeared. A pine tree's branches hung out into the lane on the left.

I hung a U-turn and pulled over to park. The dashboard clock showed 7:08. I felt that this was his hideaway, but I couldn't be sure if Keagey removed his mementoes and hid them elsewhere. I kept my eyes open, extending my senses to their fullest.

I sensed Raven Who Hops approaching from the east. I retracted my senses and waited. Raven hopped from nothing onto the passenger seat.

"*Hau, Mahtochikla.*"

"*Hau,* Raven."

"You took my advice."

"Is this where he keeps his stash?"

"You must discover things on your own, through your own effort. You may seek advice, but you must make your own decisions as to what to do."

I shifted in my seat, easing the ache in my back.

"I wouldn't want you to lose your mentoring license."

"I should ask for *Dakhota* students. They're more focused than you are."

"They wouldn't get half of your jokes."

"They take half as long to add one plus one and get two."

"Any advice?"

"Whatever you find of Keagey's must be useable by the police."

160

"We've been over that. I can't leave a trace. Otherwise, his attorneys might claim his trophies were planted."

"You haven't told me how you will do that, O Wise One."

"I'll wear gloves and a good hat."

Raven shook his head.

"Now you are thinking like a *wasiçiu*."

I didn't have a quarter to buy a clue.

"What do you have in mind?"

"Nothing that you shouldn't already know."

He cocked his head, looking me straight in the eyes.

"You offered a prayer for your task."

"Yes?"

"I understood your request for *Inyan*'s aid. The Rock is the source of all Stone People medicine. Your asking for *Wakinyan*'s help was also wise, since the Winged Ones will surely be a part of how you complete your task."

Raven cocked his head and looked at me with a beady left eye. I grew tired of waiting, shifting in my seat trying to find a more comfortable position, unbuckling my seatbelt to arch my back both ways. Raven shifted his head to level, but kept the bead on me.

"What you were thinking when you included *Inyan*'s son, *Iktomi*? Did you even think about the words that you used?"

"Shouldn't I enlist the aid of the Gods?"

"You must be very careful how you phrase the prayer. You asked for a 'glance' from *Inyan*, which is a good strategy. On the other hand, you asked for *Iktomi* the Trickster's help."

"I want to trick Keagey into making mistakes."

Yes, but the Trickster will treat each aspect of your request with equal attention."

"Meaning?"

"*Iktomi* is sure to return some trick to you."

"Won't he help me with Keagey?"

"Probably, but since your prayer was so vague, only asking for help, you are likely to receive more help than you want. *Iktomi*'s favorite lesson is how bad careless planning can be. Your prayer was poorly planned and carelessly worded. 'Please help me' is dangerous compared to 'Please help Keagey align with truth.' Can you see that?"

"I'm in trouble?"

"You may achieve your goal, but expect a trick or some pain to be inflicted on you, or someone near you."

I let my forehead rest on the steering wheel.

"Thanks for the gloom report."

"Don't get cheeky. Be on watch. Be very careful in your planning."

What could I say after finding out that I'd pinned a 'kick me' sign to my back, then asked the biggest prankster in the universe to look my way? I just sat with my mouth closed and my mind open. Raven looked at me for a while, but refused to offer advice.

"I'll leave you now. Plan your task well. Walk in peace, *Mahtochikla*."

"Walk in beauty, Raven."

I looked at the clock. 7:23. Keagey had been in the small office building for fifteen minutes. I asked my subconscious mind for an answer to the puzzle. If the answer lay within me, it would find it. 7:26. I had little to do and a lot of time to do it in.

I stretched out my senses and found Keagey's presence in the building. I extended my senses in a narrow band and moved it around me in a circle. I found a very large stone presence underground to the east of where I was parked. It felt like a granite or schist intrusion into the sedimentary rock of the peninsula.

I connected to it. It was full of ancient energy locked in a stony lattice of fused quartz and various mafic compounds, dark colored minerals rich in magnesium and iron. The stone recognized me. It let me approach. We both were quiet as our existence merged.

I thanked the Stone Brother for sharing his presence with me. I withdrew from the connection and opened my eyes.

Keagey was coming out the door. I looked at the clock. 8:41. He had been in there for over an hour-and-a-half. He got into his car and returned to Melvin. I watched him turn toward Rowe. He was probably on his way to work.

I needed to get to work, too.

I got out and walked over to the office building. I noted the address and the lack of a sign saying what the business was. The other small buildings on the narrow street had signage, but not this one.

I went back to the Jeep and called Max. After eight rings his gravel voice came on.

"West Bail Bonds. Can I help you?"

"*Hau,* Max. It's Ben."

"Hey, Chief. How's life?"

"I'm still on the little bastard job."

"I don't want to know details, but how's that going?"

"I think I've got something, but I need to find out who owns and occupies a building in Annapolis."

"You gotta go downtown for that. You go to the courthouse. It's off of Church Circle. Upstairs, they got the property records on microfilm. The recent stuff is on the computer. That will tell you who owns it. You can look up the use-permits in another place there. The librarians will help you."

"Thanks, Max."

"Any time. Call me when you're done, so I can forget some more things."

"Love having a bad memory, huh?"

"Never know when you might need it. See ya, Ugly."

"You, too, Double Ugly."

I closed the cell phone and started the Jeep. As I reversed my course and headed back into the historic district, the answer to Raven's question came to me.

I could use raccoons to search Keagey's rooms.

Now, where could I find some raccoons that could keep a secret, and how would I convince them to do a sneak-and-peek?

That was easy.

Pay them.

Chapter Fifteen

The assassin known as The Jackal roamed free for decades before he was caught. He had avoided capture by not being noticed. Other folks avoided prosecution by extreme over-exposure. Chief among them were politicians who craved the media spotlight, but routinely committed wrongdoings and crimes that they swept under the rug.

The reason that politicians aren't in jail is that they all do it. Avoiding the subject keeps folks from shining the lamp of suspicion in their eyes. Just how well politicians can hide in plain sight was revealed by my visit to the Maryland Hall of Records.

The title search went well. The property was owned by a political action committee whose function was to elect and re-elect members of the Kinkaed family. Since we were in between election cycles, it made sense that Keagey could have unfettered and undisturbed access to the building.

He may very well have a stash there, but since Keagey would have to clear out before the next election, he wouldn't have his permanent collection mounted on the walls.

Still, I needed to find out what was there. I would try that tonight. I dialed Rita and got Teresa's number. I called her.

"Maryland Educator's Association."

"Teresa Cade, please."

"One moment, please."

Time passed. Almost as slowly as when I was watching Keagy.

"Ms. Cade here."

"*Hau*, Teresa. It's Ben Pace."

"Ben! Is something happening?"

I cleared my throat as I changed my position in the Jeep.

"Teresa, would you like to do lunch today?"

"This is a surprise …"

I closed my eyes. Maybe it hadn't been Teresa's energy that had responded to mine. I was just about to make some excuse about having to be near her workplace around lunch and not wanting to eat alone when she answered.

"I don't get long for lunch, but there are a lot of places around the Historic District."

"Pick one you like."

"McGarvey's. It's a nice spot in the Market Place at City Dock."

"Maybe I could get there a little early and get us a table."

"Ask for a table in the atrium. I'll be there at noon."

Maybe more than one plan was coming together.

I hoped I could stay focused.

Quite a few lives depended on it.

Chapter Sixteen

More than two centuries ago, Jefferson and Franklin sat at Annapolis' city dock, and signed The Treaty of Paris, ending the Revolutionary War. The *wasiçius* had thrown off the yoke of a distant tyrant who played favorites, made decisions favoring local despots, who did the same, and protected those despots no matter what they did.

The one who protected Keagey had two years left in the first of her two expected terms as Maryland's Governor. When I arrived at the restaurant, I tried to stop thinking about Keagey.

McGarvey's entry room had tables to the left and a long bar on the right. In the back of the first room was the entrance to a second room on the left, where we turned. The ceiling had been removed, creating a two-story space. The only portion of the second floor that remained was on the street-side wall, where a balcony perched over the raw-bar where the oyster-shuckers cut their catch. A tree grew from the floor to the roof. It was the biggest houseplant I'd ever seen.

I'd just finished steeping my tea when Teresa walked in. She was wearing a black skirt that showed some leg above the knee, and a black turtleneck with long sleeves. Her charcoal hose outlined her legs, making her calves look great above high heels.

Thinking how I should have tried to sense her approach, I stood and looked into her eyes. I extended my hand but then remembered some Campagnella advice: "Never take a woman's hand unless she offers it."

I looked at my hand before I saw her chair beyond it. I reached over and pulled it out. Teresa nodded at the chair gesture.

"Hi, Ben. Aren't you afraid someone will see us together?"

"This isn't about that. That other thing is about not being seen with Rita. I wanted to see you for another reason."

"What?"

Just then we were approached by the server. For one of the few times, I was happy to be interrupted.

"Hi. My name is Megan. Can I start you off with something to drink?"

Teresa chose iced tea. I kept my hot tea. Megan rattled off some specials then left. I remained silent and watched Teresa's eyes.

"So, Ben, what other reason did you want to see me about?"

"I wanted to see if my memory of your eyes was right."

Teresa blinked, then smiled.

"Aren't you the smooth one?" she said as she leaned forward and looked thoughtful. "You know, this might sound ... weird ... but I had this feeling you'd call me today. I sort of woke up with the idea in my head. Strange, huh?"

"No. Early this morning is when I decided that I would call you."

"No. Really?"

I nodded

Just then our server came back with a refill of hot water for my tea and with Teresa's iced tea. *Iktomi* must prod waiters to show up just before a joke's punch line or when a conversation is getting good. Teresa chose the Old Bay Chicken Salad sandwich. I went with a well-done burger.

"Why don't you try to read my mind? I think I'd like that," I said.

I filled my mind with images of Teresa and me in a heated after-date embrace. She scrunched up her face and narrowed her eyes as she stared at me.

"You're thinking of the number six and a movie theater."

"I was thinking about asking you out on a date."

"Yes. Take me to a movie, and pick me up at six. Did Rita tell you that I said you were cute?"

"No, but she laughed when I asked for your number. Was she supposed to tell me?"

"No, she was supposed to keep her mouth shut."

"But you just told me."

"No, I didn't. I asked if she said anything. I didn't actually say that I'd said you were cute."

Her reaction confused me. Teresa must have seen something in my eyes. I didn't think I had lost my face control.

"Don't worry: you're cute enough to go out with."

I raised an eyebrow.

"Cute?"

She held her index finger and thumb an inch apart.

"About this much."

She smiled. I could feel the warmth from across the table. We drank our tea. She set hers down and looked up.

"Did you come all the way to Annapolis to ask me out? You could have done that on the phone."

"Yes, but you might have forgotten how cute I was."

"So, you asked me to lunch remind me how cute you are so you could ask me out? You're so sweet. Okay, I'll go out with you.

"Thank you."

"Where are we going?"

"I don't know."

"When?"

"Soon."

"Soon?" said Teresa. "That's pretty vague."

"I have to be vague at the moment. I'm getting close to solving Rita's problem, and I have to stay with that as it develops."

Teresa nodded, her facial expression changing from light-hearted to serious.

"This morning I was thinking about you. About how interesting and beautiful you are. My heart soared. It was just before six. I could really feel a connection to you. I tried to send you a message. It felt as if you answered."

"Wow! I thought I heard someone call my name. I woke up thinking about you. Nobody was there, so I went back to sleep."

She reached over and touched the back of my hand with her fingers.

"Perhaps we have a connection."

"I'd like to find out," she said, smiling.

Chapter Seventeen

Perfect crimes can be committed if the crooks can not be traced or prosecuted. No database on earth held raccoon fingerprints.

It was before eight at night, dark and cool. I parked at the Anne Arundel County Historical Archives. South of the Archive, an undeveloped piece of land covered by a wooded grove stretched a half-a-mile before ending on the banks of College Creek.

I walked into the grove and placed some cooked chicken and sliced apple on a rock. I moved back and performed the summoning ritual. In less than two minutes, a raccoon mother with two cubs stepped into the clearing. I spoke in a soft voice.

"Hello, Older Sister. Thank you for coming."

"Who are you? How is it that you talk to me?"

"I am a *Lakhota* priest. We speak the ancient earth tongue. I brought you an offering of food. And, yes, Wise Mother, it is safe."

She let her cubs go. They looked at her. She pushed them with her nose and they all went for the food together. She took two apple wedges while the cubs went straight for the chicken.

"What do you want?" she asked after eating the first slice.

"I need help searching a building."

"I can't leave my cubs. You will need to talk to others in the tribe."

She took some chicken. The cubs never slowed down.

"Will you send them to me?"

"Yes."

I remained silent while they ate. In a few moments, the plate was clean. She pushed the two cubs toward the forest, then turned to look at me.

"Wait here. I will send the Old One."

I waited. In about five minutes, an old white-and-grey raccoon arrived. He was big, but despite his age and girth, he walked lightly.

"Hello, Older Brother. Walk in peace."

"Walk in beauty, Little Brother," he answered. "You wish to trade with us?"

"Yes. I gave your younger sister food. I have more."

I held the bag out for him. He looked at me warily. I spoke to his fear.

"I will not harm you. I am not like other two-legged. I speak the ancient earth-tongue. Is that not proof?"

He took the sack and looked in it. He took a handful of the de-boned chicken and, without looking, threw the bag over his shoulder. Two raccoons shot out of the undergrowth and caught it. They disappeared into the forest.

"What do you wish us to do for more food?"

"I need two of your tribe to enter a building and tell me what is there."

"Why not do it yourself?"

"I cannot have been there ..."

"You want us to count *coup* on your enemy."

He looked into the forest and gave a nod. A younger but mature brown-and-black raccoon stepped from a deep shadow. Old One looked back to me.

"This one, Hard Run, is one of my best. He has a brother, Rides Back, who will be here soon. Bring back food for forty. Walk in peace."

He vanished into the shadows without a sound. A gentle breeze stirred the leaves, causing the silver spots of moonlight to dance on the ground.

"I greet you, Hard Run. I am Bear-Man."

"I greet you, Bear-Man."

I looked to him and thought I saw apprehension. It is hard to read emotions in another species.

"Is there something between us?"

"I have never spoken with a two-legged before."

"In ancient times, it was common."

"Most two-legged have no sense or manners. Some are kind and give us food, but don't want to talk or be friends."

"They treat my people the same."

"But you are two-legged."

"Yes, but I am as different from them as you from the opossum."

"I couldn't tell that by looking at you."

"Yes, we all look alike to you."

He held up a paw.

"Let me listen to the forest for a moment."

We sat in silence, alert to the sounds of any approach. After a few moments, he spoke.

"What is it we will do tonight?"

"I will drive us about a mile to ..."

173

"What is 'drive'? And 'mile'?"

"I am sorry, Hard Run. I used two-legged words. How long has it been since you and Old One came to me?"

"The time of a long run."

"We need to take two long runs toward the star that stands still. We can get there in the time of one short run if we use my smelly and noisy beast."

"The beasts that stay hot a long time?"

"Yes."

"I've always wondered about riding in one."

"Tonight you will ride twice: there and back."

A young raccoon walked up to Hard Run. He was almost full-grown, with smooth fur just turning black in the darker stripes. The beauty of his pelt made his mentor's battle scars obvious, even in the dim light.

"Did someone say my name?"

"No," Hard Run said. "Tonight we will ride in the noisy, smelly beast."

Rides Back chattered.

"Everyone will be so jealous!"

"A forager does not boast of his joys, any more than he cries about his pains. He finds food and returns. The whole tribe will ride with us tonight, even though it will be only the two of us and Bear Man inside the beast. When we return, we will tell the tribe about it."

"Aren't you excited?"

"We do not know this two-legged. He speaks our language, and the Old One said to trust him, but we must be careful. The two-legged may be tricking us."

"Hard Run is right, Little Brother. While I promise that I am your friend, your tribe relies on you. You must never completely trust a stranger."

"We must watch the way we come," said Hard Run, "in case we have to make our way home without this two-legged."

I asked, "Shall we start?"

Hard Run agreed.

We walked to the parked Jeep. While I walked through the middle of the open areas, my two companions stayed close to the bushes and trees. For the last thirty feet of open space, they waited at the forest edge until I opened a side door to let them in. They galloped over.

I cracked the window before closing the door. I walked around and did the same for the other rear passenger window before sitting in the driver seat. The rear seat was folded flat giving them the whole rear cabin in which to roam. I drove north.

"Please do not come up here. It is dangerous to climb around the person sitting in this seat. Feel free to be anywhere else. If you feel sick, put your nose into the wind at the openings at the top of the moving wall where you climbed in. Also, I need to stop and get the food. Will you wait in here?"

"Yes."

"While I am gone, do not worry about any two-legged who may see you. A magic called 'locks' keep the moving walls closed. They will be able to see you, but they will not be able to touch you. Just show them that you are brave and noble, and they will be happy to leave you alone."

I pulled into Graul's Grocery and parked. I auto-locked the doors before I went in. I returned with a 20-pound sack of fish-flavored cat food, three pounds of fried chicken pieces, five sacks of apples, and two Rice Krispy marshmallow bars. A man and a young boy were looking in my window. The man spoke.

"We were just looking at your raccoons."

"It's okay. But be careful."

The man took his boy by the shoulders and stepped back a few paces. I unlocked the car and loaded the groceries into the back seat. Rides Back stuck his head around the door to look at the man and boy. I stepped back to close the door. I spoke in the ancient earth tongue to the raccoon.

"Watch your hands, or they may get hurt."

He pulled his hands back. I closed the door.

"Daddy, he talked funny to the raccoon."

I closed the door and backed out.

"That food smells good. Can I have some right now?"

Rides Back was already digging in the bags.

"No. I must take that to the Old One."

I tossed the two Rice Krispies treats into the back.

"I brought these for you to eat on the way over. They will give you strength and energy for a short time."

I heard the bags being torn open and looked into the rear-view mirror. The two raccoons were happily eating the Rice Krispy bars. I pulled over and parked.

"We are here."

The street was quiet. It was almost 9:00 p.m. There were no cars in the lot and the building was dark. The street light two buildings north gave some

176

illumination. Nothing moved on the ground. I extended my senses and felt no humans in the local area. I got out, walked around the car, and opened the side door for my partners in crime.

"Do you need anything before we begin?"

"Water," said Rides Back.

"I'm sorry. I should have offered some earlier. I forgot that you don't have saliva glands."

They looked at each other as I pulled a bottle from the Jeep's supply and opened it for them.

When they were finished, I pointed to Keagey's building.

"We need to find a way in."

"Let's go look," Hard Run said as he loped forward.

Rides Back and I followed. Hard Run walked the perimeter of the building before speaking.

"I think I saw an opening on the other side."

He headed back the way we came. On the south side, under a towering pine tree, there did appear to be a small opening in one of the second story windows. A lot of people left windows open this time of year, airing out the winter stuffiness. Lucky for them, most Maryland towns away from Baltimore and DC still have a low crime rate.

The tree branches were too far away to use. I needed to get the raccoons up to where they could get in. I looked about and saw a length of lumber nearby, probably left over from making yard signs. I put on a pair of brown cotton work gloves. I leaned the wood against the wall under the windowsill.

"Hard Run, care to take a look?"

"Thank you, Bear-Man."

177

He climbed up my leg, up my back, then up the lumber. At the top, he spoke.

"Yes, we can enter here, but there is a barrier as a weave of thin sticks."

"The two-legged call that a 'screen'. You can remove it by lifting up on it and then pulling the bottom toward you."

I looked down as he dropped it to my left, away from the street. He slid the window further open.

"What do you want us to find?"

"Look for the room that has the strongest smell of a two-legged. Then come and tell me what you see there."

He disappeared inside. Rides Back climbed and joined his brother inside. I lowered the lumber and set it against the wall. I crouched and waited. After about ten minutes, two heads poked out of the window.

"Bear-Man."

I stood.

"Can you describe the building?"

"It's big and empty. The rooms have openings over the doors. We used them to get around."

"The two-leggeds call them 'transoms'. What can you tell me about the two-leggeds that come to this building?"

"There are a lot of old smells, but only one two-legged has been here recently."

"Where do you smell him?"

"We smell him in two rooms. One of them is small and cold, with one of those see-yourself places."

" 'Mirrors'. That small cold room is not important. What is the other room?"

"It is the size of the other rooms with a large wood box and places where two-leggeds might sit. The walls are covered by flat faces that don't move."

" 'Pictures'. How many?"

"Many."

"Were they all over, or were some of the walls bare?"

"The flat faces were everywhere but on the door."

"Did you smell anyone besides the recent visitor?"

"No. There were no other smells."

I used the lumber to lift the screen to the window.

"Set this where you can reach it, then send Rides Back down and close up."

The screen disappeared and Rides Back reversed himself down to me and the ground. After Hard Run had climbed to the ground, I put the lumber back where I found it, and returned my gloves to my pocket.

"Did you find what you were looking for, Bear Man?"

"I don't know."

I couldn't be sure, but I believed that we had found Keagey's stash house. The pictures were surely his victims. Hard Run and Rides Back couldn't smell anyone else, but Keagey might keep his souvenirs in sealed containers to preserve their smells.

It had to be his stash.

It just had to be.

Chapter Eighteen

I wasn't the only one itching to act. Keagey was actively seeking his next victim. I hoped my time would come before he raped another woman.

I was waiting across the street from An Apple Less Web Designs. For two days, John Keagey had spent a lot of time driving around, taking photographs of women. I couldn't discover any pattern. I used the voice-thrower every chance I could to goad him into action. Keagey walked out and turned toward his car. I keyed the mike.

"Johnny, can you come out and play? I want to grow strong so I can help you take on your uncle, but I need you to become strong, too."

"Haven't you been watching me the last week?"

"Yes, you took a lot of pictures. Who are you looking for, Johnny? "

"My next girlfriend. Have you seen me on the computer?"

"What do you do there?"

"I get into a group on the Internet. I sent them some money, and they gave me all sorts of information about women on AWOL."

"AWOL?"

"Any Where On-Line. I get data on women who use the phone numbers around here to connect to the

Internet. I drove around taking their pictures. Did you see them on the wall?"

"Some of the new ones are pretty."

My mind's eye saw the flaming arrow in the sky. The sign of the time was active.

"I especially like the brunette and the one with the auburn hair. They excite me. Which one do you like?" asked Keagey.

"The brunette reminds me of … someone."

"She looks like the others. When they are under me, begging me, it almost makes up for Rebecca."

"It makes you strong to dominate her. I can feel it."

Keagey moved closer to the wall and lowered his voice. I had to concentrate with all my energy to hear him.

"Rebecca would be sick to see how strong I am now, wouldn't she?"

My stomach twisted, and I resisted the urge to gag. Still, I hoped tonight would push him over the edge.

"Perhaps, after your next conquest, I will be able to help you conquer Rebecca."

"You could do that?"

"Yes. Then with Rebecca at your side, you could take on your uncle."

Keagy glanced around before he gently stroked the wall with one hand.

"I'm so glad you're here. Tonight, I will make us both strong. I'll take my time so that you can be there, too. I won't do it until I hear your voice. Then we can take her together."

Keagey started toward his car. I shut off the voice-thrower and put it the passenger seat. I started the car and pulled to the edge of the street. He was about to go harvest a girl to rape. I had to prevent it.

The flaming arrow in my mind's eye was flying lower, as if it were tailing Keagey. This was the time. I had to stay on him. Losing him would lose the girl. I couldn't take that chance.

Keagey surprised me by turning away from the mall, heading west on Defense Highway. I tromped on the gas and shot in front of an eastbound truck, swinging into the westbound lanes. By the time the truck honked, I was tucked in behind Keagey.

It was a good thing. At the first light, he turned right. I followed, hoping I wasn't too close. Keagey kept his course and drove through the roundabout at the PetSmart. I snatched my cell phone and sent to Roy Campagnella's beeper.

I hoped he wasn't too busy with racetrack business to call me back. At the tone, I pressed my numbers and the pound sign. I heard the triple beep of acceptance. I ended the call.

I stayed with Keagey as he turned left into a set condos, then turned right inside the lot. I pulled in, but turned left. I went to the next turn in the lot and turned right, taking me on a path where I could observe him. After a minute when he didn't show, I drove down the way he'd gone. I found his Mercedes convertible parked down the street to the left. I turned right, then made a U-turn and parked. My cell phone rang.

"*Hau.*"

"You called?"

"I need some help. Quickly. Do you have anyone near Annapolis?"

"What do you need?"

"My turkey has gone into the bushes. If I go in to flush him out, I won't be able to follow him when he runs."

"Where are you?"

I told him.

"My Gobbler may attempt to take a hen."

"Uninvited?"

"Uninvited. I want to let it start — without damaging the hen — then interrupt it. The turkey will run. I won't be able to get to my car before he's gone. I need to know what undergrowth he goes to so I can flush him out."

"Someone will call you."

A few minutes later, a car pulled into a garage on Keagey's block. Nothing happened. As the clock crossed the half-hour, traffic started to pick up in this workday ghost-town. My cell phone rang.

"*Hau.*"

"I hear you need a hunter for a turkey shoot."

"Right."

"Wild or domestic Tom?"

"Domestic."

"Good. So, he can't fly. Loud Gobbler?"

"Only when he gets caught. Then his family gobbles with him."

"Big Tom, is he?"

"Not him. His family's pretty loud Gobblers, though."

"Okay. You want me to sit in a blind, wait for your Tom to run past, then follow him until you're able to get there."

"Right."

I described my Tom and his escape vehicle.

"I'll be there in ten minutes."

"By the way, while you're following the Tom, I might have some hen-mending to do."

"Do what you need to."

We ended the call. After almost forty-five minutes the victim's car pulled into the garage of the condo across from Keagey's car. As the garage door started to close, Keagy ran it, dove, and rolled underneath before the door hit the ground.

It had begun.

Chapter Nineteen

I slipped down the street to the scene of the crime. I didn't have a plan for this, so I tried to figure one out as I walked toward the victim's home. I had one thing working in my favor, at least: Keagey wouldn't consummate the rape until he heard Billy's voice. That didn't make it any easier on the victim, but it would delay the ultimate degradation and pain. And my walking in on him would end it.

I reached the townhouse. I put on my cotton work gloves and tried the garage door. It didn't open. I walked to the right, around to the front door. It was locked, too. My breathing got faster, as did my heartbeat, and I started to sweat. I went quickly around to the side to a small fence gate. It opened. I went in.

A patio door allowed me to see inside without being seen. Inside, Keagey lifted a cloth off the woman's face. When he stood up, she lay still. Chloroform. What a cowardly bastard. He couldn't even subdue them on his own. My anger rose as Keagey removed her clothes. After Keagey put her panties into his pocket, I knew I had to do something soon.

My gloved hand was clenching a small wrought iron trellis. Using that, I could get to the second floor.

I climbed, threw my leg over the balcony rail, and pulled on the handle of the second set of patio doors.

They were locked.

I clenched my gloved hands as I stood there.

Deep in my mind a thought rose as if coming up from the deep of the sea. I put my hands on the upper frame of the glass door. I felt into the earth, searching for the bedrock below. The stone welcomed me and shared his strength. Clothed in stone-ness, I lifted the sliding glass door.

The aluminum lock gave way. The door lifted free from the frame. As I pushed the bottom of the door in with my foot, I let my hands drop. After the door was out of its track, I leaned it against the wall at an angle that would keep it from falling. I shed my stone-ness. My back throbbed.

The bedroom opened onto a short hallway leading to stairs. The new construction floors didn't creak. I descended the stairs, listening intently as I went. The stairs ended at a wide spot between a living room with the front door and the room to the rear with the sliding glass door.

Keagey was talking to her, telling her his lies. It sounded as if she was trying to talk through a gag. I realized that if I pretended to be her boyfriend, Keagey might not hook my face to any future events. I retreated to the top of the stairs and used my most *wasiçiu*-sounding voice.

"Honey, is that you?"

Quiet downstairs.

"Honey?"

I started making clumping sounds on the stairs. I put on the cover of stone-ness. The stairs creaked under the added density.

"Honey?"

Though I spoke in a regular voice, it seemed to boom. I'd have to ask Raven about the effect of stone-ness on voices. I looked around the corner and saw Keagey swinging something that looked like a sap at my head. I just let it hit me. The impact on the back of my neck burst the leather sack's seams, sending buckshot everywhere. Keagey looked at the broken sap in his hand, then back at me.

He wasn't wearing gloves, which meant that he must wipe up on his way out. I grinned like *Iktomi*, the Trickster.

"They just don't make them like they used to."

He took a swing at me and hit me square in the jaw. The Stone People magic made it feel as if he was brushing some crumb from my face. Keagey pulled back his hand as if it were broken, it was probably just bruised. He grunted, in surprise or pain, I didn't know which.

"Who are you? What are you doing in our house? You better drop whatever you're trying to steal, Buddy, and get out of here before I break you in half."

I glanced into the den and frowned.

"Honey? Hey, what did you do to her?"

I grabbed Keagey's jacket arm, but not too tightly since I wanted him to run.

"What have you done, you ..."

Keagey ran. He sped to the door on the other side of the kitchen. The garage door was opening before the kitchen door through which he'd escaped had closed. I hurried into the den and knelt beside the frightened woman. She jerked away when I approached her. I took out my cell phone and called the last number.

"The turkey just escaped the coop."

"Hen okay?"

"Okay as she can be."

We ended the call. I picked up a throw blanket from the couch and covered the woman.

"I am going to take out the gag, then I will free you. I promise that I am one of the good guys. Will you please not attack me or scream or run until we talk?"

Wide-eyed, she shook her head. I unbuckled the gag and removed the ball from her mouth.

"Who are you? What are you doing in my home?"

"I'm the one trying to catch the serial rapist who just ran out of here. He hasn't been convicted yet. I was hired to track him until I could get enough evidence to nail him. I saw him slide under your garage door. I came down to stop him from hurting you."

"Why didn't you stop him before?"

I took out the cell phone and called Rita.

"*Hau*. It's started, but I need you to talk to a woman whom the little bastard was attacking when I walked in on him. Don't use any names. Just tell her what we are."

I held the phone to the woman's ear. She listened to Rita talked for a few minutes. Then she looked up at me.

"She wants to talk to you before you hang up."

188

I put the phone to my ear.

"Yes?"

"Are we on now?"

"Yes. Call everyone. Tell them to bring the supplies. I'll call each of you to give you directions. I have to go now."

I ended the call and faced the woman.

"We'll need you to help us nail that bastard to the wall like a hide for tanning. Do you think you're strong enough to do that?"

"Untie me, please."

I took my ankle knife from its sheath and lifted the blanket. Her eyes went wide with fear.

"I'm just going to cut the ropes in between your hands and between your feet. You should leave the parts around your wrists and ankles as intact as possible for the police to examine."

I began to cut the rope. After she sat up, rubbing her wrists, she pulled the blanket closer around her.

"First of all, you can't remember what I look like, and you certainly don't know who I am. As I was driving by, I saw a man slip into your garage as the door was closing. I came in to help. He attacked you. Afterward, you discovered that I must have gotten in by climbing up to your second story, getting the sliding glass door open, then coming downstairs to stop him from raping or killing you. He and I fought before the assailant ran away: you heard it but didn't see it. You weren't sure if I was here to help or to hurt you, so you kept your eyes tightly closed.

"As I cut you loose, I told you I was hired to tail the bastard and that's how I happened to be near enough stop the crime. You were still terrified and not sure if you could trust me, so you never got a look at me because you were afraid I'd hurt you or even kill you if I thought you could identify me. You still weren't sure if I was with him, or if I was who I said I was.

"You didn't recognize my voice and can't describe it. When you find out who did this to you, you will know why we have to use this subterfuge."

"Can't you tell me who he is?"

"His lawyer would claim I contaminated your mind against his client. We don't want that, so we never had this conversation. All I said was that I was hired to tail him, and when I saw him get into your house, I came in to keep him from hurting you. And that's all you know."

She huddled deeper into the blanket. I took $300 out of my wallet and showed it to her.

"This should pay for a locksmith to repair the lock on the door upstairs."

She turned her head to watch me put the money on the counter.

"Don't tell the cops I gave you the money, or they will take it and keep it as evidence until the case is closed, which may never happen. You'll get a receipt from the cops for the money, and never get it back."

She nodded, then lowered her head, her face touching the blanket, as if she were trying to hide from me.

"Report the crime. Please. If you don't, we'll never be able to stop him. Tell the police you wish to press charges for gross sexual imposition, molestation, attempted rape, assault and battery."

"But I don't know who he is."

190

"You don't have to. You saw his face, didn't you?"

"After he'd already stripped me and tied me up."

"Tell them that I told you the perpetrator hit me with a blackjack that broke and lost all of its buckshot. I never touched it, so they will be able to get fingerprints off of it. Also, he ran out the kitchen door to the garage, so the only prints that should be on it will be yours, since you live here, and his."

"What about yours? On the glass door upstairs and on the trellis?"

I held up my hands so she could see the gloves. She struggled to stand without letting the blanket slip and reveal anything. She looked at me.

"Don't touch anything except the phone. Tell them you want a policewoman here to examine the ropes that are still on you. After she is done, let them remove the ropes. Then you can get dressed."

"You mean I have to stay naked while the police are here?" she said, her eyes wide again.

"It is important that the crime scene remain undisturbed. And that's why you want a policewoman. The police are a little more sensitive to victims who've been sexually assaulted. Most forces have policewomen trained to be with the victims."

She started to cry.

"I feel so stupid. How could I not have seen him get into the garage before the door closed? How could I not have heard him …"

"Don't blame yourself. That will be giving him your power. Now, call the cops. And hide the money."

She picked up the money, opened one of the lower cupboard doors, pulled out a pile of skillets, put the money into the largest one, on the bottom, then piled the rest of the skillets in the largest one, as they had been. She closed the cupboard door. When she looked at me, I nodded.

While she picked up the phone, I turned and walked out the front door, leaving Keagey's fingerprints intact.

The situation was already bad. And it was about to become worse.

Before the night was over, I would have committed more felonies than Keagey.

Chapter Twenty

Where had the turkey gone?

As I walked to the Jeep, I put my work gloves in my pocket then pulled the cell phone and dialed the guy who had tailed Keagey.

"Did the turkey find some undergrowth?"

"Yeah, the Gobbler's hidden, and it's a gasser. He's in an old whorehouse in Jessup. Been out of business for a decade. It's just off Useless-1, a little north of MD-32."

"Can you sit on him until I get there?"

"Yeah, I got a few minutes. You sure the hen's okay?"

"As good as can be expected."

We ended the call. Crownsville was on the way to Jessup, so I swung over to my home and grabbed some supplies of my own. For the occasion, I used the car corral instead of leaving my car at the bottom of the hill and walking up as I usually did. I apologized to every plant and animal on the hill as I lugged supplies back to the car.

Twenty minutes later, I was in Jessup driving down the deserted street. A black BMW sat at the curb. I slowed to a halt beside it and lowered my passenger window. The Beamer's driver window opened. I'd never seen the man before.

"Don't we know some of the same people?"

"Maybe. I'm turkey hunting myself."

"There's a big fat Tom just down the road. Need any help?"

"No, he's my turkey. I can handle him. And thanks for asking about the hen."

"No problem. Don't like hens getting hurt. Really gets me riled."

His window went up before his car pulled away. He turned a tight U-turn and disappeared the way I'd came. I never heard his engine. I'd have to ask Roy who did his friend's muffler work.

Keagey's convertible was parked in the driveway of a big home a block away. The empty street was in a general state of disrepair. Abandoned foundations of buildings, empty lots, burned-out shells of houses.

The flaming arrow in my mind's eye flew and struck the ground in the front yard of the house where Keagey's car was parked. The drums of my ancestor's heartbeats were loud in my ears. Power blew through me like a hot wind. This was the moment. Tonight would be strong medicine for Keagey to swallow, and without a silver spoonful of sugar.

I opened the driver's window and listened. No movement. I drew energy to me and made a general summoning. It took a few minutes before some birds arrived.

"Fly in beauty, Winged Ones."

"Hello, human," said an owl.

The rest remained silent.

"Thank you for coming. Are you the only animals around?"

"There is little food here. Most of us are from a place toward the star that sits still, where there is much food."

"I have nothing with me to trade, but I can bring gifts later."

"What do you need?"

I told them.

"We can do that."

I grabbed a backpack and set out walking through the sparsely treed lots. Sixty feet in, I turned left toward Keagey's hideout. I walked quickly, always keeping a tree between my goal and me. In a few minutes, only one tree remained between me and the former whorehouse.

I stopped and sent a few pulses of the summoning. Winged ones flew in from everywhere. I saw that they were all males. Two woodpeckers flew up to the front door and began tapping it with their beaks.

They kept up the racket while I moved up on the side of the house. I looked into the room on the front corner before running past. At the front corner, I peeked again. The room was empty.

I tried reversing the Stone People magic, shedding weight and rigidity. I practically flew to the wall next to the door, then stood still.

The birds were still flying in as the woodpeckers were working on the door. I took the backpack off and set it next to me on the porch. After a few minutes, Keagey called from the other side of the door.

"Who is it? What do you want?"

The birds kept it up. The door opened a crack. The tufted titmouse brigade zoomed in through the narrow opening, followed by the house finch and sparrow squadrons. I could see them flying strafing runs at his head, grabbing hair with their claws, while dodging his flailing hands.

The door flew open and Keagey ran out, down the steps and into the yard. The ravens and the owl flew mock kamikaze runs. He was shielding his face when I launched off the porch, slamming into his knees from the back. He folded like a cheap lawn chair as the birds perched in tree branches.

I slid up his back and put my knees on his shoulders. I looped my left arm under his neck as he twisted his head back and forth, flopping like a Thanksgiving turkey about to meet the chopping block. I put my right hand on my left arm and worked the chokehold.

When he went limp, I held on for another count of two. I put my knees on the ground on either side of his body. I felt for his pulse, which was stupid: I couldn't feel it through my work gloves.

I'd have to risk it. I got one side of him and rolled him over. He was limp, but breathing. I thanked the Winged Brothers while I flipped Keagey back face-down. They flew away as I lifted Keagey by his belt and carried him like a folding garment bag into the house. I dumped him on the living room floor. Lifting him had further aggravated my back. I ignored it and continued.

I went on a quick bivouac. I found a wooden chair in the kitchen. I took it to the living room. Keagey was still out. I yanked off his boat shoes and peeled off his pants. His boxers came next. I pulled his shirt over his head. Except for his dark socks and sock garters, he was naked. I left them to make him look stupid.

From behind, I lifted him at his underarms and sat him in the chair. I ran and grabbed the backpack. Keagey was still out, but showing signs of coming out of it when I returned.

I pulled a roll of duct tape out of the backpack. I yanked Keagey's hands behind him, in back of the chair. I put about six wraps around his wrists, then leaned forward to tape his ankles to the chair. As I pushed his sock down to get his left ankle bare, his leg twitched and kicked out of my reach. I hauled it back in and taped it down with about six wraps. I went around the back of the chair and taped his right ankle down, too.

I grabbed his shirt and used my ankle knife to cut it in two. I would have bitten and torn it, but I didn't want to leave my DNA. I rolled one half of his shirt and flipped it over his eyes, knotting it behind his head. I knife-cut strips off the roll of tape and used them to tape down the edges of his shirt around his eyes. I taped the knot behind his head to make sure it wouldn't come loose.

With the first round applied, I went back to his wrists and ankles, applying a dozen twists around each. As a final touch, I ran loops of tape from his wrists to the chair's under-structure. After a dozen laps, I was sure that Keagey wasn't going anywhere.

I picked up his boxers and the other half of his shirt and placed it in a plastic bag, and tucked that into a zippered pocket in the backpack. He would certainly interpret it as trophy-taking. The other reason for keeping articles of clothing is that I might need a scent of Keagey for later, though I hoped not.

Outside, I walked to the Jeep and moved it in front of the abandoned house of ill-repute. I used the time to call each of the women. I made sure their alibis were being built, then gave the address and directions. I reminded them to bring their supplies.

I took the opportunity to search the house more thoroughly. It proved one of my earlier assumptions wrong. In an upstairs room, Keagey had his trophies on display. I took about forty pictures with a digital camera. One pair of panties looked to be a real mess of dried goop. I put those in a plastic bag, too. Just in case I needed to prove my case, I would have at least one of the gruesome trophies. Even a rough guess made the number of trophies much larger than the estimates of Keagey's attacks. My anger pulsed up a notch.

Downstairs, I finished the preparations for the evening's activities. Meanwhile, Keagey was cursing me, threatening me, or begging for something or the other. I ignored him like he'd ignored his victims. Sauce for the hen is good for the Gobbler.

I went outside and sat in the car. I typed a simple-text note and let the computer's electronic voice speak it into a cheap recorder I'd bought for the occasion. In another simple-text file I placed a listing of the evidence I had found, and where to find his planning room and his treasure stash.

I saved it to a fresh floppy. I attached the digital camera to the laptop and dropped the images into a folder with the simple-text file. I returned to the house.

I ignored Keagey's whining and dug his cell phone out of his pants pocket. I put it on the front windowsill with the floppy disk and the cheap tape-recorder. I pulled a second and nicer tape-recorder from the backpack and set it on the sill next to the cheap one.

Keagey was whining. It sounded like he was telling me that he could give me money if I would let him go. A lot of money. More than I could imagine.

He didn't understand at all.

He didn't know this was about spiritual power, not political power and money.

I left him and walked outside. I could hear him crying inside. I went to the back of the Jeep and opened the hatch. I found my medicine pouches and stuffed a big pinch of horsemint in my mouth then washed it down with water. It wasn't a good way to take the medicine, but I didn't have time to make tea.

I arranged my supplies while I waited for the girls. This was going to get messy.

I took a minute to pray.

I hoped the governor didn't have her state troopers standing guard, or we'd be the ones in jail tonight. Not Keagey.

Chapter Twenty-One

There is no expression of fear on the *Lakhota* Way. Of course, we have fears, but we set them aside in order to we walk our path. Tonight I would have to be fearless and brave enough for five people.

Kelly arrived first, full of questions. I convinced her to wait until the others arrived. I continued to assemble my plan.

"Did you bring the soiled diapers?"

"They're in the back of my car."

She unlocked her car and I retrieved the bags from the back seat. I carried them to the front porch and set them just inside the front door, out of the way. Keagey heard me and started bitching and whining again. I walked back to Kelly. She was excited.

"Is that the little bastard crying?"

"Not yet. He's angry and submissive by turns."

A car's headlamps approached. I hoped it wasn't a police cruiser. When it got close, I saw Maria behind the wheel. She agreed to remain at the curb with Kelly while I carried the bag of medical supplies to the front porch. This time Keagey tried taunting me from inside the house. It was pathetic to see the limp turkey trying to question my manhood. I ignored him.

As I walked back, Lisa was getting out of her car. I got them all to stay in the front yard while I put Lisa's vacuum cleaner bags on the porch.

When I returned, Rita was just arriving.

"Sorry I'm late. I had to give Teresa a haircut."

"At a time like this?" Kelly asked.

"It's for my alibi," Rita explained.

"Don't ask. Don't tell. Rita, did you bring the hair cuttings from your shop?"

She handed me two big bags full of hair. I carried them to the front porch then returned to the women. I looked each in the eyes as I talked.

"What we are about to do is illegal. We must make sure that you cannot be recognized. If we maintain our anonymity, then we will preserve the reasonable doubt that will prevent prosecution. Understood?"

All nods, with eager looks.

"Right now, John Keagey is naked in the front room of that house, with about two rolls of duct tape wrapping his wrists and ankles to a wooden chair. His eyes are covered and taped-down to prevent his seeing anything. He's been whining, begging, threatening, and attempting to bribe me. This is not going to be easy. Any last minute changes of heart?"

Silence.

"Fine. To get your power back, we need two things. We need Keagey to surrender, to give up his hold on evil. We also need his confession, to inform the police what should be investigated. When the little bastard has confessed his crimes and had a little 'come-to-Jesus', it will be an outward sign of the inner spiritual journey he must make. It will also signal that

201

your power is there to be reclaimed. Right now, I need a volunteer who will enforce justice and administer it to Keagey."

"I can do that," said Rita.

"I'm with you," said Kelly, standing beside Rita and putting her arm around her shoulders.

"You'll be able to push him until he confesses?"

"Yes," they said in unison.

"His confession won't be admissible in court, but it will give the police information that they can use in their investigation. We need to get those details. I'll be making two copies of his confession. I'll leave one. The other I'll take for safekeeping."

I took a deep breath.

"Let's get started."

I motioned for them to follow me. I handed each one a gadget from my bag.

"There's a voice-gooser built into each mask. Put it on and try talking."

While they put the masks on, I showed them where the power switch was located.

"All you have to do is speak softly. The mask will disguise and amplify your voice. It won't sound like you. It will drown out the sound of your own voice inside the mask."

When the women talked, the electronics shifted each one's voice into a different pitch and tone, making it hard to recognize the person speaking. They sounded like cartoon chipmunks.

"You must wear it at all times. You cannot allow him to hear your real voice. It would also help if you change your vocabulary and behaviors. That will further disguise your identity."

"What do you mean?" Maria asked.

"I plan on acting like a cross between a Goombah and a Cracker. I'm not an actor, so it will not be good, but at least I won't behave or sound like I normally do."

They nodded.

"The Frenchman Edmond Locard proved with his 'Principle of Exchange' that we leave traces of ourselves everywhere we go and take traces of those places with us when we depart. Maria brought these for us to wear. They will reduce the level of exchange."

I passed out the hair and shoe covers.

"Put them on. They will minimize hair dropping and obscure the real tread pattern of our shoes. While you are inside, don't spit or sneeze. Don't touch anything that you don't have to, including the little bastard inside."

While we put on the covers, I saw a look in Kelly's eyes.

"Don't worry. Keagey is blindfolded. He won't see you. Let's take off the voice-goosers while we setup."

I passed out the surgical gloves.

"Put on at least two pairs. We don't want to leave any finger or palm prints. Wear three layers if you can."

I pulled on my work gloves, snugging them up.

"If Locard was right, we are bound to leave some trace of ourselves here. I think I have a solution to that. After we finish, we will sprinkle Rita's sacks of hair all around. We will bury any of our hairs that fall under layers of red herring hairs. The crime lab won't

203

have the personnel to process the millions that we will leave them."

There were nods all around.

"We are certain to leave some fabric fibers as well. Our solution is to sprinkle the contents of Lisa's vacuum cleaner bags all around. The crime lab will have fabric fibers and other debris from offices and homes in three Maryland counties."

"We're not going to leave the diapers I brought, are we?" asked Kelly.

"No. We will use those as part of our ceremony. They will facilitate Keagey's degradation. We will smear him with the soiled diapers."

They all looked disgusted.

"It is symbolic, but it is also an action of power." I paused. "When Keagey raped you, he humiliated you. He bragged about his power and then made you beg for him to violate you. All through your ordeal, he made you transfer power and control to him. Rape is a violent crime focused on power and control, not on sex. The final violation is just a deed of degradation to seal the deal."

I saw shades of understanding creeping across their faces as they looked at me, as they looked at each other.

"We are here to reverse that process. We will humiliate John Keagey. He will feel what he made his victims feel. He will break and beg, just like his victims. He will beg you to humiliate him. He will yield his power and relinquish any claim to have any control over himself, let alone over others. Rita and Kelly will make sure that he confesses his sins and names his victims."

"And this will return our lives and dignity to us?"

"*Lakhota* and white folks are human. We share much; we each have a common immortal spirit. We are strands woven into the same fabric of the universe. I am confident that what I would do for my *Lakhota* sisters will work for you, my fair-skinned sisters. After tonight, you will not fear John Keagey. He will have no hold over you, but you will be strong enough to frighten him if he ever darkens your doorway again."

Kelly's face had a wry smile. The others nodded in understanding.

"Each of you should take a turn as inquisitor while the rest of us watch. You may do or say anything you wish, as long as you don't reveal our identities. You may strike him with the whips I provide. This is the time to ask him anything that you want him to answer. This is the time to tell him what he has done was wrong. You will never have another chance. Don't say 'when you raped me.' Use 'when you rape a woman' instead."

They were not looking at me. Each had gone for a walk in her private garden of pain. I cleared my throat. When I had their attention, I continued.

"It is very important that you make him beg. We must help him discover regret for his evil. He must believe that if he displeases you, then his life is forfeit. Only then will he release his psychic hold on you. Only then will he give back what he stole from you, allowing you to recover it."

There were tears in a couple of their eyes, but they wiped them away and straightened their shoulders, standing tall, like their sisters.

"I don't know about *wasiçiu* mental health, but I know the spirit world and how much it influences our daily lives and the destiny of the earth. Be prepared: he will thrash around, he may foam at the mouth, he may even speak in tongues. If we do this right, he will soil himself."

Rita said, "Good."

"Remember, this is not revenge. You are not stooping to his level. We are together as a jury of peers. We are here to strip away his appearance of power and innocence. You will never be afraid of him again. He is likely to lose the will to harass women."

They suddenly all spoke at once, asking questions. I held up my hand until they quieted down. I pointed to my face. They put on their voice-goosers and adjusted them tightly.

It was time to begin.

Chapter Twenty-Two

I walked into the former whorehouse. It was dark, so I tried a light-switch. A feeble forty-watt bulb came on overhead. It provided light without attracting attention. If Keagey had chosen the wattage, he'd chosen it well. I walked over and stood behind him. I held my voice-gooser in my hand. I used the Billy voice.

"Johnny, you've been a very bad boy. A very bad boy. I don't know if I want to play with you anymore."

"Billy?" he mumbled from under the duct-tape over his mouth. "Billy?"

I put on the voice-gooser.

"No, I'm not Billy. I am the man who knocked you out and tied you naked to the chair. If you displease me at all tonight, I will cut a thousand little cuts into your skin so you bleed out."

He turned his blindfolded head toward the sound of my voice. I moved around him to a different place in the room.

"Long before you pass out from the blood loss, Johnny, I will slice your balls into little pieces. Your little nuts will only take three slices each. Maybe the left one is four slices thick. What do you think? Do you think that would be a good game to play?"

From under the duct tape, he mumbled something that sounded like a threat, something about his family, its money and its power.

I interrupted him.

"I've tracked you for over a month. I know how many times you wipe your ass when you shit. I can kill you any time I want. We ain't met till now 'cause I was waiting for you to show me this love nest."

It sounded like he was throwing obscenities at me from beneath the duct tape. He cursed me as I moved to another position.

"I'll bet this is where you lost your cherry. Yeah, your sister was working the night-shift in the next room when you rode your pencil-dick to your first pip-squeak squirt."

He turned his head toward my voice, and even with the duct tape covering his mouth, I could understand the obscenity he said that time.

"Tell me, Johnny, was your mother good that night? Or did she have too many other customers for you to get a turn? Did you have to substitute your sister instead? What? You're not going to introduce me to your mama? Too bad, I was going to pay her at least twenty bucks."

I bent close and whispered into his ear. He jumped. At least, his body jumped as much as it could considering the fact that he was taped to the chair.

"You have only one chance to save your pitiful life. And it's slimmer than your dick. A jury is about to come in the front door, and its members are going to listen as you plead your case. If you convince them that you've changed your ways, the jury members might spare your life. Then you will still be breathing when we leave."

He turned his muted, blinded face toward me. I kept whispering, confident that he could hear me.

"If the jury votes against you, I will make sure you scream for every second of the three hours that it will take you to die. *Capisce?*"

He nodded.

"Remember, like I said: it ain't me you gotta convince that you're gonna change your ways. It's the jury. And personally, I think you better start praying to whatever it is you believe in."

Chapter Twenty-Three

The front door opened. Chipmunk gasps could be heard as the women walked in and saw me bending over the naked and helpless form of their former assailant.

"Take his socks off. Ten bucks says that even when he's barefoot and naked, he can't count to twenty-one."

Score one for Rita. She had started right in on Keagey. He whined under the tape and over the chipmunk laughter.

"I'm your jury foreman. How've you been, little limp dick? You are the most undesirable piece of shit in the world. You aren't even good enough to be fertilizer."

I began my prayers. A rite of passage was in process. I reached into the backpack and pulled out four cat-of-nine-tails. I passed them out. Rita flicked hers across his chest. He flinched and made a noise of pain. Rita whacked him hard then spoke over his muffled scream.

"When you've got somebody hog-tied, you sure can dish it out, but now that you're the one who's all trussed-up, you can't take it, can you?"

Swish. Slap. Whish. Slap.

Rita drove her point home with the help of the nine leather strips, with a metal bead on each end.

He cried out each time. When he tried to speak, his words muffled, Rita hit him again. The others laughed. I made a suggestion.

"Don't just whip his shoulders. His entire body must learn what it is like to be humiliated."

"I have a better idea," Kelly interjected.

Keagey moved his head in her direction, perhaps to get a better listen.

"Just a member of the jury. You don't think there are too many members hanging around, do you?"

Kelly picked up her foot and set it on top of Keagey's flaccid lie of manhood. Beneath the tape, Keagey's voice keened in pain. Kelly let up a bit.

"We could always chop it off and throw it outside."

"We're the jury. We need to listen to his defense first."

After Rita hit him again, Kelly took a few turns hitting him on the thighs and hips. Keagey writhed. I crossed to the front door and closed it, loudly, passing Lisa and Maria in the process.

I whispered to them, "You need to take part. Otherwise, you can't get your power back."

They shuffled from the entry area into the room, but, though each held a whip, the two women hung back.

"When should we take the tape off?"

"When he's ready to confess."

"Do you think he's ready yet?"

Though Keagey nodded rapidly toward the sound of their voices, Rita shook her head.

"No, I don't think he's ready."

211

After she hit him again, she turned around, to Lisa and Maria, motioning them forward. They didn't move. I motioned to her and shook my head, pointing to the tape-recorder. She frowned and lay down her whip. We needed Keagey to tell us how many sins the police had covered up. And we needed those sins listed on the tape. After we had enough information, I'd stop recording and guide the women into having Keagey renounce his lifestyle. I picked up the tape-recorders and walked over to Rita. I lifted my mask and whispered into her ear.

"He will progress faster to submission and confession if he experiences intense pain. Something worse than a whip."

She lifted her mask and spoke into my ear.

"Leave it to me. I've been dreaming of this for a long time."

We both dropped our masks into place. As Rita stepped back up to Keagey, I pressed the record button on each tape machine. She ripped the duct tape off his mouth.

"Johnny, do you know why you're here?"

"No."

"Because you've been naughty."

"Naughty? How have I been naughty?"

"You know," said Kelly. "Now tell us."

"You mean, when I made some women love me?"

"That's exactly what we mean," said Kelly.

"I needed them to love me," said Keagy.

"How many women did you need to love you, Johnny-boy?" asked Rita.

"I don't remember."

"Liar," said Kelly, grinding her foot into him again.

"Twenty-three. Twenty-three women."

"Is that all?"

"Yes. I swear. That's all. Twenty-three."

As Rita motioned Lisa and Maria forward again, this time a little impatiently, Kelly put her foot on Keagey's thigh, but without pressing down.

"Any little girls? Little boys?"

"Little girls? Little boys? Are you crazy? I'd never do anything like that."

"So, you only want women to love you?"

"Yes. Only women."

"Twenty-three women."

Keagey said nothing. Lisa and Maria stood by the closed door. Because of the masks, the expressions on their faces were hidden, but their body language was stiff. Tense.

"Who were these twenty-three women you made love you, Johnny?"

"You wouldn't know any of them."

"How do you know?"

"Yeah, I might know some of them," said Kelly, increasing the pressure of her foot on his thigh before moving it toward his genitals.

"I can't remember them. I don't know their names."

Rita made a cutting motion at her neck and pointed to the tape-recorder. I shut it off. She grabbed Keagey's nose with one gloved hand and pinched it shut.

"I want the names."

"You're hurting me."

"You hurt all of the women you raped. Did you stop when they asked you? No, you didn't. Did you stop when they begged? No, you didn't. So, will I stop just because you ask? I think not."

She picked up the duct tape and, lifting her mask, began pulling off pieces, tearing them off with her teeth. I rushed over to her side and grabbed the torn tape from her hands before she could cover his mouth and nose with them. Kelly and I both shook our heads and her as I handed her my knife and cut the tape. Rita stared at us a moment, almost as if she didn't even recognize us. Then she slowly nodded as I crumpled the taped with her saliva and skin cells on it and stuffed it into my boot.

She cut piece after piece of tape until Keagey's entire mouth and nose were covered. She was calm again. In control. When she finished, she handed me the knife and I put it away. Kelly held out the tape-recorder and shook it in front of Rita, but Rita just stood there, watching Keagey. The other girls looked at me. It was obvious that with his mouth covered, he couldn't confess. With his mouth and nose covered, he couldn't breathe. Was Rita trying to frighten him or had she lost control? I didn't know. I looked at the others. I shook my head and shrugged.

At first Keagey started to mumble and shake his head, twisting it around the room, searching for the voices which were silent now. Rita lowered her mask as she watched him.

Then Keagey began to struggle harder. Rita watched, her arms crossed over her chest. Kelly took her foot off him. He started to rock and shake the chair. He fought against the tape around his limbs.

His body began to convulse. I reached out to tear the tape from his mouth and nose, but Rita hit my hand away. Keagey threw himself and the chair backward. His body lurched and bucked. It shook and jerked. Rita moved her mask's speaker to his left ear.

"Give us the names, you sonofabitch," she said, "or I won't even let you beg. I'll just let you fucking suffocate. I'll leave your mouth and nose taped closed, and then we'll all leave."

He soiled himself. I tossed his pants over the mess. Then he began gagging and throwing up. Choking, coughing, and gagging with all that tape over his mouth and nose, he'd begin to swallow his vomit. Then the women wouldn't have justice or healing. They'd have nothing but murder. I went over to where Keagey lay fighting on the ground and, with my gloved hands, tore the tape off his mouth and nose.

Rita tried to stop me, but Kelly helped me to right his chair. We didn't clean him up. He tried to breathe through the gagging. Rita walked over and shoved the tape-recorder near his chin.

"Give us the names of the women you raped. All of them."

From under his blindfold, tears started to roll down his face. He was crying and gasping, with an occasional gag. Good, he was starting his journey to the other side of the road.

"Names."

"All right, all right."

I started the tape-recorders as Rita began again.

"John Keagey, tell us the names of the women you raped."

"Becca-1, Becca-2, Becca-3 ..."

Rita took off her mask and looked at me. She raised her shoulders and held out her hands as if asking me what to do.

"Rita Montgomery, Allison Thompson, Janie Wilson, Becca-4, Joy ..."

Rita put her mask back on as he told us the names, dates, where he'd grabbed the women, and where he'd raped them. He told us which souvenirs upstairs were theirs. He even told us which item belonged to each of the "Beccas."

Lisa slumped to her knees. I put the recorders down on the floor in front of him as he continued. Maria helped me take Lisa outside. Once on the porch, Maria and I settled Lisa on the steps. I removed my voice-gooser. Maria took off her own, then helped Lisa with hers.

"The confession part is always intense," I said. "Why not just stay here for a little while and get some fresh air?"

Maria's eyes were wet. Fresh tears followed the wet tracks down Lisa's cheeks.

"He's more than a monster. He's pure evil. He really doesn't care, does he?" asked Maria.

"He doesn't see his victims as human. He sees them as prey. They feed his ego and his self-esteem. They also allow him to hurt someone, a woman he obviously can't hurt in real life."

"Becca."

"Someone named Rebecca," I said. "I'm going back in. When you feel better, come inside. You all need to finish this together."

I entered the front room. Rita and Kelly were standing motionless while Keagey droned on. I couldn't read the women's emotions through their voice-gooser masks, but I could read Keagey's.

He had begun gloating. Now he was telling us the real names of Becca-1, Becca-2, and all the other "Beccas." He embellished his tale with personal details, including his favorite moments from each rape. I wanted to kill him.

Keagey talked until the tape ran out on the little recorder. I stopped the other one too, then stopped him. I walked over and put my mask next to his ear and lowered my voice.

"You made your victims beg you to fuck them. You said if they didn't, you would kill them. Okay, we'll put that shoe on your foot. Beg your jury not to smear your body with shit and piss, or I swear I'll kill you. The jury's prevented me from killing you so far. But I don't think they'd stop me now."

Kelly and Rita went to the diaper bag. Rita took the one on the top. Kelly dug through them until she found the one she wanted. Maria and Lisa made no move to join us. Kelly stepped up and shoved her diaper into Keagey's forehead, then dragged it down his left cheek. It left a thick brown smear. Rita stepped up and painted the other side of his face brown. I went to Lisa and Maria.

"His humiliation is a necessary step. Just touch one to his skin, then you can drop it."

They walked forward with me. By the time we got back to Keagey, Rita and Kelly had already used a dozen diapers on him. He was smeared from head to toe and they were working on his back. Keagey just sat there, saying more names, dates, times, locations.

Maria smeared the diaper on Keagey's right front shoulder, then dropped it. It seemed as if a weight slid from her shoulders. She turned and walked away.

Lisa surprised me. At first she hung back. I was about to push her forward when she stepped into Keagey with fists flying. We all stood there in shock as she tapped about a hundred-and-fifty beats per minute on his face. That turned off the litany of victims' names.

I stepped forward, catching her wrists. Kelly was right behind me, with Rita closing fast. I scooped Lisa up and carried her toward the front door. The other two stepped aside to let us past. Maria watched us go by her and onto the porch. I closed the door behind us and took off our masks. Lisa looked at me.

"He raped me. He raped all those other women. And he doesn't care. He doesn't care one little bit."

I held her while she cried into my shoulder. Lisa held her fist tight by her face on my shoulder. As she calmed down, she pulled herself away from me. I picked up a trash bag from the porch, dropped my gloves in and then held it open for her.

"Drop your gloves in and put on some fresh ones."

"Ben, look, I'm sorry for going off like that."

"I think it was a healthy reaction on your part. You did fine."

I set the trash bag down then fished a fresh pair of brown cotton work gloves out of a bag on the porch. When I got back to Rita, Kelly and Maria, I saw that they were quiet. Looking at Keagey.

Listening to him. I picked up the bag of diapers, collected the used ones, and handed the bag to Kelly, who took it back out to her car.

I handed the bags of hair to Rita and Maria. Lisa came back in with Kelly. I handed them the bags of vacuum cleaner lint. I did a complete wipe-down of the window sill and doorway. I wiped anything that I was suspicious might hold a latent print of ours, including most of the front porch.

When I was finished, I went outside and took off my voice-gooser. One by one, they came out. I took their masks and put them in a travel bag.

"Give me your hair and shoe covers and gloves just before you get into your cars."

I held out a trash bag to capture the debris. When we were finished, we walked to the cars in the street. While they helped me load everything into the Jeep, I gave them their post-op debrief.

"I want you all to go home and re-connect with your partners. Share, bond, and heal. Tomorrow, go about your lives as if nothing happened. Don't listen to the radio or watch the television news. It doesn't concern you. If anyone comes to you and asks where you were tonight, stick to your alibi. If you'd like, tell them you would like to thank whoever did it. Your sincerity while telling them your true feelings about rapists will sell them on your alibi. Now get going. I'll be in touch in a week."

I went back in and picked up Keagey's cell phone.

"Who is it? Who's there?"

I pressed 911 send and the end-game began. When I heard a human speaking, I pressed play, pocketed the good tape-recorder, and left.

Chapter Twenty-Four

I sat in meditation, searching for how it had gone wrong. I had left Keagey for the police to find, but he had vanished. There wasn't a peep about him in the press. Campagnella said his cop contacts didn't even know that it had happened. The Kinkaeds must have him sequestered somewhere. 911 tapes can't be erased, but I was sure a subpoena wouldn't find a record of the call that I had placed.

I checked Keagey's condo. Ordinary dust had accumulated on his doorknob and inside. I called An Apple Less and asked for him. They said he was on vacation. I sent a troop of raccoons into the stash house. It was stripped clean.

I could start looking for him, but how many Kinkaed compounds were there in the US and in islands that were no longer virgin after the Kinkaeds had gotten to them. I could search for months and never find him.

Even worse, Maria and Lisa had not recovered as I had hoped. In fact, Maria showed signs of depression. My careful planning had turned into buffalo chips. I looked around the hilltop clearing. The Tall Brothers wore shirts full of leaves that whispered songs as Tate, The Wind, walked the night sky.

Twinkling Old Ones danced a slow path across the depth of space. The sounds of scurrying feet came from the bushes. It seemed that I was the only one going nowhere.

My legs had vanished in meditation, affording me an opportunity to escape my shell. I anchored my soul to my body and stretched my mind into the earth. None of the surface stones would talk to me. I passed through colonies of Igneous Stone People embedded into the older Sedimentary community. The younger stones acknowledged me, but none offered conversation.

Falling further, I reached the mass of the earth's mantle. The heat of the magma below, combined with the pressure above, caused the Stone People of this strata to flow and mingle, their souls stretched and melted. Like some cosmic session of musical chairs, they stayed in flux until Earth Mother thrust them upward in yet another intrusion, cooling into the colonies I passed on my way down.

I searched for one who would talk to me. They paid no attention. I followed some light-hearted veins of quartz that were mingling with some saucy layers of feldspar. I heard a lot but learned little. I gave up. I floated through the layers, stopping near the surface near a large schist. Everyone was too busy discussing a recent ground movement to answer my question.

I pulled myself past my anchored legs and into my body. Opening my eyes, I breathed in, sharp and deep, accelerating my heart rate to support my awakening. I let my mind search for the unseen. Only my woodland cousins were close enough to be noticed. Peace and beauty saturated the hilltop, but it had yet to penetrate my agitated heart.

I felt Raven Who Hops approaching from the west. Perhaps he had been visiting the Utes.

"*Hau*, Raven."

"*Hau*, Little Bear."

"So, I'm 'Little Bear' again?"

"Yes."

"John Keagey has disappeared, avoiding prosecution for the other crimes we uncovered. The Kinkaeds are on alert, and I appear to be no nearer to my goal. The only thing that worked was the alibis for the women. The police were looking for three women who assaulted Keagey. Their count was off, but they were on the right trail. They checked on the women I protect, but decided that they were not the ones who were there. I didn't get them into trouble, but everything else is not good."

Raven hopped in front of me and settled down.

"I don't understand what went wrong. We got Keagey's confession on tape, we left him tied up in the house with his stash, with the police on their way. I didn't expect the confession to be admissible, but the upstairs trophy room should have been accepted as evidence."

"Did you really expect two hands to hold back the wind?"

"I expected some impact. I can't detect any change."

Raven bobbed his head twice.

"You changed the physical world, and the spiritual world was affected, but not enough become realigned. You aren't done."

"I don't know what else to do."

"You make the same mistake your ancestors made: you expect the *wasiçiu* to be like you, men with honor. You exposed their hypocrisy, expecting them to admit it and accept defeat, but instead they just re-buried everything you uncovered."

"I walked the best path I knew. What else could I have done?"

"Think larger than Keagey. Your struggle with the Kinkaeds over Keagey's abuse of the women is an echo of the *Lakhota* struggle with the *wasiçius* over their abuse of the Red Man."

"That's a great point of philosophy, but how does it help me right now?"

"Your quest will not progress until the people are with you. Then the world will change. As long as the *wasiçiu* can hide behind closed doors, nothing will change."

I stilled my soul and thought about my grandfather, Vernon Two Trees. *Wakan Tanka*'s power was with him. His children went grey before he did. We bow-hunted on the morning of the day he died. I was just big enough to carry the elk's forelegs back to camp while my father and Papa carried the rest. We shared elk steaks then slept under the stars. That night, Papa went to join our ancestors. I asked myself what Papa would see if he were in my shoes. What would Papa think, say, and do?

I was quiet, waiting and feeling. A presence I had not felt for a long time came near. I closed my eyes and looked within. It was Papa. My task must be important for him to make the journey. He didn't speak; instead he made gestures in Indian sign language. I spoke in my mind and Papa nodded, then made more signs. We talked like that for a while. Papa didn't answer my last question. Instead, he turned to leave. I opened my eyes. Raven cocked his head then leveled it. Being with Papa had re-centered my soul. I spoke from my renewed strength.

"The ones that relied on me didn't receive their healing. Their turmoil disturbs and wounds me."

"Yes."

"I must take care of my wounded before I can rejoin the battle. Their affliction is spiritual. To heal them, I will perform the rite of *Inipi*."

"Yes, the *Inipi* restores souls. That will be good for your sisters, but what will you do about Keagey?"

"I need to find a way to expose his crimes beyond what the Kinkaeds can cover up. I don't have a plan for that yet."

"I have faith in you. You will think of something."

"I wish I had your faith in me."

"It's human to have doubts, but *Lakhota* shun doubt. Stop worrying about results and concentrate on perseverance. Saturate yourself with The Way."

I said the blessing.

"I walk in beauty. I walk in truth. I walk in peace. I walk in strength. I live in eternity but feel the moment."

Raven and I shared some silence. I felt the approaching presence of *Taku Skanskan*. From the south, a faint blue light spread across the hilltop.

Raven changed, taking the form of a man. He towered over me, more than nine feet tall. Jet black hair flowed down his back. The firelight shone on his deep reddish brown skin as he looked down at me.

224

His eyes were charcoal black. He made a motion for me to remain seated.

The blue light of *skan* was brighter toward its center and was moving toward us. It came to rest in front of Raven. His loincloth held an ornate knife on his hip. He took it and held it out to *Taku Skanskan*. The Power Spirit accepted the blade and as Raven let his hands fall to his sides, the blade floated in the glowing blue light.

The blade scribed a slow circle, then came to a rest pointing at me. My vision expanded inward and I stood near the top of *Mahto Paha* under an overhang looking into a sunset. Raven's knife hung in the air beside me. I knew what was expected. I took the knife in my right hand while pinching up a small piece of skin from my ribcage with the other.

While saying the sunrise blessing, I thought of my quest for justice for the four women and for the Red Nations. I asked *Wakan Tanka* to hear my prayer. I cut off the piece of skin, sublimating the pain, persevering in my prayer for justice.

I dropped the skin over the cliff in front of me. Switching the knife to the other hand, I prayed the sunset blessing, and cut a small piece of skin from my other side while praying for justice. I dropped it over the cliff, too. I dropped the knife, and it floated free.

On the mountain, the sun was still above the horizon, but sinking — glowing yellow against the blue but darkening sky. Indigo crept in from the sides, pushing the blue to the center, while the sun shrank then vanished. I was once again on the hilltop with Raven and *Taku Skanskan*.

Raven's knife still hung in the air, now pointing up. Again it rotated a slow circle, stopping when it pointed toward the center of the blue light. It made a few quick twists and two small pieces of blue light separated from the whole. They floated toward me, one just ahead of the other, two thin strips, about the same size and shape as the skin I had cut from my sides.

Raven spoke, "Open your mouth."

The first of the pieces touched my tongue and melted. It refreshed like water from melting snow and smelled of sweetgrass. The ache in my back went away.

The second of the slivers of light melted on my tongue. This time it was hot and pungent like a broth. Heat coursed through my veins and I felt weariness fall from my shoulders. I closed my mouth.

Stillness held me for the next few minutes. Raven was still as well. I couldn't tell what was happening, but my meager skills in the spiritual realm made me aware of a conversation between my spirit guide and the Power Spirit of *Wakan Tanka*, The Great Mystery.

After the moment passed, the blue light in the center shrank, pulling the lighter blue light in on itself, until it vanished. I blinked my eyes, and Raven stood beside me, once again in bird form. I looked around the clearing. Nothing was visible but the firelight dancing on the tree trunks that rimmed the hilltop.

"Did I dream it?"

"Feel your sides."

I pulled on the skin and looked. A small slice of skin was missing from each of my flanks. The wounds oozed blood that was beginning to clot. I reached down and lifted my legs from crossed leg to straight and began to rub the blood back into them. The pins-and-needles sensations began.

"I was on *Mahto Paha*?"

"Yes. You offered a piece of your life, which was accepted. In return, you received small pieces of pure *skan*. It is very rare for The Lord of Power to visit anyone in this way."

"Was it a blessing?"

"It depends on how you look at it. It can be a blessing, but some would consider it a curse as well. You have been given an increased measure of power, but with it comes responsibilities. Your life is now even less your own. You will serve everyone else before yourself. Some people would consider that a major loss."

"The Way requires one life for the many. I am not holy alone. I am holy only within the *Lakhota* nation."

"Your heart is right. You are ready to continue your task." With that, he hopped a few times and leaped into flight.

I stood and stretched. I bent over to touch my toes and didn't feel any back pain. On the other hand, my hamstrings were plenty tight. I walked to my lodge and entered. Passing through the great dome to the center one, I found my cell phone and began to contact the women who had come to me for help.

It was time to complete their healing journey. After that I would find a way to help Keagey to complete his.

Chapter Twenty-Five

Tonight we would have *Inipi*, the sacred rite of sweat-lodge purification that frees the spirit to soar. Physical, mental, and spiritual poisons would be drawn from us and we would leave *Inipi* attuned to the Great Father's universe.

It was the night of *Can Wape To Wi* — the Green Leaves Moon, May, was full. At the Rez in North Dakota, further north than we were, green leaves were just beginning to cover the trees. Here in Maryland, they had been out for over a month.

I had been preparing for two days. The sweat-lodge was rebuilt. The ceremonial hides were repainted and re-sewn, then stretched over the lodge. My cousin Tishton came down from the Rez to be my fireman.

Together we re-dug the fire-pit, then built the six-foot-tall double *tipi* stack of cordwood and kindling, with twenty-seven stones in the middle. The effort triggered my back-ache, but it was good to share the preparation for *Inipi*.

When the sun was at zenith, we lit the white sage smudge, purifying the lodge, altar, and fire-pit. With the last of the smudge, we lit the fire stack, connecting it in prayer to *peta-owihankeshni*, the fire of no end.

"They come," said Tish.

"Yes."

"*Mitakuye oyasin,*" said Tishton, speaking the sacred *Lakhota* phrase that acknowledges that we are all children of the Great Father. "I won't remember their names right."

"Perhaps your horse face will make them forget their own names."

"They're your friends. They will forgive my looks, too." He paused. "Is she coming?"

"Who?"

"The one you want to talk to under a robe."

"Who said I wanted to start courtship rites?"

"A lizard told me."

"The lizard was wrong. And, no, she won't be here tonight."

The car approached.

"We should go meet them."

We walked from the sweat-lodge to the car corral. Lisa got out of her car and walked toward us. She was dressed for *Inipi* in a blue jean skirt and light blue top. Blue was a good choice; it was the color of *skan.*

"Thank you for coming, Lisa. Your outfit is fine for the ceremony. Do you have a change of clothes for afterward?"

"Yes, right in here."

She patted a gym bag that hung by her side. She gave Tish an appraising look.

"This is my cousin, Tishton. Tish, this is Lisa."

Tish tilted his head forward.

"I am glad to meet you."

Lisa held out her hand.

"Nice to meet you, too."

They shook hands before she turned to me.

"You said this is part of what will restore my life. To tell you the truth, I am nervous about conducting a pagan ritual."

Tishton grunted. I led them to some hides laid on the ground outside the sweat-lodge, with a picnic basket.

"We aren't pagan, Lisa. Some believe that our Great Father is the same 'God the Father' whom you pray to. And your 'God the Father' is the same as the Jews' 'Elohim'. Those are only different names for the same spiritual force. "

"It's just … different."

"Is it?" Tishton asked as we sat down.

He would be fine in this conversation. He'd studied comparative religion as part of his degree in philosophy. I listened to their debate while I passed out bottled water.

Another car was coming uphill. I left Lisa and Tish to their discussion. Walking over, I saw Kelly drive in, followed by Maria in her car. They parked, waving before walking over together.

"*Hau*. Thank you for coming."

"Who's that with Lisa?" Kelly asked.

"My cousin Tishton."

"Where's Rita?"

"I don't know. Perhaps she is on her way."

Kelly took Maria's arm.

"Come on, hon; let's go get spiritual."

They shouldered their gym bags and followed me to where Lisa and Tish sat on the hides. Maria wore a floral patterned cotton skirt and a white blouse.

Kelly's skirt was navy blue with a kelly green shirt. I smiled, then noticed that she was wearing earrings.

"You can't wear metal in the sweat-lodge."

"Why not? How does metal affect the spirit world?"

"It'll affect you. The metal conducts the heat and will burn your skin."

She removed them, putting them in her bag. After Rita drove in, I turned and waved. As Rita got out, the passenger door opened. Teresa stood there. Behind me, Tish grunted. He'd figured out that the extra person was the one the lizard had told him about. It was a good thing that the subtleties of *Lakhota* guttural sounds were lost on the women. I turned and looked at Tish, who obviously relished my discomfort.

I didn't need or want Teresa here tonight. I was guiding the *Inipi*. I didn't have time to be distracted with worry about her possible culture shock. The journey of the four through *Inipi* was more important than whether Teresa would react negatively to my life in the *Lakhota* Way. She would find out in time. Tish offered his wisdom.

"*He tuwa hwo? Hankasi waye?*" he said, asking if the extra person was his female cousin.

I walked to the approaching women. Teresa's khaki skirt and navy blue shirt would be fine, but Rita was dressed in sweats. That was against tradition. I went to them.

"*Hau*, Rita. *Hau*, Teresa."

"*Hau*, to you, too."

Rita hugged me, then kissed my cheek. Teresa did the same, but lingered before pulling away. The proper form of greeting for a woman to use was '*han*,' but Rita was here for *Inipi*, not language lessons.

"Rita, I asked you to wear a modest skirt and blouse. It is traditional for men and women to dress for *Inipi*. It is a matter of respect. In the *Inipi* lodge, we conform to *Wakan Tanka* and his Power Spirit. We come not as we want, but as he wants. Women wear a skirt to symbolize the union of the womb and their walk. The man wears only a loin-cloth to symbolize his vulnerability to all manifestations of Grandfather."

"I've got a skirt and blouse in the bag. I'll change."

Rita went back to her car, to the passenger side, and bent down so no one could see her. After she returned, now dressed appropriately, Teresa slipped her arm through one of mine while Rita took the other. We started toward the others. I looked at Teresa.

"I don't mean to insult you by asking this, Teresa, but why are you here?"

"I wanted to know more about your culture. I thought this would be a good time to start learning."

"I won't be able to spend any time with you until afterward. *Inipi* is a sacred rite of purification, and my heart will be focused on guiding it. Rita and the others need to be set free. The *Inipi* will do that."

"You go ahead and concentrate. I promise I won't get in the way. Forget I'm there."

"*Inipi* is usually open to everyone, but Rita and the others are bound together through a shared harm. Together they punished the one who hurt them. They must go though the renewing together."

I stopped our walk and turned my head to Teresa. She looked at me.

"While you know them, and you know what happened, you are not one of them in this matter. Your presence may inhibit some. They need to feel completely free. I must ask you to stay outside during this ceremony."

"Can I observe?"

"Perhaps we will share an *Inipi* at another time."

She sighed before I turned to Rita. When we reached the picnic area, Rita and Teresa greeted the others. I introduced them to Tishton. Rita explained that Teresa would not be participating in the ceremony and told them the reason why. I reached into the picnic basket sitting on the hides and passed out bottled water.

"Drink up. We will be losing a lot of it. During *Inipi*, you should drink whenever you're thirsty."

I looked around the group.

"Everyone skipped lunch?"

They nodded their heads.

"We will eat afterward, but, for now, try to accept the hunger as part of the path. If you had eaten, the heat would make you sick. Since you haven't eaten, your intellect will be sharpened for you to see your path."

The eyes that watched me showed different emotions. Rita looked ready. Lisa looked anxious. Maria looked sad, while Kelly looked curious. I could see nothing in Teresa's eyes: I didn't know what that meant.

"Tishton won't be joining us in the lodge," I said. "He is our fireman. He will purify us and pass in the stones. He will also be our safety watch."

I pulled my doeskin shirt over my head. I ignored their curiosity. I reached into a pouch tied to the right hip of my loin-cloth and removed the *Chunumpa*. As I assembled it, murmuring prayers, Tish explained.

"It is a *Chunumpa*, a sacred pipe. When a person speaks with visible breath, it is a binding spiritual oath. *Wasiçiu* call it a 'peace-pipe'."

"What if we don't smoke?" Lisa asked. "Will it make us sick or intoxicated?"

"No. We use red birch bark mixed with common tobacco. Not marijuana."

With the assembled *Chanumpa* cradled in my left arm, I spoke.

"Clear your minds and open your hearts. Enter the sweat-lodge only if you are ready to be cleansed. Anger, jealousy, and fear will melt away in its heat. The pipe helps us send our prayers to Tunçila, Grandfather, but you don't have to smoke. Just hold the pipe in front of you and breathe on it, then pass it on. Don't worry about how *Inipi* is performed. I will explain it as we go. Any questions so far?"

I gestured them to follow me toward the lodge. We approached from the side, stopping between the door and the altar.

"The path between the altar and the door of the lodge is sacred. Before you can take that path, you must be centered in your spirit. Each of you should find a place to pray alone."

I looked at the setting sun.

"Meet back here in ten minutes, and we will begin."

"Are we going to get naked?"

"No. That would be disrespectful."

"A friend of mine went to a sweat ceremony in Oregon and everyone got naked."

Lisa looked anxious. Tishton shook his head and walked away. He removed his shirt as he took the sacred path to the altar, beginning his fireman duties.

"No, we don't get naked, take drugs, or have an orgy afterward," I said. "New Age people do sweats, but they aren't *Inipi*. This isn't recreational spirituality. We approach *Wakan Tanka* seeking a re-birthing. We are modest and respectful in Grandfather and Earth Mother's sacred house. Now, go and prepare. Think about the healing you seek. Remember who you were before, and who you want to be in the future. Go and tell God what you want. When you come back, we will seek his answers together."

As they separated, I stood where I was, about 15 feet from the circle of power around the sweat-lodge. I turned inward, shutting out the world, letting everything go. I would not steer events. I accepted the evening and whatever *Taku Skanskan* had in store for us. I stood drawing his presence into me, saturating myself with his peace and beauty.

When I felt that it was time, I opened my eyes. Lisa stood in front of me, watching. I said nothing. I waited for what would be. Kelly and Maria were walking towards us, as was Rita. Teresa sat on the hides, watching.

"Why are you and Tishton so different from us?" Lisa said.

235

"We are just like you."

"You feel different. I mean, I feel different when I am around you."

"You feel the Great Father. You see it in us because *Lakhota* don't live in the present. We live in eternity."

"I wish I were as … spiritual as you are."

"Grandfather is the source of all spirituality. Come. Do you know what you seek tonight? You may tell me if you wish."

"I just want to feel clean again. I always feel so dirty, but I can't wash it away."

"*Inipi* is very strong. Have faith."

Kelly and Maria had stopped to watch from about six feet away. I waved them over. Rita joined us soon after. I grunted the beginning sound. Tish met my eye, then lit the white sage and sweet grass smudges, bringing them toward us. He walked the twenty feet to us, praying in soft tones.

"This is *Inipi*," I said. "A spiritual journey of re-birth and renewal. You are safe here. Grandfather watches over us. Tishton and I will not let anything bad happen. Your are here for healing, so trust in Grandfather, *Wakan Tanka*, the Great Mystery and his power. Just do as much as you can at each step of the ceremony."

Tish started at the four corners around the group, then moved in to smudge each of us.

"The smoke purifies us and begins the blessing of harmony," I said.

I reached into my hip bag and pulled out a handful of little pouches. I gave each woman three.

236

"These are medicine. Tishton will lead us to the altar, where you will untie a bundle and rub the herbed tobacco onto the altar as you say your prayer to The Great Father. Then Tishton will smudge you again. Turn clockwise one circle. Say '*Mitakuye Oyasin*.'

"*Mit-a-ku-ye* ..."

"*Mit-a-ku-ye O* ..."

"*Oyasin. Mitakuye Oyasin.*"

"*Mitakuye Oyasin.*"

"Or, you can say it in American, 'we are all family'. Say it as you crawl into the lodge. Inside, crawl around clockwise, then sit and wait for me."

I made my eyes pleasant in the torch-light.

"We shake hands before we start our journey."

I motioned them to follow Tish to the altar. One at a time, the women did their part. Rita, Lisa, Kelly, and Maria prayed at the altar, then crawled inside, while I prayed out loud in English.

"Oh, Grandfather, *Wakan Tanka*, you are and always were. We do your will as you taught us. In placing rocks at the four directions, we know you are our center. Sacred rocks for helping us do your will. *Wakan Tanka*, this is your eternal fire that you gave to us on this island. We do your will by building a sacred place in a sacred manner. Your eternal fire burns and through it, we shall live again by purification, coming closer to your power. Send your Power Spirit to us tonight. Cleanse us with *Inipi*. Re-birth us into a new life on this island, your earth."

With that, it was my turn for personal prayer at the altar. I crawled inside and straightened the sage covering the small altar hole inside the lodge. I talked to my sisters.

"Take one of your medicine bundles and tie it to one of the cords hanging from the ceiling."

We did it together. My bundle was right over the sacred furrow cut into the earth at the center of the lodge to receive the fire stones. The women's bundles were around mine.

"This lodge is symbolic of our Earth Mother's womb. Tonight we will be re-born when we crawl out into the world. The entire floor is covered with fresh sage. It will combine with the steam and our body oils to produce a fragrance for Grandfather. It will also purify our hearts."

When I gestured in the dim light, the women looked around.

"There are water bottles all around the outer wall. Drink whenever you want. If you get too hot, splash some water on your face. Leave your bottles behind you to keep them as cool as is possible."

I said the sacred *Inipi* blessing as Tish passed the stones in. I removed each of the seven from their leather sacks and placed them in the sacred furrow. I gave each one a sprinkling of spice as I set it down.

I lit the *Chunumpa* and offered it to the four corners. I drew breath from the *Chunumpa*. As I exhaled, I said the *Lakhota* blessing of power.

"We are here seeking you," I said in American. "We await you. We sit in beauty. We sit in peace."

I took another breath of the pipe and passed it to Maria who was on my left. Tishton closed the door. In the darkness, I took a ladle of water and dribbled it over the stones, which sang their steamy songs of power and strength.

"We will have four cycles of sweat. Each will be of a different temperature and duration. This one will be warm and about 45 minutes long. The last one will be ten minutes and very hot. The flap of the lodge will open only to send more stones in."

A rich darkness bathed the walls as the women, watching me, waited in silence.

"Reach out and touch your neighbor. We are here together, for ourselves and for each other. We all need healing for something. We all want that healing, for ourselves and for each other. Whatever we do here will be blessed as long as we seek divine power and love. Continue holding hands if you want to. It is not required. Don't be afraid to cry, laugh, or express whatever emotion you feel. We are here together. We are all one family, and all things on earth are our relations."

I felt Rita put the pipe by my leg. With that, I moved aside for *Taku Skanskan* take over. I was quiet until a prayer came into my head. A few times I spoke in *Lakhota* to the spirit guides that came to minister to us. Each of my sisters had one, though they were unaware of their Guardian Angels as they walked among us.

Where each angel stood, the roof of the lodge became transparent, stars framing their heads. The angels were tall and dark-haired, like Raven was when *Taku Skanskan* whisked me to *Mahto Paha*. I preferred the animal forms myself. Looking above me, I saw Raven Who Hops watching it all from the roof of the lodge.

The flap opened and five more stones were handed in. I relit the *Chanumpa* and showed my breath.

"Thank you, Grandfather, for your visit. We are here in a sacred way. We seek our part of your universe. We are here in the way you taught, seeking to know our part on this island. We would know your power, peace, and strength. We are here on our journey with you."

I sprinkled the spices and sang the second song while dripping water on the stones. Each stone was the size of a human head. For this cycle, I dribbled water four times. My new sisters were good. There were confessions that went into the ground to be forgotten. There was a lot of crying. The water released the heat of the stones, bringing waves of emotional heat rolling from us.

I refilled the *Chanumpa* with a song. It was ready for the next use. I thought of how this *Inipi* was turning out. It wasn't *Lakhota*. It was more like a Protestant tent revival, but also a little Catholic. My sisters hummed tunes that meant things to them, just as, without their knowing it, the angels had come because Guardian Angels were important to them.

Toward the end of the second cycle, they hummed "Amazing Grace" twice. I knew the powerful song, written by a former slave-trader who came to the realization that his profession was wrong, but I didn't hum along. For my sisters, that song was part of their cultural iconography.

This wasn't my *Inipi*. It belonged to Grandfather and my sisters. It wasn't important that it be *Lakhota*, just that it be real spirituality. Only that would cause the healing to flow. We prayed and journeyed together through two more cycles. During the third cycle, two sisters complained of heat fatigue. I suggested that they wet their hair and drink more water. That helped and kept them all in the heat, focused on their personal search for connection to our Grandfather. The last cycle was the most intense.

It lasted about ten minutes and was very hot. I took strength from it, but my sisters less so. Lisa cried with deep sobs. The rest were not much quieter. I told them to let everything go with the steam Grandfather was strong enough to take it from them.

Then I opened the flap and crawled out, carrying the *Chunumpa* with me. I stood back and prayed as my sisters crawled from the lodge, plastered in sweat. When they were all standing beside me, I spoke.

"Don't talk to each other just yet. You are still in a journey state. Go into the house and pick a bedroom in the back dome. Each one has a shower. Clean up and change clothes. When you come out, Tishton and I will have food ready. We will continue in a spirit of prayer through the evening meal. When you go home later tonight, remember this time before you fall sleep. Whenever you feel stress or fear pulling you away from your renewed center, return to tonight and remember where your heart connects to others and to Grandfather."

I spoke to Rita.

"You can take Teresa with you if you would like."

Rita looked at me through teary eyes. Rita motioned Teresa over as she walked to the domes. I looked around. Tish had lit the outdoor torches and turned on some lights in the house. These gave enough light for the women to walk to the domes. After my sisters had left, Tish spoke.

"What kind of *Inipi* was that?

"The kind they needed, apparently. You could sense their journey, couldn't you?"

"There were plenty of spirits coming and going. Who were they all?"

"I think they are the ones the Christians call 'Guardian Angels'. They did some annointings and some pass-through cleansings, nothing malevolent. Grandfather has never allowed an *Inipi* to be violated."

"Should I go inside your house and get a buffalo robe for you and Teresa ?" said Tish, grinning widely.

"You know, I can't remember my own name after looking at your Horse-face."

"By the way, Bear-face," said Tish, leaning in, "I think your doe has her hunter in her sights."

"You're imagining things."

"Am I? You were in the *Inipi*. I was watching her. Her head was bowed, her hands in her lap. Like she was praying. How do you know that her prayers weren't being passed to *Whope*?"

"Teresa doesn't need to pray to anyone to be beautiful or to catch herself a husband."

"Your meat may already be drying on her rack, Bear-face, and you don't even know it."

I said nothing, letting him get what he could from my brown eyes before I walked, easily and securely, despite the dark, to my outdoor shower, wishing Keagey were as easy to find in his darkness.

Chapter Twenty-Six

Sometimes the way ahead lies in an opposite direction. It was a Tuesday afternoon, the 18th day of *Wipa Zunka Waste Wi*, or the June Berries Moon, and I was picking wild blackberries in an open field when Raven Who Hops landed on a rock pile near me. He bent his head and grabbed a few berries with his beak from the vine nearest him.

"Delicious."

"*Hau*, Raven."

I pointed to the cars in the parking lot next to the field.

"Nature stares the *wasiçius* in the face, but they buy their berries at a store."

"Their TV doesn't tune to our channel."

"They probably think meat is born boneless on Styrofoam wrapped in plastic."

"You're getting better. Did Tishton help you write that?"

I continued picking berries, and Raven continued eating them from his side of the berry patch.

"Do you know anything about the women?" I asked.

While I waited, a few grasshoppers took flight lessons in the spring air. If beaks could smile, Raven would have done it. I picked berries in silence. A whole earth and I had nowhere else I needed to be. Raven   loved teaching me patience. I never knew how long he would make me wait before he spoke.

"I visited their Guardian Angels. They had good reports on your sisters' progress."

"Even *Iktomi* the Trickster won't meddle in Grandfather's *Inipi*."

"With the women on their way to health, all you have left to do is to rebalance the local flow of the universe."

Raven cocked his head and squinted at the sun then looked at me.

"What are you going to do?"

"I'm going home to wash these berries and eat some of them."

I watched Raven wait. I spoke slowly, making him the one that waited this time.

"And there's that Kinkaed-Keagey thing."

Raven twisted his head. He flapped his wings. I grunted a starting sound, signaling my shift to a business mode.

"I'm still trying to think up a way to expose the Keagey cover-up. And I need to link it to *Lakhota* exploitation somehow."

"Are you asking for my help?"

"I don't know. I guess not."

"As you wish. If you need something, call for me. I'll be with you as soon as I can."

"With the few *Lakhota* there are alive today, you'd think that the Christian Guardian Angels would be the ones working overtime and not our own Spirit Guides."

"It's more complicated than that. You need to plan your strategy for shining light into the dark corners of Keagey's world."

"Any suggestions?"

"I thought you wanted to figure it out on your own."

"That was before you offered to help."

Raven cleared his throat.

"First, you need to find Keagey."

"I know."

"Then why haven't you found him?"

"Do you have any idea how many compounds, properties, and houses the Kinkaeds have on the east coast? Where can I get an army of bloodhounds?"

"Have you asked your winged brothers?"

"They don't see in a way that would help them recognize Keagey in person from a photographic image of him. Is there a bird with a great sense of smell?"

"Vultures. They smell a kill on the wind and track it to the source. You can put some organ meat in your yard and a few Turkey Vultures will show up in less than an hour, even if you put it under some trees. They are an honorable people. They will help you if you ask. Fresh meat is a good idea."

"I'll get the Keagey scent ready as well."

Raven helped himself to a few more berries. He did a little bob-and-weave. I sat down on the grass.

"What rhymes with grudge?" said Raven after he'd swallowed enough berries.

"You read the *Drudge Report*?"

"No, but his Guardian Angels do."

"How will this help me?"

"That's for you to figure out." Raven said.

"Now you hold back."

"I'm not holding back. I think the *Drudge Report* is one place for you to get your story launched."

Raven Who Hops grabbed a last beakful of berries before he leaped into the sky. He vanished before his wings could beat twice.

Round two had begun.

I had a place to start for finding Keagey. This time, my plan would include a media spectacle that couldn't be swept under a rug.

I had no idea how to keep us anonymous, but I would have to try.

Nobody said realigning the path of the future was easy.

Chapter Twenty-Seven

I had never met a Vulture before.

It was after 5:00 p.m.. My hilltop would have light for another two hours. I sat cross-legged near my front door, watching the piles of chicken livers and thighs that I bought on the way home from picking berries. It had only been fifteen minutes, but already there were two Winged Brothers circling high overhead.

I sat motionless. The wait wasn't long. A large black bird with a bald head and neck glided in and hopped into a shuffling walk. I continued to do nothing. As the Winged Brother walked around the piles of meat, another flew in along the flight path and joined the circle-walk around the food.

The circle shrank until the two Turkey Vultures were able to peck at the pile, then pull away. When they were satisfied that the pile wasn't going to jump up and fight, they proceeded to toss back big beaks full of meat. I spoke in the ancient tongue.

"Peace and power, Winged Brothers."

They both hopped away from my voice, ready for flight, but hearing nothing else, they stopped and looked back. I began the summoning ritual, but made my presence small and peaceful. Both birds swiveled their heads toward me as I spoke.

"Peace and strength, Winged Brothers."

The smaller of the two put one eye on me and one on her mate.

"He thinks I am male."

"He's a two-legged. What would he know about anything?"

"I bring food for you, inviting you to council."

"Why should we speak?"

"I am a sky-child of the Great Father, who is also called the Great Mystery."

"He is our Grandfather, too. What do you want from We Who Work Alone."

"I am *Lakhota*, which means Association of Friends. I am honored to know you, We Who Work Alone."

The female spoke, "I think it's trying to be friendly."

"Strange behavior."

"Perhaps he is sick."

"At least he didn't call us 'Buzzards.' What an ugly name."

"And I don't think he believes we look like turkeys either. Stupid birds. He is different from the other two-leggeds."

"Perhaps we can listen to him. To see what he wishes."

Speaking about me in front of my back must be permissible in their tribe.

"I need a favor from you. In return, I will do a favor for you."

The male spoke while the female resumed eating.

"What is this favor you seek?"

"I want to locate a certain two-legged who has gone into hiding."

"We don't do the living."

"I'm not asking you to do anything but find him. Your sense of smell is very keen. You may smell him in the wind."

"This is a strange request, but I think it can be done."

He looked to his mate. She swiveled toward me.

"What do you offer us for this service?"

"I can make meat for you."

"That is a good offer. Perhaps you can offer more than chicken?"

"I hunt. What I can't make for you, I can acquire."

She said something in Vulture speech to her mate, then resumed eating.

"We will accept your offer. Please provide a rabbit and a chicken or other bird for us every fifth day of our search. We will find him if we can. May others join us in hunting your prey?"

"Yes, but not more than eight or so. If too many of your kind come here, it may make some two-leggeds nervous. They may do stupid things."

"We've noticed. We prefer not to eat eagles, but when a two-legged shoots one, we are there to clean up the mess."

The female finished eating.

"Let us smell the two-legged's scent."

I opened the bag and extracted the torn shirt piece and boxers. I wore a clean cotton glove to keep my scent to myself.

"Don't try anything tricky or nasty."

"I am your friend."

The male hopped up and put his bloody maw near the shirt. His nostril holes pushed air in and out.

He spoke something in Vulture. His mate hopped over and smelled Keagey, too. I sensed the presence of Raven Who Hops, but didn't move. The big birds shuffle-walked away.

Raven hopped over and said something in Vulture. Both of them spoke back at the same time. They conversed for a few moments, then Raven spoke in the ancient tongue.

"I will vouch for him. I am his Spirit Guide."

"That would explain his good manners," said the female.

"Thank you, Good Mother," I said. "I will tell my own mother that I brought her honor."

There was some more discussion in Vulture. I put the piece of Keagey's shirt and boxers back in the plastic bag and stood. This time, my movements did not alarm the black-feathered couple. I walked over to where the meat had lain on the ground and scuffed dirt over the dampness that remained.

I looked at Raven and the Winged Ones Who Work Alone, who were conversing in Vulture. I left them and entered my lodge. Raven Who Hops had suggested the Turkey Vultures. I had confidence in his guidance.

They would find Keagey.

And soon.

There was little time to prepare the spectacle to use when Keagey was found.

Chapter Twenty-Eight

Keagey had been found.

I was on a reconnoiter to confirm the sighting. If it was, indeed, the little bastard, I would have to go with my plan as it was — unfinished.

The new moon of *Canpa Sa Wi*, the Red Cherries Moon, hung black in the sky, just visible if you knew where to look. To the *wasiçius* it was July, named after another Roman emperor. Red Cherries sounded better to me.

I lounged in a large poplar tree at the edge of a park in Cape May, New Jersey. I was stretched out along a thick branch about 45 feet above ground. My head was aligned with an opening in the foliage that allowed me to see into the backyard of one of the ocean-view homes across from the park. A few hours before, the same branch had been a perch for my turkey Vulture friends.

Earlier in the morning, they had brought news of their find. I packed some supplies and tracked them to a park near the lighthouse in Cape May. That was hard to do with my driving on roads while they flew the thermal drafts.

I had to stop the car outside Milton, Delaware and send them a summons so I could explain that I couldn't just fly across the Delaware Bay as they did. They finally understood that I needed to cross the bridge where the two shores meet to close the Delaware Bay off into a river.

From there, I turned south onto the piece of New Jersey coastline that ran in the direction of the Red Road far enough to form a bay with Delaware and Maryland. That was good. The Red Road was the path of peace, a good road.

It was a long haul down the coast and my Winged Brothers and Sisters had to stop and rest along the way. I hoped they had found Keagey, but part of me hoped they hadn't. Cape May was too far to run a successful solo kidnapping operation, and crossing state lines added to the felony complaint. I could do without the complications.

When I got to Cape May, my Winged Brothers and Sisters rested high in a tree at the center of town. I got out, stretched my legs, and used the public facilities. When I returned, the Turkey Vultures flapped their wings and took off, turning west toward the Lodge of the Thunder Beings.

I had a few glimpses of the beautiful Victorian-era homes in various styles and colors. I felt the pull. This road ran straight and flat toward the lodge of the Thunder Beings. More than other roads, this one was linked east-west to the Black Road. It was a fearful road, a road of troubles.

A few minutes' drive took me past a big piece of land marked with billboards claiming it was a Nature Conservancy project. How nice. All those *wasiçius* buying land to protect it from other *wasiçius*. I wondered if my people dressed as bears and wolves, would they help us protect our lands, too?

252

After another few minutes drive, I followed my guides left onto a side street that took me to a big car-park in front of a lighthouse and a collection of out-buildings. This was as far south and east as you could journey in New Jersey without getting your feet wet.

The north end of the parking lot had a sign warning of dire consequences if someone disturbed the wild bird wetland habitat. Nobody had ever cared or warned others of dire consequences if the *Lakhota* habitat was disturbed. Environmentalists seemed to like all animals except humans.

Across the car-park and to the southwest was an area that bordered a sizeable bird sanctuary. It was separate from the wetland habitat to the north. Half a dozen homes of modern design lay between the park and the ocean. They had views of the ocean, the park, the lighthouse, and the bird sanctuary.

The price of one of those houses would feed my whole tribe for years. I couldn't even imagine the size of the bribes required to build on such a fragile ecosphere.

I made myself stop thinking those thoughts. The *wasiçius* could do whatever they wanted to each other and to their land. This wasn't my culture. If our ancient traditions were true, this wasn't even our planet. Besides, I had a job to do.

My two Vulture friends sat on a branch in a tall poplar tree at the edge of the sanctuary. We all rested for a while before I sent a gentle summoning call. They swiveled their heads in my direction. I got in my Jeep and drove off, looking for a place to meet. I headed east, retracing my route. After a few miles, I saw a sign for a weekend farmers' market. I turned

253

north on the road and after a half-mile, pulled to the side of the road beside a farm field full of immature soy.

I unloaded the sacks of raw market meats, dumping them on the grass beside the road. I put the trash into the Jeep, wiped my hands on a cloth and then drove the Cherokee a little distance down the road. As I walked back to the meat, my hired trackers from They Who Work Alone flew in for their last payday.

It would be a few minutes before the local talent got wind of the free feed. It wasn't free to my friends: they had earned it. Before I left the parking lot by the lighthouse, I had seen Keagey's head over a backyard fence. I wasn't sure, but it looked as if he was jumping from a diving board into a backyard pool.

"*Hau*, Winged Brothers and Sisters. Thank you for finding him."

They knocked their beaks together before the female turned to eat. The male spoke to me.

"Should we wait to clean up after you confront him?"

"No. He's not that sort of enemy."

A glance to the sky revealed two pairs of birds a few miles downwind.

"You should eat before the locals swoop in."

"Not a problem. You have brought plenty. Besides, those are my relatives. They're just waiting for you to leave. Anytime you want another favor, let us know."

I looked back over my shoulder.

"I'll do that."

I returned to the park, took a rope and my backpack, and then started toward the poplar tree. It was a quiet July afternoon, just heading toward a sunset. The park was deserted. I went to the side of the tree away from Keagey's place. The lowest branches were too high to reach. I made a heavy knot on the end of the rope and tossed it over the lowest branch, then used a pair of leather work gloves to make the climb. It would have been faster to use the pole-climber leg spikes that I had kept from my days with the telephone company, but I didn't want to harm the Tall Brother's skin.

After a minute and several pounds of back pain, I sat resting on the lowest branch. I thanked Grandfather for this tree being here for me to climb. Soon I was high enough and had worked my way to the side of the tree facing Keagey's hideout.

I took my digital camera from the backpack and snapped some pictures of Keagey doing dives into the pool. I zoomed in for close-ups of Keagey's face as he took another try off the diving board. He seemed relaxed. His tan was good, too. He must have left his conscience in his other pants.

Thoughts ran through my head like deer before a fire. I was hot to find a plan to blow the whole Keagey cover-up wide open and into the headlines as well as a way to make it advance the Red Nations. So far, all my thoughts had been for naught. Every plan I made offered me nothing but ways for it to fail. No matter what, I couldn't alert the prey prior to closing the snare. I didn't want to track him down again after another police-assisted flight from justice.

Chapter Twenty-Nine

I sat on into the twilight, when Keagey went inside. I debated going to my Jeep, but decided to wait in the tree for inspiration. The breeze combed the Tall Brother's leaves, moving their branches. It murmured a song about a seed flying far to take root and grow. That got me to thinking of my friend Gentle Wind. She was younger than I, and was attending Georgetown Law in DC. I hadn't seen her for a few years, not since the last time I was home for the Summer Dances.

I left the tree and made my way to the Jeep. While I was loading my stuff into the rear hatch, a police car cruised by, the officer giving me the stare that they use to make people act suspicious. I let him get what he could from my blank expression.

After the cop left, I finished loading my gear and drove the four-hour route home to Crownsville. On the way, I punched the number for the Tribal Police back on the Rez and asked for my cousin Two Feathers. He goes by his *wasiçiu* name, John Campbell. I waited.

"This is Campbell. May I help you?"

"*Hau*, John. It's Ben."

"*Hau*, Cousin! The Great Mystery still guiding your feet?"

"Yes."

"Why don't you come back and work with your own people?"

"When I'm ready, I will."

My cousin made a noise into the phone.

"So, what d'you need?"

"Your sister's phone number."

"She's got a boyfriend, Cousin."

"I just need some help with a little project I've got going."

"I got Sara's cell phone number. Will that do?"

I grabbed a pen from the console and wrote on my palm as I drove, steering with my knees. We ended the call. I stored her number in my cell phone, then called it. After three rings, a woman's voice answered.

"Gentle Wind, it's Ben."

There was a short silence.

"Ben Pace?"

"*Hau.* How's law school?"

"A lot of work."

I cleared my throat.

"I need a favor."

"What?"

"I need a crew of protesters to picket a place. Some police and politicians are covering up a serial rapist's crimes. I need two groups: some women who will protest the cover-up of the rapes, and some Indians to protest the government's cover-up of the rape of the Red Nations."

"Who is it that you want to get the connection?"

"Everyone."

"Who's the serial rapist? Anybody I know?"

257

If the Keagey or Kinkaed names came out before the protest started, the liberal Democrats in the women's group would probably choose national party politics over every woman's right to be safe from rape. The Kinkaed family was powerful in US politics, but rape is wrong, no matter who does it or what kind it is. And rape, whether of a woman, of my people, or of our land deserved justice. As much as Keagey's victims did.

"He's not famous, but his family is rich. You'd need to look further out in the family tree before you found fame or power."

After a pause, she spoke.

"I know some people who can arrange it. Where are we doing it? Bethesda?"

"No, Cape May, New Jersey, and I need them real soon."

"Then you'll need to cover their expenses and make a contribution to their organizations. You might even need to pay each person something."

"How much we talking?"

"At least $5,000 for the local chapter of the National Womyn's Council. Probably about $2,500 for the Inter-Indian Council. Plus gas and food money."

"Why the difference in the amount of contributions?"

"The women have to pay dues to the National Womyn's Council network."

"I'll get the money. How soon do you think we can get them?"

"When do you need them?

"Next weekend?"

She laughed out loud. I waited. She got quiet for a moment.

"You're serious."

"I just found the rapist stashed in a swanky compound. I don't know how long before he moves again. This guy raped a lot of women, and he used his family's money to buy off everybody, even the cops. I need to get him now, while I can, before they move him again. I need to make a big enough stink in the media that it can't be hidden again."

I hoped that this plan worked better than my last one.

This time there was sure to be open conflict.

Chapter Thirty

H e raped us."

Rita looked at each of the people gathered around her. Kelly, Lisa, Maria, and I stood behind her as she faced the small crowd in the car-park of New Jersey's Cape May Light. The ones in the back stepped closer while others cocked their heads.

"First, he raped me, then two women who aren't here." She gestured toward us. "Next he raped Maria and then one who killed herself."

Rita gestured toward the other two, as Lisa took a small side-step toward me.

"Then he raped Kelly and later Lisa."

Gasps and murmurs were heard throughout the crowd. Most of them were women, and about a third was from various Indian tribes.

"His family is rich, really rich. He had a whole firm of high-priced lawyers from Baltimore who beat the DA in court. It didn't matter that he did it. Family money paid for his crimes to disappear. Unpunished."

Rita's voice broke. She sobbed under the strain of emotional disclosure. I stepped to her side. She looked at me, then back to the crowd of faces. Her voice was strong again.

"After he got off on a technicality, he began stalking us again."

"Didn't you get a restraining order?" asked a woman in the front row.

"We couldn't get anyone to listen. The lawyers that we could afford couldn't outwit the ones his family hired. He was free to harass us. Free to do disgusting things at our homes and leave the evidence there. Free to scare us when we went to the grocery store. He always made sure there were no witnesses."

When Kelly stepped up to the mike, Rita held her hand.

"One time he walked up to me outside my home and told me that he was going to make me his 'girlfriend' again."

Tears rolled down her angry face.

"He told me he still has my panties and … and … that he … he masturbates into them."

The crowd's reaction was stronger. Emotional fires were being stoked to a temperature that would ignite a strong protest. Rita put her arm through mine.

"Through some connections, I got Ben's name and phone number. We went to him to ask if he would help us."

I took the microphone.

"These brave women helped me track down their rapist. We found his secret hideout where he stored his trophies. We got him to confess — on tape — to raping over twenty other women. Double jeopardy prevents him from being tried again for what he did to the four who are here with us, but the new evidence tied him to the other rapes. We turned everything over to the police."

261

Several people nodded their heads in agreement, while others grunted in approval. I paused to let their emotions build.

"There was enough evidence there to convict him on several of those rapes. It should have been enough to bring new charges against him. New trials. But do you know what happened?"

The members of the crowd turned their heads to watch the emotions that played on the faces of my sisters. I waited through their tense silence until their eyes came back to mine.

"Nothing happened."

The crowd shifted uneasily. I nodded as I held their eyes.

"Nothing happened," I said again, slower, for emphasis, moving my hands over them as if my hands were wings covering them all. "Despite our call to the police, despite all the taped evidence left with the rapist for the police to find when they arrived and found him, nothing happened. Oh, the police took all of the evidence, but nothing else happened. Nothing in the papers. Nothing on the televised news. Nobody in law enforcement who wasn't at the scene knows anything about it."

"No!" several people cried out.

"Police bullshit!" said others.

A few of the Indians grunted their anger. They were almost ready to create some good footage for the newscasts. We needed national exposure to pull this off.

"I spent three months searching for him, day and night, before a bird told me that he was hiding in Cape May."

One woman in the front row winked as if I had told a joke. A few of the Indians nodded their heads in understanding.

"Before you arrived this morning, I watched him have breakfast on his back deck. He hasn't left the house." I looked to the leaders of the groups who had come to our aid before I continued. "Get your people ready, and in about ten minutes, we will go and protest around his house. It's the pale grey shake-shingle one that sits near the lighthouse out-buildings."

"Should we try to stop him from leaving?" said Patricia, the leader of the National Womyn's Council.

"No. We aren't trying to get him, and he's not the problem."

"He's not?"

"We don't want to get ourselves arrested. That takes the attention off him and what he and his family did and puts it on us — the victims."

I looked from face to face.

"Our problem is his family and the political and judicial influence that their money buys. What we need is to use him as an object lesson to stir the conscience of society, not get ourselves arrested for bothering a man who was found innocent by our judicial system."

Some of the audience members started to nod in understanding.

"We will be video-recording the whole protest. We need to make so much noise against injustice that we make the evening news. If it's a slow news day, we may get nationwide exposure. His family won't be able to sweep his crimes under the rug again. Then the police will have to enforce the law against the rich just as they do against the poor."

The crowd watched the emotions that played on the faces of my sisters. Some of the people in the crowd began to murmur. Patricia, head of the Georgetown chapter of the National Womyn's Council stepped up to the microphone. She'd brought many of her loyal followers with her. They gazed up at her in adoration.

Now it was time to see what she could do for us.

"Thank you for coming. Each of us is here for our own reasons, but what matters is that we are here together. They win when we are alone, but we win when we join together. We may not be able to win this war, but we can damn sure win this battle! Let's make today count. Rape is wrong. Cover-ups are wrong."

She pointed to Keagey's house.

"His family and their money are covering-up the rapes. All citizens are guaranteed equal protection by the US Constitution. Women are citizens, aren't they? Where's our equal protection?"

They almost went wild. It was time for my friend Jim to speak. I touched Patricia's hand and indicated Jim.

My friend Jim Franks grunted in ascent. I gave him a nod as I went to the microphone one last time before the crowd dispersed. Though they were restless and excited, I managed to get their attention.

"Since I helped my new sisters with their problem, they wanted to help me with one of mine."

I stretched out my hand of greeting to Jim.

"This is my friend, Jim Franks. He holds the pipe of Georgetown's Inter-Tribal Council. He will explain."

Jim stepped forward and clasped my arm. His blue-jeans held a crease for the occasion. He wore a collared shirt with the Cheyenne Council logo. He smiled at my new sisters before he turned to face the throng.

"Thank you for letting us stand with you against your enemy. The evil done to these women is wrong, but the greater evil is that those with money go unpunished while the innocent and the poor suffer."

They erupted in applause. His Head man status among his people was obvious. The Power Spirit was with him. I stepped back, leaving Rita and Jim standing together. Rita watched him with the interested eyes that her sister had for me when she thought I wasn't looking. The urge to look at Teresa was strong, but I resisted. Jim's voice held a low rumble, as the promise of distant thunder.

"We are also here for another purpose. Yes, we fight for all women. No woman deserves to be violated. But we also fight against a similar injustice. The US Government repeatedly violated the Indian treaties. Just as rapists steal a woman's dignity and self-esteem, the government stole our hunting grounds. Just because some dirt farmers coveted our lands. Our lands, not theirs. Where the buffalo, elk, and deer were free."

Some of the women began nodding.

"Just as rapists plunder a woman's sacred place and take away her safety, the government plundered our sacred places, looting gold from our sacred and holy ground. We cared little for this metal that drives some white men crazy with greed. We cared more for our children, their spirits, and their destiny."

The women began looking at each other, nodding, talking to each other. Jim looked from face to face as he spoke.

"We fought them. Just as these women fought their rapist. Just as all the other women he attacked fought him. We fought so that we could fulfill our duty to protect the mystic path. We are the appointed caretakers of this land and the spirits who live here."

The women began to stir. They were ready. But we had to make sure that they remembered to protest both injustices: rape against women and rape against the Red Nations. Their spirits had to be joined to each other's as well as to ours.

"My cousins and I are here, not as mere men or women, not as Cheyenne or Miniconjou, not as *Lakhota* or Crow, not as Cherokee, Mohawk or Apache. We are here as citizens of this country, of this earth. The US Government has lied, cheated, and stolen from all of us here today, and others like us, for over 150 years.

"How long did it take the women to be given the right to vote? When was it that women were no longer considered the 'property' of their husbands? Why do women who have gone into the work-world still get paid less than their male counterparts for the same jobs? Why are women expected to work jobs, take care of the children, and do all the cooking and household chores? Why aren't absentee fathers forced — by the government — to financially support their own children?"

There were cheers and shouts as some of the women raised their fists and shook them.

"Why are women who are raped considered 'responsible' for the crime committed against them? Why is the way a woman dresses considered an 'invitation' to rape and violation? Why is her private sexual history displayed for all to see, yet the rapist's hidden? Why are men not punished when a woman says 'No' or 'I've changed my mind' and the man forces himself on her against her will? Why are women blamed for rape, discrimination, and violation?"

There was a hum among the women, an angry hum. The women's spirits were connected to each other's. Their spiritual energy was strong and powerful. Now Jim had to take that energy and the women's rage against injustices they had suffered and join it to our own.

"Why are the Red Nations forced to live on land that the government 'gave' to them instead of on the land the Great Father meant for us all to share? Why are the Red Nations blamed for their poverty when there are no jobs for them? Why are the Red Nations blamed for alcoholism when it is the government who gave them the very thing that addicts them — and takes subsidies for doing it? Why is the color of the Red Nations' people's skin an invitation to theft, discrimination, and violation?"

Some of the women began to applaud and cheer. Others shouted angry words — against men. Against politicians, the justice system, law enforcement, and the government. Jim raised his arms, his hands open to gather the women's spirits together.

"All of the justice system's lies and government cover-ups must stop. Raping women is wrong. Looting the trust funds of the Red Nations is wrong. Covering up these crimes is wrong."

The women surged forward as they cheered and applauded. They shouted names at the government, at lawyers, at the rich, at all unpunished crimes. The four women on the stage with us were openly weeping, as were some of the women in the crowd, though their weeping seemed to come from both pain and anger. The women's spirit energy was so powerful that it hit me like a huge ocean wave, its undertow threatening to pull me under. Jim held his hands to his breast, over his heart.

"I take your pain and suffering into myself. I will fight for you as any honorable man would. I join my spirit to yours. Now, let us go and, with our loud voices of protest, stop the crimes against the Red Nations. Let us shout to everyone that the crimes against women must stop."

I bowed my head and thanked Grandfather. The Kinkaeds would no longer be able to hide Keagey's crimes behind money and high fences. The government and law enforcement agencies would not be able to deny their own crimes, thefts, and lies either.

Against women.

Against the Red Nations.

Chapter Thirty-One

I n the front of the crowd, standing together, were Lisa's sister Emily, Maria's fiancé Robert, Kelly's friend Linda, and Rita's sister Teresa. When we cleared the crowd, they came forward to support their loved ones.

Teresa inserted herself between Rita and me, with an arm around each of us. She kissed my cheek after she kissed Rita's. I wanted to linger in her arms, but now wasn't the time. After a quick look into her eyes, I stepped away to where I could see them all.

"Did each team bring a video-camera with charged battery packs and blank tapes?"

Everyone nodded.

"I need Rita, Lisa, Kelly, and Maria to be the camera operators. It will hide their faces from the other cameras and keep Keagey from seeing them." I looked at my four new sisters as I said, "You need to wear your camera as a mask."

I turned to the others.

"Your job is to be lookouts. While they are looking through the camera, they won't be able to look around. So, your job is to keep an eye out for interesting developments that would be good to have on video. You should also look out for where they are walking. We don't want them stumbling. Does everybody understand?"

They all nodded.

"I want one team on each corner of the protest. Shoot anything near you. Don't try to save tape. You might miss a shot. Don't worry about whether another crew is getting what is in your area. Just make sure to get what's near you. Let's go."

The teams went to their cars to get their camera bags. I stood near my Jeep. A familiar presence approached me. He spoke.

"*Hau, Mahto.* There is much strong energy here." Raven bobbed his head then cocked it. "People are waiting for you."

"Spirits, too. Besides the *Lakhota* ones, I feel several Cheyenne and Apache spirit guides. Why can I not see them? Why will they not show themselves to me?"

"They follow their custom to remain invisible and speak only to their students. *Lakhota* guides show themselves because we like the feel of fur, hide, and feathers."

Raven lifted his head, as if he were listening to something far away.

"Events are about to spin out of control, *Mahto*. You will be tempted to step in and take charge. Do not. Feel and join the spirit of the moment, but do not try to control it."

"But Keagey …"

Raven shook his head.

"The Red Nations …"

"After we are done here," said Raven, "you should apologize to your mother and father for becoming an idiot after leaving your aunt and uncle's home."

"You became my Spirit Guide about that time. I just wanted to become like you. I'm glad it all worked out."

"I have several good replies, but never mind. Just listen. I'll spell it out for you. Walk as a bear, but wear the Stone People's magic. When it starts to spin out of control, use the magic to stretch time. That will slow the progress of events. The emotions that will be enraged and come into conflict today must not be allowed to go too far. If they do, everything we've worked for will be lost."

"I don't know how to stretch time."

"You'll manage."

"Do you have an instructional brochure with lots of pictures? That would come in handy."

"You'll have what you need," said Raven Who Hops. "I've arranged a private lesson for you."

"Now? When things are starting?" I said. "You could have dropped by last night for a chat. That would have been helpful."

"How about afterwards? We could find some fresh berries and discuss the weather."

"Discuss the weather? Oh, you mean ... eat together? You and me? You mean, I've learned enough that we can share a meal together?"

"Right now you need to go."

"Raven, I don't know what to say."

"Don't say anything. Go."

Raven hopped across the roof of the Jeep then leaped into the air. I tracked him into flight, where he joined a sky full of turning birds. Eagles, hawks, and ravens flew with owls, falcons, Turkey Vultures and seagulls. It wasn't normal for those birds to fly together. I doubted the *wasiçiu* would notice.

It had, indeed, started. The women and Indians were already moving across the parking lot toward Keagey's. I fast-walked toward my camera crews.

"Let's go everybody! You know where you need to be and what you need to do. Be brave! The Power of everyone here is with you today!"

I made eye contact with Robert and then looked to Linda who was with Kelly.

"Make the calls."

Linda was already busy with her cell phone. They were calling the radio stations in Cape May and the television stations in Atlantic City to report a huge and rowdy protest going on at the lighthouse. If asked, they would pretend that they were tourists who happened to see it and were concerned about it.

We hurried to catch the crowd headed toward Keagey's. The Georgetown chapter of the NWC got there first. They filled the sidewalk in front of Keagey's house, their raised signs proclaiming it unfair that a rapist should live in comfort while his victims lived in pain. They held their signs high.

RAPE IS A CRIME
RAPE IS A VIOLATION

NO MORE COVER-UPS
PROSECUTE CURRUPT COPS

RAPE IS WRONG
WOMEN DESERVE PROTECTION

RAPISTS ARE CRIMINALS
GIVE BACK WHAT WAS TAKEN FROM US

RAPISTS DESERVE TO BE PUNISHED
ONLY COWARDS HIDE BEHIND DADDY'S MONEY

The women were on their second lap around the sidewalk when the Inter-Tribal Council arrived. The Indians set up a longer circle by putting more space between their marchers. Their westbound leg was on the grassy median, and the return route was in the street.

THE GOVERNMENT STEALS
THE GOVERNMENT LIES

THE GOVERNMENT RAPED THE RED NATIONS
RAPE OF THE RED NATIONS IS A CRIME

THEFT FROM THE RED NATIONS IS CRIMINAL
GIVE US BACK OUR LAND

GIVE THE RED NATIONS WHAT YOU PROMISED
KEEP YOUR WORD TO THE RED NATIONS

HONOR THE TREATIES TO THE RED NATIONS
COWARDS & LIARS HIDE BEHIND POLITICS

NO MORE RAPE OF THE RED NATIONS
STOP THE LIES

STOP THE INJUSTICE
STOP THE THEFT

STOP THE RAPE

A Lexus sedan that probably belonged to Keagey was trapped in the middle of the circling Indians. His Mercedes hadn't been seen since he disappeared from public view. I stopped where I could look in Keagey's windows while appearing to watch the protest.

> "What do we want?"
> "Justice."
> "When do we want it?"
> "Right now."
> "Who deserves it?"
> "We do."
> "What do we want?"
> "Justice."

Keagey showed his face inside the big front porch window. He cracked his glass storm door and stuck his head out for a few minutes before jerking his head back inside. He pulled a phone from his pants pocket. Whipping it out just seemed to come natural to him. He talked to someone, waving his free hand while he talked. After he closed his cell phone, he stuffed it back into his pocket.

We had engaged the enemy.

He had made his opening response.

All we could do was march and hold up our signs and chant protests until we saw what Keagey had fired in our direction.

approached Patricia, who had the bull-horn. She handed it to an apprentice who kept the beat going on the chant. She turned to face me.

"Are they on their way?"

I waved to Linda who nodded her head then hunched her shoulders. I mouthed the words "Thank you" to her. Robert saw my wave and nodded his head. He smiled big. I struck my palm with my fist, then raised my eyebrows and cocked my head. Robert laughed as he hunched his shoulders like a football player. I turned back to Patricia.

"The Cape May radio stations are almost a sure thing. The Atlantic City television stations are not as sure. We sold them well, but it depends on how many other stories there are."

"We sent our press release to the DC and Atlantic City stations. You'd think that would be enough to get the crews out," she said.

"Protests used to be big news. Now, we'll just have to wait to see if they show up."

If no one came, Keagey would be able to go deeper into hiding. I ignored my own fears and spoke to hers.

"They will come, if for nothing else than to use a traditionally Democrat event to push the Republicans out of the top news story slot."

"I hope so."

"In the meantime, can I suggest a new chant? This one's getting worn out, don't you think?"

"What do you have in mind?"

"How about 'Arrest police who break the law'. 'This rape is the final straw'."

"We'll try it."

"I'll check on our camera crews to make sure we're getting your good side."

"Just make sure that you get us copies of the tapes."

While Patricia suggested the new chant to the troops, I moved toward Jim. He was on the street-side leg of the Indian protest march and heading toward me. My movement must have caught his eye, because he turned his head toward me. I made the expression for a question. Jim's eyes tracked to behind me, as if I should look.

I heard a car approaching. Cars had been arriving in a steady stream since we had arrived. People jumped out and headed for a day at the beach. They parked close to the beach or the shore side of the lighthouse.

So far, nobody had ventured over to where we were on the road from the Lighthouse buildings to the tiny cluster of homes perched on the exclusive stretch of beach. Perhaps when the news crews arrived, we would generate a crowd of observers.

"Arrest police who break the law."
"This rape is the final straw."

From the new sound, another car was headed in our direction. I saw a minivan cut a tight turn right where the road met the parking lot, drawing a bead on our position. It had WFIB 94.5 FM emblazoned on the side in letters big and bright enough to be seen from another state. Jim's voice spoke from behind me.

"Perhaps we should handle this?"

Patricia joined Jim.

"I'm not good with public relations," I said.

"Now's not the time to learn," said Patricia. "We need to work the reporter to get what we need."

"I leave it to the experienced," I said.

We touched hands as we passed, wishing each other luck. They continued on to meet the new arrivals as I headed toward my camera crews. I had asked Lisa and her sister Emily to take the street side on the end, closest to the car park, and Maria and her fiancé Robert to film from the same end, but closer to the house. I reached them first.

Maria was happily recording the event for posterity, oblivious to my approach. Robert saw me.

"A radio station got here."

Maria looked up from her task.

"Here to check on us worker bees?"

"No, here to talk strategy. Get whatever you feel should be caught on tape, but make sure that you get anything that happens on the lawn, the porch, or in the house. The others may get something, but you can't rely on that. If there's more than one thing happening toward the house, then focus on the ones closer to the house. Remember, whatever you do, don't cross his property line. Stay on the sidewalk."

"You got it, Boss," said Robert with a smile.

"Things are bound to heat up. When they do, I want you both to stay clear. The pictures are not as important as you and your safety."

"You mean, we're going to get hurt?" Maria asked, lowering her video-recorder.

"No, I don't think so," I replied.

Robert pushed the camera back into position.

"He's just asking us to be careful, hon."

"Okay. I'll be a good do-bee," she said to Robert as she placed her eye against the viewer. "Besides, I've got you here to protect me."

He put his hand on her shoulder.

"I need you both to be careful today. You have a wonderful future. Be heroes to the children you will have together. Today will take care of itself. Robert, just kiss her or put your hand on her back or do whatever it takes to keep her filming. Keep her safe when it starts."

I nodded goodbye and then moved to Lisa and Emily. I had put Robert and Maria where they were because that was bound to be the most active corner. It was the closest to Keagey's house, the lighthouse, and the parking lot. If there was trouble, it was sure to be in that direction. I knew I could count on the big Scot to make sure Maria was safe.

I had put Emily and Lisa where they were for the same reason. Emily was formidable when someone threatened her little sister. They could hold their own without me, which was good because I would be on the other side of the protest when the figurative bullets started flying.

"Hi, Ems. Hi, Lisa."

They both looked over, smiled, and chorused "Hi." We went over their tasks, but their emphasis was on the rear action. I left them with the same admonition to keep safe and to let others be the heroes today.

Down the street with Kelly and her friend Linda I repeated the briefing, then turned to take my place with Teresa and Rita.

"*Hau*, Redman," Teresa said.

"Only men say '*hau*.' Women say '*han*' as a greeting."

"*Han*, hon," she said, smiling.

"*Han*, Ben," Rita added.

"*Hau, Tanksi*," I said to Teresa before I turned to Rita. "*Hau, Tankse*."

"Are you sweet-talking us?"

"I just called you each 'sister'."

"Then why didn't they sound the same?" Teresa observed.

She was such a clever one.

"We have two words for 'sister'. I called you 'little sister' and Rita 'big sister'."

She narrowed her eyes and pursed her lips as she stared at me.

"Listen, guys. We've got something more important to do right now," said Rita. "You can continue your *Lakhota* lessons later."

"My spirit guide, Raven Who Hops, told me that things are going to spin out of control soon."

"I wish I could have met him," said Teresa.

"Spirit Guides are very private. Even if you were with me for decades, you may not see him, let alone meet him. Besides, that's not what's important. Didn't you hear what I said that my Spirit Guide told me?"

"Yeah, That things are about to get out of control. That sounds pretty good to me.

"Do you mind?" said Rita, sounding stressed and exasperated. "We've got a major protest on, trying to focus some national attention on the little bastard, and you two are doing the hormone hokey-pokey."

"We have to stay focused," I said.

"I am staying focused," said Teresa.

I went over the details I'd told the others.

"You'd better stay here with us," Rita said.

"Why?"

"Because if you are across the way, she'll just stare at you and not be my look-out."

"Rita! I can't believe you said that."

"If you stay here and hold her hand, she might actually be useful for something."

"Rita Louise Cade! I can't believe how you just run your mouth! And after you promised to keep everything I told you a secret."

"That was before I knew I was risking my life ..."

I stepped to Teresa's side and took her hand.

"Will that help your concentration?" I said.

"Yes. And I forgive you, Rita," she said while looking into my eyes.

For a moment, as I put my arm around her waist, pulling her close, I forgot about the protest. She snuggled in as if it were a cool crisp day in *Can Wape Kasna Wi*, the Falling Leaves Moon. I turned my head to Rita. Though she shook her head, she was smiling like a wolf on a warm rock.

"You owe me a date with Jim."

280

"With Jim?"

"He's not married, is he?"

"Just start filming, okay?" I said.

"Sure thing."

I looked over the protest. Lisa and Emily had moved to film the radio interview of Patricia and Jim. I wish I'd thought of that. I hoped they had it from the beginning. Keagey peered out of the window a few times, but so far, not much was happening.

Teresa took the opportunity to put her head on my shoulder and her mouth near my neck. Her hot, moist breath tickled. After a minute, I felt the faintest touch of a kiss near my ear.

"What are you doing?" I whispered.

"Letting you know that if you're interested, so am I."

"And you're picking now to do it?"

"This may be the only chance I'll ever get."

"Teresa, are you sure you know what you're getting into?"

"No, but I think I can take the chance with you."

"What are you two whispering about?" said Rita, turning around, the video-camera on us.

I held my arm up in front of my face.

"The protest. Film the protest."

With a suspicious look on her face, Rita grunted as she turned the video-camera back around, saying, "You definitely owe me a date with Jim."

I leaned closer to Teresa.

"Do you know about the Lakhota practice of a young brave putting a robe over his and a maiden's heads?"

Her voice became a little husky.

"No, is it kinky?"

"No, but it says a lot about my culture. It means that privacy is hard to find in a tribe. We are closer as a society than your culture. We have few secrets from each other. There is a lot you should know about my culture before you get too involved with me."

"Then let's just enjoy being superficial while I get to know you better," she whispered.

"Are you seducing me?"

"You haven't dated much recently, have you? Don't worry. I like it that I'm your first girlfriend in a while."

I didn't have to speak. Her head rested on my chest, where my heart was pounding like a war drum. If she weren't deaf, she knew that she had gotten to me. I put my hands on her shoulders and pushed her a little away from me.

"Is something wrong?"

"No. But this isn't the time. Or the place. We're here for another purpose. And my spirit guide said things were going to get out of control. And he didn't mean with us."

"Okay," said Teresa, staying slightly away from me, but looking disappointed.

So far, not much was happening.

Then, without warning, everything changed.

Chapter Thirty-Three

Three big, black Mercedes sedans rolled through the parking lot. They were quiet: only the sound of high-grip performance tires on clean pavement betrayed their approach. They must have used Campagnella's muffler man. The Mercedes drivers parked their cars in slots behind the radio station's SUV.

The numerous men that jumped from the cars all wore khaki slacks and teal green shirts. They moved together in a knot and without a sound, across Keagey's lawn and up onto his porch. Without stopping to ring the bell, the one in front simply put a key into Keagey's door lock and entered, leaving the door open behind him for the ten others who followed.

They had "private security" written all over them. We must have rattled Keagey's cage enough for him to call out eleven *Goombah* babysitters. The door key meant they probably worked for his uncle, one of New Jersey's two U.S. Senators.

Their arrival spurred the energy of the NWC protesters. They started a new refrain.

> "Hey, Ho, Hey, Ho."
> "This here rapist has to go!"

The Indians reacted as if the goon squad was the second coming of George Armstrong Custer and did some war whooping before rejoining the main chanters' refrain.

We didn't have time to discuss the development or the changing atmosphere of the protest. Just then, three Cape May Police cars rolled in. Their patrol cars boxed-in the private security cars and the radio station's SUV. The officers exited their vehicles and moved towards us.

Two of the police approached the radio crew where Patricia and Jim were still in interview mode. I couldn't hear from this distance, but it seemed as if the police officers knew the radio folks; they shook hands with Patricia and Jim. Patricia showed them the permits for the protest. The officers nodded politely after examining the permits. Score a big PR point for the Cape May Police. They appeared to be approaching the situation with an open mind, asking questions before they started beating people.

Two other officers walked over to Maria and Robert. They appeared to say something and made a few hand gestures, after which Maria went back to filming the protest instead of the policeman and woman who stood near them.

The remaining two police came toward us. One stopped in the road behind Lisa and Emily, the other continued to stand behind Kelly and Linda. He was a big brute, at least seven-feet-tall and built like stacked weights at a gym. I hoped his mere presence didn't terrorize the two women to the point where they forgot their filming mission. And I hoped the officers didn't lose their tempers and go off half-cocked on any of us.

Keagey's door opened and a few of the teal-dressed protection team came onto the porch. The door remained open, with a few teammates in the doorway. Sound and movement in the parking lot made me look as two big vans rolled in, each one with a deployable crane microwave dish on the roof. One was blazoned with the WCAN station symbol and slogan. The other proclaimed that WTIZ Atlantic City was "where the news comes first."

Too bad honesty wasn't even in the race at most news organizations. From the *NY Times* down to the student papers in schools, more sins were hidden than revealed. More crimes than the Maryland Police covered up. I hoped that these news crews were after a story and not just stooges for the Kinkaed political machine.

WCAN rolled in on the west, while WTIZ took the east. Competing meat-puppets, each with a camera jockey, rushed in to get what they could. The WTIZ blonde wannabe model bounced up to the radio crew and pulled one of the Cape May police over in front of her camera. Meanwhile, the male Chippendale from WCAN and his camera crew dragged Patricia and Jim away from the Radio Jocks.

One of the protestors had an African drum that he used to add punch to their chants. To my disappointment and chagrin, the protestors had shifted back to their original chant.

> "What do we want?"
> "Justice."
> "When do we want it?"
> "Now."

Things went well for a while, but my heart and spirit were uneasy, and not only because of what Raven had said. A few minutes after the TV news crews switched targets, Patricia's head snapped toward me. Even at this distance, I could see that she was angry. Jim didn't react like Patricia did. On the other hand, what Red Man would reveal his inner feelings?

Patricia turned and stomped our way.

The wannabe-model must have told her that Keagey was a member of the Kinkaed family.

Chapter Thirty-Four

Patricia swooped by the front of the protest and gathered her followers. She led them over to us.

I stepped in front of Rita and Teresa, whispering, "Keep filming."

I clothed myself in the walk-of-a-bear magic. I felt my hands and feet grow large and heavy. They didn't actually change size and shape, but the power and mass of the bear was mine. Patricia arrived with her entourage. The Indians continued their marching and chanting.

"You lied to me."

"I have never lied to you. My words have been straight."

"You didn't tell me that the man you are accusing of rape is the nephew of the Governor of Maryland as well as one of the US Senators from New Jersey."

"What difference does that make?"

"He's a Kinkaed."

There were gasps and murmurs in the crowd standing closest to her.

"You didn't tell us that."

"You asked if his family was well known, and I replied that the Keageys are not well known, only rich. That is the truth."

"You should have told us! Lying by omission is still lying."

"You must have been raised in the Catholic Church."

"This is not a goddamned joke."

"It is not a lie, Patricia. Crimes are matters of evidence. Guilt should not determined by skin color, nor innocence by family ties or wealth. You didn't care earlier who the serial rapist or his family were. Why should it matter now?"

"You just don't understand how the political system works, do you?"

"Corruptly," I said.

"The Kinkaeds are an important family. We can't do anything that may hurt their reputations."

"You're not. You're exposing Keagey as the serial rapist he is."

Patricia stomped one foot, looking frustrated as she crossed her arms over her chest, and glared at me.

"The Kinkaeds officially and politically stand for women's issues. We have to support them."

"Officially and politically they may stand for those issues. But personally, they don't care about women at all. They manipulated the trial to get a serial rapist freed because he's a member of their family. They released him — to continue raping women — despite all the evidence we left them to prove his guilt, because he's a member of their family. Doesn't that make any difference to you? What if his family was named Johnson or McDonald or Davidson?"

"The Kinkaeds are incredibly powerful."

"They misuse that power."

She turned an angry look on Jim and then on me. Behind her, the supporters looked nervous and frightened. Some of them had started to slip away.

288

"Who are you? God? That you pass judgment on other people?"

"Rape is wrong, whether it is of women or of the Red Nations."

"Will you stop with that 'Red Nations' shit? You should have told me who he was."

"Again, I ask you, why does his family's name make a difference? He raped women. At least twenty. They deserve justice. Even if it is from a judicial system and a government that raped the Red Nations."

"Again with the 'Red Nations' broken record," said Patricia.

"Do you see some difference between the two kinds of rape that I don't?"

She looked around her troops. More were leaving. She cursed and shook her head.

"Equal justice under the law, right?" I said. "Isn't that what we're protesting about? That the rich shouldn't get away with crime while poor minorities go to jail in their place. That no rapist — whether an individual man or an entire government — should get away with rape, degradation, and violation. Equal justice for all. Isn't that what this protest is about?"

Patricia stared at me. I could feel her fierce anger and deep sense of betrayal. My bear-ness allowed me to notice it but not to be attacked or wounded by it.

"What does any of that have to do with your lying to us about his Kinkaed connection? Now that we know you've told one lie for your own purposes," she said, giving Jim and the Indian protesters the same angry look, "how do we know that you aren't lying to us about Keagey. For some vindictive reason of your own that I haven't figured out yet."

She cocked her head at me, fixing a beady eye on me just as Raven Who Hops sometimes did, before she continued.

"I'm beginning to think that he's innocent, and you're simply trying to blacken his name, along with the reputation of the Kinkaeds."

"Here, hold this," Rita said in a loud voice to her sister.

Teresa took the camera. Rita turned Teresa and the camera back toward Keagey's house. Rita stepped closer to Patricia. She raised her shirt, taking her bra with it. She pointed to her left breast, where a ragged scar, as long as her finger wandered around it.

"He cut me with the tip of a knife while he ordered me to beg for my life. He didn't wear a mask, disguise his voice, or pretend that he was anyone else. He insisted that I use his real name. He made me beg him to fuck me. He tied and cut me, making me beg for my life, and then he raped me, in more than one way, making me beg him to fuck me. Making me say that I loved him. That I wanted him. And all to prevent him from killing me after he raped me."

Even Patricia's face got as pale as those of her followers. We were like a silent circle within the circle of the Indians' chant.

"Cover-up. Cover-up. Lies so low."
"Cover-up. Cover up. Lies real fast."
"Stop the cover-up is what we ask!"

Rita's rebuttal knocked the angry look off Patricia's face. Rita pulled her bra and shirt down. I sensed her strength as, like the young Ali, she danced around Patricia — figuratively — then jammed her left arm forward for the TKO.

"You must be one of those 'skin-deep' women's rights people. You wear it like a shirt over your real agenda, which is to sell us out as soon as you can for political gain."

"We're leaving!"

"Come on. Prove me wrong. Stay here and protest how Keagey's guilty ass is free because the Kinkaeds ordered the evidence destroyed. Stay here and tell the world that no man can rape a woman, no matter who he is. Tell the world that the government can't rape the Red Nations with impunity."

Patricia used a condescending tone to dismiss us. "You have no idea how real politics work."

"Unjustly," said Rita. "Unfairly."

"You're saying that because you couldn't present enough evidence at his trial to prove him guilty beyond a reasonable doubt. Sounds like 'sour grapes' to me."

I put my arm out so Rita wouldn't lunge toward Patricia and scratch her face to shreds. Jim had extended his arm out the same time. Rita's clenched fists remained at her sides, her breathing shallow and fast as she cursed Patricia. Jim and I kept our arms in front of Rita. She didn't need to be violated any more by being arrested for assault and battery. Patricia turned to her people.

"Come on. We're leaving. And we're keeping the money. I already cashed the check."

Rita shouted at Patricia's back as she and her remaining team departed.

"At least I haven't sold out to seek favor from misogynous men who are guilty of every crime I can think of."

She went to Teresa, took the camera, and started filming again. About half of the NWC members didn't follow Patricia. She turned and spoke to them.

"What do you think you're doing?"

"Rape is wrong, no matter who does it."

"The government did commit a terrible injustice to the Red Nations."

"Rape."

"Yes, the government raped them. And lied to them."

"Violated them just as this Keagey violated his victims."

"It makes me ashamed to be white."

"This Keagey deserves to be punished."

"Yeah. Who cares what his name is? I don't."

"Not if he's a serial rapist."

Patricia glared at them.

"The Land Rovers are leaving in a few minutes. If you're not in them, you'll have to find your own way home."

"We have room for you," I said to the braver members of her crew. "No matter where you live, we'll get you home safely."

"You have our word," said Jim, "as honorable men who fight injustices against the Red Nations and against women."

Chapter Thirty-Five

G o ahead and leave if you want," said one.

"Our belief in the cause hasn't changed," said another.

They turned and came to Rita.

"That bastard should pay, no matter who his family is," said another.

The Georgetown women who had decided to stay with us returned to their places, but we lacked enough people to make a good line. The Indians moved onto the sidewalk and added the women into their loop. The chanting got louder. Jim was standing with Maria and Robert.

Keagey's porch was starting to get crowded with the Teal-Team. Most of them appeared to have no necks. Maybe they had once been World Champion Weightlifters. Or Super Bowl-winning former football players. Either way, my bear-ness might not be strong enough to protect all of us from them.

They seemed to be waiting for something. That something soon arrived. Eight New Jersey State Trooper cars pulled up. They put their cars in a broad arc behind the Cape May Police and the TV vans, blocking their escape routes. Nobody was going to make a quick get-away.

The State Troopers donned their equipment before coming our way. Nightsticks swung on their belts, slapping their thighs as they walked towards us.

Two were carrying shotguns. I hoped they shot bean-bags and not buckshot.

The Teal-Team left the porch and formed a skirmish line. They moved forward as a group, looking intimidating as they stopped at the edge of the lawn. The line of protesters fell back toward the street, giving the goons plenty of room. The Troopers moved up behind us, making a line on the street side of the protesters. I feared that this sandwich maneuver meant we were toast.

The reporters and film crews took up positions in the back, between Lisa and Kelly. A crowd of people had gathered from their cars and the beach to see what all the fuss was about. This event was shaping up for a good chance at some local press coverage, but it probably still lacked the punch for a national news story. Besides, quite a few of us might get seriously hurt.

The protesters stopped marching and chanting. Jim walked to the front of our group. He spoke to the Teal-Team *Goombah* in the middle.

"May I help you?"

"You can all leave right now."

"Maybe you have noticed that we don't have sleeping bags or tents. You can relax. We won't spend the night. And we won't be back tomorrow."

The one on the right of the one Jim had spoken to cleared his thick throat.

"Don't youse play smart with us, Tonto. Youse leave right now, and nobody gets hurt."

Jim raised an eyebrow.

"Tonto?"

This was going to get uglier than I'd imagined. I stood to the side, making the car park the backdrop for my view of the Jim versus the rent-a-cop debate. A movement caught my eye. A dark-complexioned man and a US Marshall were moving through the crowd towards us. I didn't think they were on our side, and we appeared to be very out-numbered. And we had no weapons.

I looked at the man with the Marshall. My heart soared. He was a squat Indian with bushy eyebrows. I doubted he was a Kinkaed. Their visit must be something that Jim had cooked up. This had to be the time when trouble would burst the dam of tensions around me.

Raven had told me to use the Stone People's magic. I had to lock-and-load. I took a moment to root myself into the earth. I sensed bedrock below the sidewalk and topsoil. I dropped my presence to its level. It was an ancient colony.

"Greetings, Stone People," I said silently.

The ancient granite block closest to me spoke.

"Greetings, Topsider."

"Do you have something to tell me?"

"You need to learn the importance of your continuing lessons in Stone Dreaming."

"Lessons? Yes, they're important, but today, right now ..."

"After today, your bones will know the importance of your lessons. Not just your mind."

I stayed silent. I held down my fear. No fear. No fear. It was the *Lakhota* way. It was my path.

"You would ask to use our magic to alter the subjective time-streams of the topsiders that are about to fight."

"I don't know how to use your magic yet. How could I use it?"

"I will come with you back to the surface. Don't worry how. Let me perform the joining."

He stretched his spirit and came around to my back. I felt him put his hands into my arms and run them forward into my hands. His head moved forward to envelope mine. His body sank into mine. I now wore him as a hunter would wear a deer skin.

"Let's go," he said.

I tried to rise, but couldn't.

"I can't lift us."

"Is this better?"

Our spirits zoomed to the surface and reattached to my body.

"I slowed topside time while we talked. You haven't missed much. Jim is waiting for us."

"Jim knows what I am doing?"

"Jim is further along his path than you are in yours."

I opened my eyes to see Jim looking at me. His eyes narrowed a tiny bit.

"Tell Jim you are ready," my new friend said.

I let my eyes widen for a small moment. Jim's eyes went to neutral and he turned to face his opponent. The Teal-Team spoke.

"Are youse listenin' to us, Tonto? Youse need to leave. Right now."

"My name is Jim, not Tonto. And we are on a public sidewalk, practicing our Right of Free

Assembly and our Right of Free Speech. We also have the necessary permits to allow us to do so legally."

"Youse ain't got those rights on this here sidewalk."

"Would you prefer that we step into the street to continue our protest? You can't violate our civil rights. They're protected by the Bill of Rights. Which is attached to the Constitution, in case you didn't know."

"Funny. Very funny. Tonto thinks I don't know what the Constution is," he said to his partners. "Ya see, Tonto, youse don't look like no Geronimos, so youse and your buddy-Tontos better leave. Youse lost them civility rights when youse came into my backyard."

"Your formidable elocution reveals how truly erudite you actually are, Sir."

Half of the *Goombahs* tried to figure out what Jim had said while the rest instantly took offense. The non-Indian women in the line of protesters gasped then backed up, but with the Troopers lined up behind them, they stopped, with nowhere to go. They stepped back into the Indians, who put their arms around the women.

The motion started a chain-reaction. The two lines of Indians joined and put their arms up and around each other, making a long line of 30 people. The Red among them started a low humming of the ancient war song of all people.

"Now is the time. Let me operate through you," my Stone Brother said. "Relax. I'll do it all."

I felt the weight of the Earth on my shoulders. My vision seemed to swim for a moment before settling. When I returned to the present, Jim was speaking to the head goon.

"How are you going to do that with all of these State Troopers and Police watching?"

The middle one with the better grammar answered.

"Who do you think I was talking to on my cell phone when the Troopers got here? They are with us."

"Youse shouldn't oughta fuck with the Kinkaeds on their home turf."

"As for the Cape May Pinkertons, they'll kiss the ass of anyone with money who doesn't screw up the tourist business. The residents like quiet, and you're causing a scene. Our job is to make you go away."

He seemed to be drawing his words out, as if he was speaking slower than before. It was the Stone People's magic. I wondered how my fellow Indians were taking this. As usual, we were hiding any reactions from our enemies.

"What if we insist on exercising our civil right, especially since we have the legal permits, and refuse to go away?"

"Then they will look the other way while the boys and I put you into your cars and you drive away. If you don't play nice, we'll put you in the cars unconscious and drive you to the state line where you can sleep it off in a visitor's center."

"What about the crowd?"

"When it's over, we'll tell them we were filming a scene for a TV movie. They'll buy it. And don't worry about the news. They know they have to play ball or suffer the consequences. They want raises and a chance at a national gig. We have them handled."

He gave a head flick and the Teal-Team stepped forward, shoving our line of protesters back into the State Troopers. I pulled Teresa and Rita back with me, escaping the crush. I looked to Kelly and Linda. They were behind the Troopers.

I couldn't see Lisa and Emily through the throng. I caught a glimpse of Robert above the surging line, grateful that he was tall. He was moving away from the turmoil. I assumed that Maria was with him. I hoped for Lisa and Emily, but I couldn't leave Teresa and Rita alone at the front of the fight. A quick glance back showed that Kelly and Linda were okay.

The State Troopers retreated as the Teal-Team drove the Indians into the street. The goon on the right spoke again.

"Why don't youse towel-heads just go back to Iran or Iraq or wherever youse come from? Youse ain't wanted here, you fucking foreigners."

Without moving forward, to avoid heightening the crisis, Jim raised his voice one notch.

"I am Cheyenne. My ancestors walked this land before your people came down from the trees. Your grandparents probably escaped from prison in Europe to come here. Why don't you go back to where you came from and get the hell off of my continent, you ape-faced dick-wad foreigner."

"I ain't no foreigner, youse Tonto-piece-of-shit."

Goon number two stepped up to Jim and unloaded his right arm into Jim's stomach. Jim bent then straightened up.

"You hit real good for a sissy."

"Fuck you!"

He hit Jim in the mouth. Jim touched his face and looked at the blood on his fingers. He spat on the ground by goon number two's shoe, who took another swing at him. Jim ducked the punch and spun the goon around and shoved him into the head goon.

Everything broke loose. All of the goons were knocking the Indians around. The red women were hauling the slower moving white women behind the red men for safety. The men were shoving the Teal-Team goons into each other, in an attempt to counter their number advantage. Despite this effort, the goons were making no-neck headway into our group.

From behind us, the State Troopers stepped forward and started grabbing the women. I heard the ones closest to me yelling.

"You're under arrest for disturbing the peace."

They started yelling the Miranda Warning.

What a horrible joke. The goons were guilty of assault and battery, but we were the ones being arrested.

I bet they had a Kinkaedian judge waiting for us.

Chapter Thirty-Six

The squat Indian I had seen with the US Marshal moved through the fight like a sky-diver through air. He walked unimpeded to the middle of the mayhem, with a Trooper trailing in his wake. The Indian reached Jim, who was being held by goon number two while the head goon worked him over.

"Who's in charge here?" the Indian barked in a voice that reminded me of my Boot Camp Drill Instructor.

Everyone stopped what they were doing and looked. The Trooper that had trailed in the Indian's wake stepped in front of him and shoved a nightstick into his stomach, doubling him over. As he went down, the Trooper cracked him on the back of the head with the nightstick.

A gunshot from a powerful gun broke the air. A command voice rang out.

"I'm US Marshall Joe Gibson."

He came forward from the edge of the crowd.

"Step back, right now!"

He pointed his gun at the Trooper who had nightsticked the Indian.

"You just struck a US Senator's Chief of Staff. All he did was ask who was in charge and you assaulted him."

He pointed the gun in the face of the Trooper.

"Drop the stick and hit the deck!"

The State Trouper complied as the Indian got up, shaking his head. The Marshall spoke to the Indian.

"Luther, are you okay?"

"I've got a headache, but I'll live."

"Get his cuffs and lock his hands behind his back."

Marshall Joe Gibson pointed his gun at the two goons holding Jim.

"Release that man and step back, or I'll blow your kneecaps off."

They dropped Jim, who stood up.

"Are you well enough to help me?" Marshall Joe asked.

"Yes," Jim replied.

"Fine. I am appointing you a field-deputy to assist a Federal Marshall in dire circumstances. Take that Trooper's weapon and point it at his leg. If he makes a move to escape, hit him hard with the gun. Don't shoot him unless you have to."

As Jim took the Trooper's gun, Luther looked around. He spoke to the crowd.

"I work for US Senator Dan Nighthorse Campbell. He was aware of Jim's plan to bring his group to this protest and asked me to file a report on the day's activities. You can be sure that I will. Joe?"

Marshall Joe stepped to Luther's side.

"I discharged my weapon. I will now have to file an official report that will be investigated. The FBI reviews every weapons report filed by a US Marshall. This is now a Federal case, and your New Jersey machine can't help you.

Marshall Joe pointed his free hand at the head Cape May cop, who had been sidling towards his cruiser.

"You," said Marshall Joe, pointing at the cop, "get over here."

The Sergeant came forward. I took the opportunity to maneuver Rita and Teresa through the crowd to be close enough to catch the central part of the action on videotape. Marshal Joe, a stern look on his face, spoke to the policeman.

"I noticed that you and your officers did not take part in this. I also noticed that you didn't, in any manner or form, attempt to stop from escalating into violence. I want you to have your men separate these groups. I want the protesters on the street. I want the private security on the porch with the geek who is there now. Get everyone on one side or the other. If anyone tries to enter the house, shoot him in the leg. I want the Troopers in the middle of the lawn with all their weapons here on the sidewalk. Got that?"

The policemen nodded. The protesters still looked frightened. Many of them turned their faces toward Jim. Marshall Joe spoke again.

"If you and your men don't want to go to prison and lose your pensions, I suggest that you start acting like police officers right now!"

The police leader started barking orders to his men. The TV crews seemed to be getting it all. Just in case they missed anything of importance, my four crews were still recording. Marshall Joe stepped back toward the street to keep an eye on the action while the Cape May Police did their duty.

"Luther, how are you doing?"

"Okay, but I'll have some great bruises for the camera to keep as evidence."

"Give me a minute."

Marshall Joe pulled out a cell phone and pushed some keys.

"Yeah, this is Gibson. Look, all hell broke loose here in Cape May. I need the FBI or anyone else you can get to me fast. Hell, send me some Coast Guard if they're close. I need back-up. Quick!"

He listened then spoke.

"I've got 11 rent-a-cops for A&B for a start. I've got one New Jersey Trooper in cuffs for A&B on Luther, and seven more who are probably guilty of a lot more than the police brutality that I witnessed. I'm willing to bet that there's RICO charges in this that may go as high as the US Senate and the Maryland State House."

He listened some more.

"Okay. Fine. Just tell them to hurry."

He holstered his cell phone.

"The Cavalry is on the way. Oh, sorry. Forgive me for not thinking when I said that. Our back-up help is on the way. You are pressing charges, aren't you?"

"Damn right. This Trooper is toast. If we squeeze him good, maybe we can really clean house."

"You still won't get a Republican Senator in the New Jersey delegation."

"We can hope," said Luther, and he smiled. "I have some cameras to talk to. I'm going to make this one big."

"You're such a political animal."

"No, I'm a good citizen. We have a rapist who used influence to escape justice and over a dozen people whose civil rights were violated. I was beaten for trying to protect those rights. I'm going to walk over there and lay out a line for the press to follow. I'm going to give this story legs and make sure it runs. I'm going to make Dan proud of me and two years from now, I'll be an Apache in the US Congress."

I noticed that Luther already knew about the rapes. There were things going on behind the scenes long before I found Keagey. Luther and his group seemed to be as ruthless as the Kinkaeds.

But who was I to judge him? I had chosen to fight the system from the outside, and I hadn't been very effective at it. Luther was trying to get inside the power structure itself, where he could carry on the fight in a more successful way.

If Luther was in it just for himself, I guess it didn't matter what party he was in. Politics was a dirty business. Since Luther was going to carry our causes to national attention, I kept my opinions to myself. Marshall Gibson broke my reverie.

"While you are on your way, send those amateur camera crews over here. I need them to do something for me."

"You've got one of them behind you."

Marshall Gibson turned to look at us, then back to Luther.

"They might have your strategy on tape. You okay with that?"

"Jim tells me that the man behind you, Ben Pace, can be trusted. Ben?"

"Walk in peace, Luther."

"Walk in beauty, Ben."

"Perhaps we can share the Meeting a New Friend ceremony when this is over?" I asked.

"We will, Ben. I have some lawyer friends that will want to represent you in your upcoming civil rights trial."

"My friends on the cameras were not harmed. Neither was I. Perhaps we can just be witnesses for the others? I've also got a tape recording and some digital pictures that you should see."

"Good. We'll work out the details later. Here's my card."

He turned and left. Marshal Gibson looked at me.

"Your people have the civilian cameras?"

"Yes."

"Here's what I want you to do. Have each of your crews film every person. Start with the private security and then shoot the troopers. After that, I want you to film every one of the protesters. By filming them last, their contusions will have time to swell. Have them turn a full circle for the cameras. Get close-ups of any cuts, scrapes, or bruises, any soiled clothing. I'll have your four separate tapes of the victims, just in case. Can you do that for me?"

I nodded before I turned to direct our part of the mop-up. We had done it. Luther would make sure we had a national platform to register our grievances.

Against Keagey.

And the *Lakhota* against the US Government.

I looked to Rita, Maria, Kelly, and Lisa. Our long road was ending, even as another was beginning. Some paths had merged along The Way. Others had diverged. But I could sense that each had reclaimed her own personal power. Each had retrieved her dignity and self-esteem. Each felt whole again. Their spiritual energy was strong once again.

Though we were no longer on the same Path, we were all threads of the universal tapestry, woven together irrevocably. Beautifully. Joyfully.

In a tapestry that could never be unwoven.

We would all be forever related.

Chapter Thirty-Seven

The road to the Rez lay ahead. My heart sang a happy tune each time I looked at Teresa sitting in the passenger seat. We were heading northeast on Interstate 70 and Pittsburgh was about three hours ahead.

It had been a week since the Cape May uprising. At least that's what the news was calling it. It was a week into *Wa Suton Wi*, the Ripening Moon, what the *wasiçius* call August, named after another Roman emperor. Later this moon I would dance in the sun before *Wakan Tanka* until four eagle claws ripped from my chest. I would seek his wisdom and blessing on my life-path.

If I were lucky, he would merely notice that I was serious about dedicating my life in service to my God, my nation, my tribe, and my family. Grandfather owed me nothing and was not impressed with a mere five years of dedication. He would wait until I proved that I was solid before granting me more power to help my people.

It was a twenty-eight hour drive from my Crownsville hilltop to my parents' lodge on the Rez. Teresa and I were making it a four-day journey, arriving at the Rez at around 2:00 p.m. on the last day.

Another three hours would get us home to the family compound. After that I would have five days to prepare for my Sun Dance.

My eyes nourished themselves on Teresa. It was good that it was Wednesday morning because the traffic was light. Since the road was straight, I could safely look at Teresa for a long moment. She caught me watching her.

"What?" she asked.

I pushed my eyes back to the road and played dumb.

"What?"

"You were looking at me. I saw a look in your eyes. What were you thinking?"

"Nothing."

"What were you thinking?"

"I was thinking about pulling the car over and kissing you, but I'm driving and we have a long way to go. We shouldn't stop."

She unbuckled her seat belt and turned so her knees were in her seat.

"Keep your eyes on the road."

She leaned over and brushed her cheek on my thighs, then up my stomach before kissing my lips from below. After a quick but enticing kiss, she pulled away.

"Can you still see the road okay?"

"Yes, your hair falls down so I can see over it."

She proceeded to kiss me as if I'd never been kissed before. I was just able to keep the Jeep headed in a straight line as Teresa took me to places I'd never been. We passed three exits before she stopped. I glanced at the speedometer. I had slowed from 70 to 45 miles per hour. I resumed my speed.

"I've never been kissed like that."

"Maybe it's time for us to get out that buffalo robe."

That's only for when we don't have any privacy, like when we're at home on the Rez."

"Oh, I see," she said, kissing me one last time.

I felt taller, but I had to adjust my trousers before I felt comfortable.

"Will I still be alive four days from now?"

"Don't worry: I'll keep you alive. I want to see how we turn out."

"I'd like to see that too."

When I'd pledged to accept the future, I had hoped it wouldn't all be selfless sacrifice. With Teresa by my side, heading to the Rez with me, I knew that I could also be happy. Truly happy. With my woman under the blanket. She gave me another short kiss before resuming her seat and seatbelt.

"Ben, I forgot to tell you."

I hoped that it wasn't something about a jealous ex-con ex-husband or a stalker ex-boyfriend.

"Rita called me just before you picked me up. Maria and Robert are engaged! She called Rita to tell her the news and about the ring, so Rita had to tell me."

"That's wonderful! I'll have to call them both! I hope I get an invitation to the wedding."

"Don't worry. Maria couldn't say enough nice things about you to Rita. You'll be on her list."

"Good, I'm glad."

"Not as much as I am."

"What do you mean?" I asked.

"I'm just glad that I met you."

She leaned over and kissed my cheek softly.

"All those years I dated cowboys and now I find that I was really looking for an Indian."

"I looked over at my woman and smiled.

"Rita told me to thank you. Your friend Jim and she are having their third date this weekend."

"I had nothing to do with that."

"Jim told her that you gave him her phone number."

"Jim asked me for Rita's phone number before we left Cape May. I didn't do anything else. Not even ask him why he wanted it. Rita got her own date."

I took my mind off Jim and Rita, off Teresa sitting beside me, off the feel of her kisses and my desire. I straightened a little in my seat to stretch my back.

"When we get to the motel room, I'll give you a nice, long back massage," said Teresa. "After."

She was making it difficult to concentrate on driving. Difficult to think of my people on the Rez. Would they treat me as an outsider since I'd lived away from them for so long? How much would I have to sacrifice until they accepted me as a medicine man? Would they ever accept me?

"Rita heard from Kelly," said Teresa, looking out the side window at the passing scenery. "She's doing much better. Her friend Linda got her involved with her church. The congregation's big and she's made a lot of new friends. I think she'll be fine."

I glanced over at her, but she was still watching the passing landscape.

311

"Any news from Lisa?"

"The last Rita heard, she and her sister Emily were dating a set of identical twins. One's a mechanical engineer, and the other is a waterman."

"What's a waterman?" I asked.

"A man that makes a living doing anything he can with his boat. He crabs and fishes and runs a charter service whenever anyone wants to fish the Chesapeake Bay. He's been doing it since he was a teenager. His father did that work, too. Meanwhile, the engineer is nine-to-five, and as regular as clockwork."

I smiled without looking at her.

Her face was clear and bright in my heart.

She reached over and held my hand.

We shared the silence for a while.